A Moment

Book 1 in the Cliffsides Chronicles

TES

STARGAZER PUBLISHING

A Moment

JES

Dedication

T o my dad, who always told me that I write a book in every birthday card, and to my husband, who told me to stop talking about writing a book and just do it.

A moment. That's all it takes to cleave your world in two. Your instincts kick in. Take over. React. They are supposed to save you, but they fail you instead. One moment everything is possible. The next? Life as you know it has ended.

Chapter 1

Gabriella - Present Day: 1999

I pull up to the old Darla's Dine and Drive to pick Kasha up from her shift. You can smell the hot oil and fried food before you even park your car. It is one of those sticky smells, one that you feel is coating your skin, your hair, and the air in your lungs as you enter the aroma's atmosphere, which is now coating you in week-old oil, too.

Crossing the little two-lane highway that runs through our small town, I turn left into Darla's parking lot. There is a group of teenagers and a few couples sitting outside at the old wooden picnic tables, immersed in their early afternoon treat, most of their faces familiar. I try to ease my Camaro over the shoddy, crumbling speed bumps while avoiding the potholes. It's no use; I scrape the underside of Carly's front bumper. Again. Grimacing at the sound, I send a whispered apology to my car: "Sorry, girl."

Kasha is waiting out front for me, with her hostess apron still wrapped around her middle. She has always worn it higher up on her waist than the other girls, saying that it accentuates her hips and makes her feel like Marylin Monroe, but that is the only thing Norma Jean about her. If anything, she looks more like she stepped out of a Garbage music video, with her laced-up combat boots, fishnet stockings, pleated miniskirt that I wouldn't be caught dead in, and an open, oversize flannel. Her long, thick, blonde hair is plaited in tiny braids across the top of her head, like a Viking shield-maiden, which forces the rest of it to hang loose over her shoulders. Creeping my rumbling car closer to where she is waiting, I notice she has two milkshakes in her hands. Yes! I love my girl and not just because she consistently is able to score us Darla's shakes free of charge. Though it does help.

I reach over to turn down the music on the radio and settle Carly into neutral as Kasha hands me a shake from the open passenger window. Kasha whips off her apron, tossing it in the back.

"Thanks for the shake," I say. "It's chocolate and strawberry, right?"

"Who do you think I am? An amateur? Of course it's your weird combo shake."

As Kasha holds on to the roof, she kicks her legs over the top of the door and slides down into the passenger seat, stating, "Man, that was a shit day. Please get us out of here. Let's go enjoy these delicious cups of sugar and calories up at The Hook."

"You know, the door does work," I point out. "I fixed it last spring, and it opens perfectly now. You could just get in like a normal person."

"But where's the fun in that? Plus, getting in 'normally' would totally cramp both Carly's and my style. Wouldn't it, girl?" Kasha says as she gently pats the dash, like Carly is a puppy and not a 1989 V8 Chevy Camaro.

Smirking, I start to take a sip of my shake.

When the straw is halfway to my lips, Kasha exclaims, "Oh! I almost forgot!" After leaning forward and fishing through her oversize black tote, she tosses an oil-stained brown paper bag of Darla's fries at me.

"Girl, you know I love you."

"I know." Now it's Kasha's turn to smirk.

I pop a warm fry into my mouth and quickly follow it up with a slurp of shake, mixing the warm, salty, oily flavor with the cold creaminess of my chocolate-strawberry shake. I close my eyes for a second. Mmmm, perfection.

"You are so odd," Kasha says as she pops the straw of her vanilla shake into her mouth.

For someone who is as flamboyant as Kasha, she loves her food as plain and boring as can be. Laughing, I shift my car into first, keeping my left foot hovering over the clutch as I maneuver through the treacherous parking lot.

We leave the splintering and faded old Dine and Drive in our rearview mirror, and I head out onto the highway. The folks sitting outside Darla's continue to chat quietly, sipping their shakes and munching on fried chicken and fries from red plastic baskets. They don't even bother looking up as I shift gears, Carly growling in response.

I rescued Carly five years ago from being shipped off to the scrapyard, when I was eighteen. She was a real clunker, but I couldn't stand to see such potential be torn apart because someone was too lazy to do the work. I had saved up my money from the local Pump and Go and purchased her from Gary, my boss. Gary was a big man, mostly in the gut. He had a permanent five o'clock shadow, thinning, dark hair slicked across his shiny bald spot, and grease stains consistently marring his white tank and dusty blue coveralls, which were always folded and tied at his waist.

Both Gary and my pops had told me that the Camaro was a waste of time and money. After all, what would I know about rebuilding a car?

I told them "I'd learn," and I did. One painful monkey wrench and knuckle smash at a time.

Pops continued to rave at me for a couple days, followed by a silent spell when he realized that this was something I was going to do with or without his blessing. Mom just smiled and shrugged and tried to convince Pops that I needed to find my own path and that included making my own choices... and mistakes.

Gary was more than happy to take my money.

I spent the next five years remaking my girl into the beauty I knew she was deep down. Her engine and chassis were still in fine shape, but I did need to drain and replace all the engine fluids, the hoses, belts, and wiring, which had lived at the mercy of time, neglect, and some local rodents who had taken up residence in the engine compartment. The next thing I did was drain the brakes and replace the pads and discs. It took a lot of swearing, bloody knuckles, broken nails, and grease-ruined jeans, but my girl was ready for the road. Sort of.

Her body had been another story. Sanding down the old brick red paint, with Gary's sander he didn't know I "borrowed" from the garage, I was able to then fill in the damaged areas with some Bondo. Letting the putty solidify, I then sanded it smooth. Again, sounds simple. It was not. For months my car looked like it was one of the drives at the local Putt-Putt Golf, covered in mounds and depressions. It wasn't a good look. Rebuilding the car made me feel good. Accomplished. Then after mom passed away, distracted.

I pick up speed as I steer the Camaro up the winding mountainside road. The sun beats down on us, and the wind pours in from the open windows, whipping at our faces. Kasha's hair is wild in the wind; strands from my usual dark, loose bun blow in my face. Kasha reaches over and turns the stereo all the way up. Music blasting through the speakers, vibrations of the V8 in our seats, and the summer elements on our skin, we feel... free. Like anything is possible.

I downshift as I approach The Birds' Nest. It's a local spot teenagers hike up to sit on the cliff's edge that dangles over the curving road. High schoolers spend hours there, drinking, making out, and throwing things over the top of road and into the ravine below on the other side. Kids are dumb, but it would be a lie if I said I never took part in some of the stupidity that comes along with adolescence.

Passing the area that has always given me the heebie-jeebies, I continue to climb the hill. Between the abrupt drop off below and teenage idiocy above, I have never been able to shake the ominous feelings that The Bird's Nest gives me. I begin downshifting the engine, right as the road seems to disappear in the near distance. It is such a sharp left turn that if you weren't used to driving Hill Canyon, you would think that the road was never finished and turn around. If you take the turn carefully, though, it will spit you out onto a great dirt overlook.

The curving road and dirt path are shaped perfectly like an old fishing hook. Hence the name, The Hook. It has always been Kasha's and my special spot, for as long as we've been able to get up there independently. It's where we go to be alone. To yell at the wind and cry to the stars. To share our secrets and dreams and, of course, Darla shakes.

I slow the car down as I pull off and onto the dirt road, setting it in park. I reach down and pull back on the emergency brake, feeling it slowing click into place until it is taut, and cut the engine. It is a beautiful day. The air is warm and dry, with just the right amount of breeze pulling through the canyon, keeping the summer heat from becoming too thick and heavy. Taking a moment, I try to recline my seat back and fail. Oh, that's right. My seat only folds forward. I still need to buy a new recliner mechanism. Ugh. I climb out of the car and onto the hood with my shake and fries. Tipping my head back and gently resting it on the windshield, I can feel the heat of the sun on my face, throat, and chest. Closing my eyes, I listen to the breeze in the canyon trees, the birds chirping and some insects or rattlesnake grass buzzing, I can never tell which it is. I have the faint sense that Kasha has come out to join me on the hood.

Peeling my eyes open, I roll my head to the right, taking in Kasha who has been unusually quiet since we parked. There is still a fine layer of silt floating in the air from when we pulled in, giving everything a sparkling, golden glow and a dusty smell. She is looking out over the drop-off in front of us, silently sipping her shake.

"What's up? Was it really that shit of a day?" I ask, perplexed by her somber mood.

"No, not really. It was just another typical day, you know. It's just..." She trails off, still looking over the beautiful cliff ahead of us to the view of endless rolling hills covered in sycamore and oak trees. The sky is a crisp blue, with hardly any clouds in sight.

"What?" I ask.

"Don't you ever feel like our time here should come to a close? You know, like a chapter in a book? That we are destined for more than spending our whole existence in a small, dusty town?"

This is a conversation the two of us have had many times before. This time, though, I have begun to feel the way Kasha does. There is a sense of impending change that has been sitting in my gut, and it is getting harder to ignore.

Kasha continues. "I'm just scared of turning out like Darla, you know? Working at the Dine and Drive for fifty years, till I'm old and wrinkled. And not the good wrinkles that come from laughing and too much time in the sun. The ones made from dust and stress and working everyday just to make ends meet. I am afraid of living my whole life in a small town when there is an entire world out there waiting to be explored. Or at least the beach and cliffsides."

Here Kasha gives me a sideways glance and smirk; she's been trying to get me to go to the cliffside for years, but I haven't been able to leave my pops after Mom. Even for just a trip. Where Kasha has always fantasized about leaving South Brook and doing more with her life than what a small town can offer, I have daydreamed about continuing the small and simplistic life. Just... I never have wanted it here. I have always had a pull towards the sea.

"I would like to visit that at least, with you. The cliffsides." Kasha says. "I don't know, maybe have a romance with someone we didn't go to kindergarten with?"

At this we both start giggling. My shake threatens to come out of my nose, which makes us laugh even harder. I reach up to my face, to try and staunch the cold pain now shooting through the roof of my mouth.

"What do you mean?" I ask in mock shock. "Jamie Key isn't your kind of guy?"

"Are you kidding me? First of all, he was rotten in kindergarten, still a jerk in middle school, and high school did not offer him many improvements in the 'charm department.'" Here Kasha makes air quotes. "There is Chris Roberts, though."

"Ewww. No, thank you," I state matter-of-factly. "There is no way I would end up with someone like my pops for a husband. No offense to my dad, but I already have one former jock turned beer-bellied alcoholic in my life. Thank you very much." I shove my straw into my mouth to make the point that the topic is now closed. End of story.

"Come on, you don't think those good looks will last?" Kasha asks with a smirk on her lips. Just one sideways glare from me and we both start giggling again.

"How is your pops, anyway?"

My dad was once the dreamy guy every girl in South Brook tried to nab. A baseball player in high school, he had a full head of dark brown hair—still does, actually, though it's more salt than pepper now. He was always good with his hands and could still be found whittling all sorts of woodland creatures up until a year ago. With as many options as he had, it was my mom, Martha, and only my mom that Jewel Pinkard had big, brown eyes for. She was the quiet girl growing up, and she kept to herself, avoiding the big crowds and parties. That was never Mom's jam; she would rather be outside drawing, walking, or trying to identify all the different kinds of foliage around South Brook.

One afternoon in the fall of '73, during their senior year, Martha's best friend, Liz, ran all the way over from the Quicky Mart after work to tell her some news. She found Martha with her hair loose. Long waves ran down her tiny back, and a yellow gardening apron was cinched around her waist as she sat in an open field near her house. Martha was quietly humming to herself as she delicately documented some wildflowers she had found.

Liz grabbed her by the arm and, plopping down in the golden grass next to her friend, tried to catch her breath enough to say, "Martha, you are not going to believe what I heard!"

Mom was never one for gossip, nor could she care less about the drama that circulated South Brook High on a regular basis, so with as little enthusiasm as she felt, she said, "I don't know, Liz. What did you hear? And how did you know where I would be, anyway?"

"Oh. My. God," Liz pants out. "First, of course you'd be in this open field, where else? Anyway, I heard from Tom, Jewel's best friend, that Jewel totally has the hots for you."

"Ha. Ha. Very funny, Liz. Now if you don't mind, I would like to get these flowers categorized before the sunlight leaves me." Bending her head back over the wildflowers she collected, she continued to draw them in her notebook with the most intricate detail, colored pencils splayed out on an old kitchen towel next to her.

Grabbing her shoulder, Liz exclaimed, "No, you don't understand! He likes you and wants to go out. He wants to know what you think. I've been asked to ask you. It is all very exciting!" At this she gave Martha her biggest smile, awaiting her response, high on the thrill of the gossip.

Martha set her pencil between the pages of her book, slowly and gently closed the covers, and placed it in her folded lap. As she turned to look at her best friend, she saw with no small satisfaction that her calm demeanor was giving Liz a conniption fit. "Well, I suppose if he wants to know what I think, he'd better ask me himself."

With the finality of her tone, she picked her sketchbook back up and continued to document the details of the *Nemophila menziesii*, more commonly known as Menzies' baby blue eyes, a tiny flower with periwinkle blue petals and a white center.

The conversation was over, at least temporarily.

The next week, Jewel Pinkard approached Martha Goode and asked her to a game of Putt-Putt and dinner. They enjoyed each other's company so much that they attended senior prom together that spring and were inseparable for the rest of their final year of high school. In the summer of 1974, they were married. I came along a year and a half later.

Mom and Pops' joy from their relationship was contagious. It was the marriage that everyone was envious of, the relationship that people aspired to have. Even if their honeymooners' love made you ill, you still invited them to your party because their joy lightened the whole room. They danced in the living room together listening to music, from Duran Duran to The Cult to Doobie Brothers. Mom would often tell Pops how good he looked, and he would come up to her and wrap his arms around her middle while she was trying to wash the dishes.

These are the warm, happy memories I have of my parents. This was the comforting, joyous, infectious love I grew up with; a childhood filled with hope and hugs and laughter.

It all ended as abruptly as a screech on a record player. One day, Mom collapsed in her garden, doing what she had loved. She was unresponsive and unable to be revived.

"Oh, you know," I say. My mind drifts out of my memory fog and back to Kasha's question about my dad. "He hasn't been the same since Mom died. It is like a part of him died that day, too. He is still drinking, too much in my opinion, not that I can say anything. He says he's looking for work, but he refuses to take a job out of pity. Not that that is the reason they are being offered to him, but to him it is. If he isn't blackout-drunk, he is heartbreakingly sad or so silently angry I just stay clear. He's not even working in the shed on his creations anymore. It is just so frustrating. I lost her, too, but it's like my grief doesn't count. Like I'm not still here, too. I don't know. I am just not sure what to do anymore other than just be present for him."

Kasha is silent as she listens. I know she understands the complex dynamics of a broken family. Her dad ran out on her mom and his five children when Kasha was still running around the yard barefoot. Her mom had to take on a second job at night just to be able to put food on their table. Jacob, Kasha's older brother, dropped out of school to work at the local welding shop to help support the family. One day he couldn't take it anymore and left, too. Things had improved as the Owens clan had gotten older and more self-sufficient. Kasha and her three younger siblings had practically raised themselves, creatively finding ways to make things work.

"It's hard. You know his grief is not your responsibility, though, right, Gabs? It's been just over two years. You need to put yourself first sometimes, too."

I glance down at my black-and-white Converse All-Stars. The side plastic is starting to crack and peel. I pick at the frayed hole in my blue jeans, just above my knee.

"You're right. I know you are. It's just harder than it seems."

"Most things are."

"Besides," I mention at a near mumble. Trying to convince myself just as much as trying to convince Kasha. "Somedays, I feel like he does show improvement. Slightly at least. I mean, he has started talking more." After a pause, both of us staring off into the faraway distance, I add, "Well, not about anything you know... important. It is more superficial stuff. But still. I feel like it is an improvement. I am not fully invisible."

We finish our shakes and quietly watch the sun set through the trees, lost in our own thoughts and crossroads of decisions. Once the light in the sky starts to dim, signaling dusk's approach, we climb back into the Camaro. I flick on the headlights and head home.

Chapter 2

Martha - Two Years Earlier: 1997

They say that it is the woman's job to hold the family together. I never gave that much thought until Mom passed away the spring before my nineteenth birthday. I never realized how much of the glue she was, holding our trio of a family together, until that glue was no longer there. How hard it was to step in and fill her shoes. As much as I tried, I could never be that glue for Pops and me. A three-legged stool will topple over if you remove one of its legs, no matter how sturdily it is built.

We called ourselves The Triad. Although that may sound like a gang of corrupted, immoral bad guys from the new witchy TV show *Charmed*, the term actually came from my sixth-grade music class.

Our local school is a K-12. Being such a small town, they just packed all the grades into one location. It's a huge, red-and-tan-brick building that's located at the center back border of the grassy quad, and there are three longer single-story buildings sitting along the other sides of the quad. Climbing the small hill behind the big building that house the core classes for sixth through twelfth grades were more rows of single-story buildings and a few portables turned into classrooms. This is where all the lower grades were located. There's a big, grassy field with differently sized play structures and a blacktop equipped with handball courts, a bike path, and basketball hoops. In the side buildings to the east and west of the big brick building and the main quad, the art courses were housed. Because the school was determined to have their students well rounded, regardless of our small size, we had to take a different type of creative arts class every year, starting in sixth grade.

In sixth grade it was music, seventh was fine arts, eighth theater, ninth ceramics, and tenth grade was creative writing. Then starting your junior year, you could choose which area you wanted to focus on for the duration of high school.

My sixth-grade music teacher, Mr. Bennet, not only taught us how to read and play music on our instrument of choice, but he believed it to be fundamentally important to understand what made the music what it was. It was from him that I learned what a triad was. It immediately reminded me of our little family, and I told Mom and Pops about it that night at the dinner table.

A triad is three musical notes stacked in thirds, creating a chord. Those notes are known as the root, the third, and the fifth, with the root being the lowest note. When stacked together with the others, it creates the harmony.

That was our family. A triad. A simple harmony that came together, with Mom being the root, the base and foundation of our familiar song. The nickname stuck, and since that day we referred to ourselves less as the Pinkards and more as The Triad.

Folks say that I look just like her, my mom. She was thin with long, light brown hair that rested at the small of her back. I can see the similarities between our posture, bone structure, and mannerisms. We both had a slightly crooked smile that went up on the left sides of our mouths and a smattering of freckles across the bridges of our noses. But where her hair was lighter and she always wore it loose and down, mine is a deep brown, like Pops', that I keep pulled back from my face in a ponytail knot. Mom's eyes were hazel, but mine are a gray-blue, something I inherited from my grandmother. Mom loved nothing more than to be outdoors, in the sun of an open field or in her garden, with dirt under her nails and a pencil behind her ear. She never went anywhere without her notebook and pencils. I, however, always prefer being on the back of a horse or working with my hands, using tools and being awed by how they help shape something from nothing; how they assist in a job that otherwise would have been near impossible to complete. I suppose I am more like Pops in that sense. A simple blend of my two parents.

My parents were married for just over two decades, before God called Mom home. They were happy always touching in some small way, making the atmosphere in our home feel light and airy. Their legs would rest next to each other's while watching TV on the couch. Their toes would touch under the dinner table during our evening meals. Every time one walked past the other, they would give a light kiss or trail their fingers down their arm or across their back. When my friends would discuss arguments that their folks would have, I would sit and just listen, having no frame of reference. If my parents ever did fight, they never did it so that I noticed or even picked up on the aftermath of a disagreement.

Our weekends consisted of Pops sitting at his workbench under the lean-to, whittling some creature out of a scrap of pine from one of his projects, while Mom sat in her garden nearby, weeding or documenting the different plants and their stages of growth in her journal. I would have been building some elaborate ranch for all my wooden horses, using sticks and stones I had found around the yard. Things were simple. Happy. Everyone was content to just be near each other.

Mom's drawings were remarkable. She would draw a flower or plant that she would find, in such delicate detail, adding color, with notes and descriptions in the margins. Her script was just as lovely as her drawings, with its gentle, liquid flow. We had notebooks upon notebooks all piled and stacked on the shelves in our home, some with loose pages sticking out, giving them a deckled edge. There were drawing pencils and colored pencils loose or dumped together in a glass from the kitchen on shelves or end tables. Mom had a unique system to her organization even if Pops and I could never figure out what it was. It was a common occurrence to find pencil shavings and dirt on the bookcases instead of dust. She would say that appreciating the tiny, beautiful details of life was what made it worth living.

Every Wednesday evening after dinner we would have family music night. This was when we would each take turns choosing and playing any song we wanted. The music would be loud, the lights dim, and we would either dance in the living room, moving the coffee table off to the side, or we would quietly sit and listen to the lyrics and melody of a favorite song.

Kasha asked me once why Wednesdays? Wouldn't it make more sense to stay up late and play music on a Friday or Saturday night? Her logic made sense, but when I asked Mom, she would say to me, "Gabriella, darling, we need to celebrate the ordinary. Wednesday is just another day that has nothing special for itself. It sits right in the middle of the week, holding no complaints about the start of the week or fresh memories from the weekend. It doesn't have the impending hope of the approaching weekend. Wednesday just is. That is why it should be celebrated." So, Wednesday nights at the Pinkard house were music nights.

Mom was like that, always pulling the beauty out of the mundane.

One particular Wednesday night, as the evening of dancing, laughing, and music started to wind down, Pops played Duran

Duran's "Ordinary World." Once the opening guitar and synthesizer kicked in, he slowly walked over to Mom. Taking her hands in his, he pulled her up from the couch to her feet. They gently brought their bodies together, with her arms around his wide shoulders and his wrapped around her narrow waist. They danced together quietly, eyes closed, lost in their own world, swaying tenderly together in the living room. I sat on the couch, legs folded underneath me, blanket draped across my lap, and just watched them for a minute, taking in the joy and love that they created together. Then I quietly got up, wrapping the blanket snugly around my shoulders, and went to bed. Eyelids heavy, with a warmth in my heart and a smile on my lips, I drifted off to sleep. Content.

A few months later, while working in her garden, Mom complained of a sudden severe headache. She felt nauseous and dizzy. She mentioned the possibility of coming down with something and that she was going to go inside and lie down for a bit. As she went to stand up, she collapsed. Her pencils scattered in the dirt, and her journal pages flapped in the breeze as she fell to the warm earth, unresponsive.

Pops and I dashed over and tried to revive her, to wake her, get her to talk, to open her eyes, anything. Her breathing and heartbeat were both so shallow and light that they were hard to detect, but they were there. We clung to that. Pops scooped her up as I dashed inside to grab the keys to the pickup, adrenaline and instincts kicking in. My heart pounded as we raced to the hospital, and we prayed she would be okay. Prayed for no traffic on our way to the hospital. Prayed that the doctors could help.

After we came to a screeching halt in front of Saint Luke's, the nurses came running out of the automatic glass doors with a gurney in tow, clattering over the curb. They placed Mom on it, strapping and securing her in place. The doctors and nurses were asking Pops questions that my brain could not register. Everything sounded like it was underwater. The sun was too bright and hot reflecting off the black asphalt of the parking lot, and no matter how hard I tried, I couldn't focus.

Pops was shouting at me, "Gabby, Gabby! Gabriella!" My eyes finally adjusted and focused on him, and the world came crashing back with the full force of a tidal wave. The sounds, the frantic movements... He calmly but firmly grabbed both my shoulders. "Gabby, I need you to go park the truck. I am going to follow the doctors inside. Meet us when you are done. The receptionist will tell you where to go." I just nodded at him and jumped in the driver's seat as he ran after the doctors. After Mom.

The doctors said that it was a ruptured brain aneurysm. That a brain aneurysm is a bulge in a weakened blood vessel in the brain. That most aneurysms are small and don't cause any type of damage. They are more common in women between the ages of thirty and sixty. Unfortunately, for some, these aneurysms can rupture. This bleeding happens fast, only lasting a few seconds, but the damage can be irreparable.

We sat there in those uncomfortable chairs with the metal arm rests and scratchy floral-print cushions and continued to listen to what the doctor was trying to tell us. The air-conditioning system kept clicking on and off.

Click.

Silence.

Click.

Silence.

The florescent lights had a slight humming sound to them, and the lack of natural light with the strong smell of disinfectant was starting to give me a headache. Or was that the stress? I should probably get something to drink... *Mom... Oh, God, Mom... What was the doctor saying?*

Pops and I apparently did a great job getting her help as fast as we did. They were able to rush her right into surgery where they attempted to attach a surgical clip in her brain, also known as an endovascular coil, intended to seal off the ruptured vessel and stop the bleeding, but her blood pressure was too low. It dropped further during the operation. They tried to revive her... They did everything they could.... So sorry... she's gone. The world no longer spun. The lights stopped flickering and buzzing; people no longer spoke, all frozen in place. Midmotion, files and Styrofoam cups of bad coffee in their hands.

I was numb.

Then, the next second, I shattered.

Chapter 3

The Funeral: 1997

The next week we buried Mom at Sycamore Springs Memorial Park.

At the far end of town, past the school and hospital, Sycamore Springs sat with its tiny office building just off the gravel road leading into the complex. It was a small one-story building, painted white with green trim and a brown roof. It had a few rosebushes that looked like they'd seen better days out front, in raised, red-brick gardens. Behind the office the burial plots were spread out up the sprawling hills; sycamore trees scattered throughout the property, offering shade for those mourning their loved ones. A tan-gravel path weaved in and out, crisscrossing up the hill, allowing a walking trail for people to find the burial site of their family member or friend. Old iron benches were laid out for places to rest, remember, and grieve.

South Brook is a small town of approximately four thousand people, with one main road in and out. Jenson Road was named after South Brook's founder in the 1800s, though all the locals just refer to Jenson Road as The Highway. Charles Jenson came out west with the rest of the pioneers who had gold lust in their eyes and adventure in their bones. The story has it that Jenson never made it farther north than South Brook because he fell in love with the valley nestled between steep, rolling hills covered in oak and sycamore trees. The little river that runs southwest of the current highway offered plenty of fresh water from the steady supply of runoff from the Sierras. It transforms from a calm creek in the summer and fall to a river rushing over the riverbed's boulders in the winter and spring.

Having the dream to stake a claim of his own, Mr. Jenson did just that and placed a literal stake in the ground where our town hall building sits now. The stake is still there, now encased in concrete, with a wire cable fence around it.

Creating something out of nothing but the beauty of the land, Charles Jenson had South Brook offer a good resting point for folks to stop on their travels from Los Angeles to San Francisco, a place for them to water their horses, get a meal and a solid night's sleep before setting out again on the dust covered road.

Jenson Road is still the only road in and out of South Brook. The town is spaced out along either side of the fourteen-mile stretch before it bends toward a large expanse of empty land leading to more populated areas along California's Central Coast.

Pops and I bump along in his old Chevy pickup, heading north to the Memorial Park. The silence stretches the distance between us in the cab, making the air feel tight. I find myself with nothing to say, what feels like a permanent knot stuck in my throat and an invisible weight on my chest. I turn to look out the passenger window, watching the town roll past. There is the Pump and Go, the tiny gas station and mechanic shop. Gary is standing out front, his faded, blue coveralls tied around his bulging middle, pumping gas into some lady's fancy, dark blue sedan. He sees us pass and quietly raises his hand into the air. The town knows today is the day we place Martha Pinkard in the ground. I raise my fingers, which are hanging out the window, in response. I'm not sure if he notices. I don't really care. It seems that is all the energy I can muster at the moment.

Next, we pass Darla's Dine and Drive. There are fewer people out today as the outdoor wooden picnic tables with their dusty, faded-yellow umbrellas sit empty, but it is still early, I suppose. I crane my neck, looking passed Darla's to the twisting incline that is Hill Canyon. I am going to need a serious getaway up at The Hook with Kasha after today. I'm thinking I'll even ask her to sneak her brother's old flasks out with her.

The town continues to whip by... The Hitching Post, our local watering hole. The vet clinic, the town hall with the old wooden stake out front, The Quicky Mart where Mom used to work with her best friend, Liz. The South Brook School of the Arts, our local K-12. Saint Luke's... My eyesight starts to blur. I can't tell if it's from me zoning out again or from the tears that threaten to fall. I turn to face forward again, sparing a glace to my left, at my pops. His hands are tight on the steering wheel, and he's staring straight ahead, mouth formed in a grim line that turns down slightly at the corners. Even if I had anything to say, the energy in the truck would not permit it. I rest the back of my head on the seat rest, closing my eyes, trying to imagine I am going anywhere but where we are actually headed. Anywhere but here, as the truck cruises and bumps along the highway, closer to Mom's final resting place.

The funeral service is a small affair, with only a handful of people to watch us lay Mom to rest. It's how we wanted it. It's how she would've wanted it. No fuss.

Everyone is clad in black, wearing drawn, heartbroken expressions and holding white flowers in their hands. There are so many flowers, ranging from roses to lilies, to carnations, to daisies, all white with long, green stems. The contrast with the black and the variety of the flowers is beautiful, something that Mom would have appreciated. I can't help but think that the people of South Brook knew her well.

The casket hovers over the empty plot, supported by two long metal poles that run underneath it at either end, keeping it suspended. To the right of the casket is an oversized portrait of Mom sitting in the middle of an open field of swaying grass and tiny wildflowers—her happy place, a pencil shoved behind her right ear. Her hand is up to try and shade the sun from her eyes. A genuine smile appears on her face, and a few strands of hair blow across her throat. If Heaven has a personalized location for each of us when we die, that image would be Mom's Heaven.

There are a few chairs situated under a popup shade canopy for those that want to sit, but very few choose to sit. Most people stand nearby, heads bowed in solemn silence, weight shifting slightly from foot to foot, everyone lost in their own private battle of grief. I can hear their thoughts practically shouting out of their heads, as if they are saying them out loud. *She was so young... So tragic, leaving behind her family... Especially leaving Gabby as a young woman just starting out, when girls at that age need their mothers... I hope Jewel will be okay... A brain aneurysm, how rare... What are the odds... So hard...*

I sit in the front row of three chairs, under the shade, but the sun still hits my toes and ankles. My eyes are drawn to my feet. How odd, I think. I am at my mom's funeral and all I can think about and look at are my toes in my strappy, black sandals that I found buried in the back of the closet. I am wearing a black V-neck dress that has an overlayer of lacy fabric, classing it up. It ends just above the knee and has long sleeves that stop halfway between the wrists and elbows. Kasha and I bought it at a secondhand store. "Every woman needs a little black dress," she told me with a devilish grin on her face. "You never know when a situation will arise." With our heads wrapped around a sexy dinner date with a guy, sipping white wine, little did we know that the first time I would wear it would be for a funeral. My mom's funeral.

Forcing myself to look up from the surprisingly riveting view of my feet, my eyes sting as they are temporarily blinded by the afternoon sun. Everything just feels so wrong, like I am in a nightmare that I can't wake up from. I catch myself starting to panic, the grief rising from my center like a tidal wave, when Kasha, sitting to my right, grabs the hand that was balled up in my lap. She gives it a fierce squeeze that almost hurts, snapping me out of my soon-to-be episode. We don't have to look at each other for me to know that she would do anything for me; with that simple gesture, she has already helped me immensely. Silently and firmly, keeping her fingers woven through mine, she moves our joined hands to the center of her lap. She won't let go. I know that she will never let go of me. Never let me fall alone. The idea helps bring me peace.

The clergyman that works at Sycamore Springs, Mr. Rogers, is a tiny man, short and frail, with a head of messy, gray hair and slouching shoulders. He has been the town's minister long before Kasha and I were even born. He's handled all the funerals, weddings, and baptisms in South Brook for the last forty years.

I have always found it amusing that he is the embodiment of his name, Mr. Rogers, just like the old TV show from my childhood, always caring for those in his neighborhood. My mouth wants to smile at the memory, but the action seems too hard.

He has the Bible delicately sandwiched between his knobby hands, resting at his center, when he starts speaking. "I plan on starting today's service for Martha Pinkard with the reflection of her love and with the grace in which she chose to live life. Martha was a gentle, creative soul who loved the beauty of the little things, the forgotten things, the mundane things in this world. She was a walking reminder for the rest of us to embrace life and to focus on the positives, to see simplicity in the details and to love with our entire souls, as God intended. Martha is now at peace with our Lord and Savior.

"Proverbs 3:5 states, 'Trust in the Lord with all thine heart; and lean not unto thine own understanding.' It is more than difficult to lose someone dear to you. It makes it even harder when that person was as kind and gentle as Martha Pinkard. I am not here to tell you not to grieve, not to feel emotions, not to cry. Emotions are God given. Jesus himself said in Matthew 5:4, 'Blessed are they that mourn, for they shall be comforted.'

God gifted us with tears to help us in our time of sorrow. Allow yourself to cry, to feel.

"The time may also come when you may find yourself questioning things. That is okay. Question. However, remember to choose something wonderful to focus on, things you know, the memories that bring you joy. That was how Martha chose to live her life. Honor her memory by following in her loving footsteps and adhering to God's word: 'A joyful heart is good medicine, but a crushed spirit dries up the bones.' Proverbs 17:22.

"As we begin to conclude our time together this afternoon and start to share stories of our fallen loved one, Philippines 4:7 reminds us, 'And the peace of God, which transcends all understanding, will guard your hearts and mind in Jesus Christ.' May God rest her soul. Amen."

"Amen," the small gathering echoes.

The pallbearers lift the straps, allowing the support struts to be removed before they slowly lower the casket into the ground. People begin to lay their white flowers on the coffin as is it descends into its final resting place. I wait until everyone has stepped away, approaching on liquid legs. My left arm is looped through Pops' elbow, giving us both the support we need. I place my small bouquet of white Lisianthus on the center of the casket. Near where her heart would be.

I was about twelve on a particularly warm Mother's Day morning, when Mom and I were planting flowers in pots on our porch. This was the spring before our big family trip to the coast. Her gardening gloves coated in dirt, trowel resting on her knee, she told me that, "The Lisianthus flower, Gabby, is also known as prairie gentian, with its long, delicate stem supporting double leaves and a full head of oval-shaped petals. It is a heat-loving flower that, much like you, loves the warm summer nights." She says this with a loving smile forming on her face and a twinkle in her eye. "It also symbolizes the bond between mother and daughter, a lifelong connection. That is why every year from here on out, I want to plant Lisianthus with you, my precious daughter. It was God's blessing when he gifted you to me. Always remember that our bond is stronger than any amount of time, distance, or obstacle that life may throw at us."

My memory starts to fade as I notice Kasha hugging me.

"I'll see you back at the house, okay?" she says.

"Okay," I manage to whisper, giving her a slight nod.

Turning, Pops and I start the short walk down the weaving gravel path to our truck parked at the base of the gently sloping hill.

A half hour later, we pull into the dirt drive of our small ranch-style home. There are already people there unloading food onto our kitchen table. I wonder what Pops and I are going to do with all that food; our freezer can only hold so much. I am overwhelmed with all the hugs and stories of Mom and the wishes of 'You have our deepest condolences.' I take a glass of water and head out to the swing that hangs off our back porch, needing to get away for a moment. Kasha is already waiting for me, quietly rocking back and forth on the swing. I plop down next to her, taking a sip of my water, then setting it on the ground at my feet.

"I love you," she says.

"I love you, too."

With this I lie on my hip, folding my legs up to my chest, head resting in her lap. Kasha strokes my long, dark hair down the side of my head, fingers combing my scalp. The rhythm of the swing and the soothing motion of her fingers in my hair starts to lull me to sleep. I feel my eyes grow as heavy as my heart feels, and I drift off into a welcome unconsciousness.

I wake a few hours later with an old afghan blanket draped over my body and a couch pillow wedged under my head. Tucked under the corner of the pillow is a note:

Finish your water, get some rest, and do not hesitate to call me. I am and forever will be there for you. xx K

Grabbing my water glass and securing the blanket around my shoulders, I head into the now quiet house. I am not hungry but figure I will have a pounding headache in the morning if I don't eat something. I end up shoving a handful of cheese from a leftover platter into my mouth. I spot Pops silently sitting in the living room. He appears to be molded into his recliner, beer in hand, gazing off to nowhere.

"Hey, Pops, I am heading to bed."

Setting his beer on the end table, he uses what appears to be all the strength of his body to place his hands on the armrests and hoist himself up and out of the chair. He looks like he's aged ten years today. Closing the short distance between us, he grabs me in a strong embrace, holding me as if I am a life raft in the middle of a stormy sea. We stand like that for a few minutes, just feeling.

Placing a kiss to my forehead, he says, "I am proud of you, Gabby, and I love you, baby girl."

Tears fill our eyes, falling freely down our cheeks. "I love you, too, Pops."

"Night."

"Night."

I turn and walk down the hallway to my bedroom, not even bothering to take off my dress as I collapse into bed. I pray for sleep to take me again, and I embrace the awaiting darkness, where things don't hurt.

Chapter 4

Present Day: 1999

The day starts off like any other. The alarm clock on my nightstand starts buzzing promptly at six, my eyes still crusted shut from the night's sleep. I reach over and start pushing random buttons on the top of the clock until it stops beeping. I stretch my body out as far as it seems it can go; I have one leg on top of the sheets, and the other is twisted underneath, the pillows lay askew on the bed. I lie there for a few minutes, letting my eyes adjust to the morning light creeping in through a sliver in the navy-blue curtains, making the world seem brighter than what it should be. I allow myself a moment of meditation before I take on a new day. Lying on my back, I take a few deep breaths. It's amusing how you can wake up, a clean slate ahead of you, but your head is still filled with thoughts, to-dos, and problems that need solving from the day before.

I saw a motivational poster hung at our local library once, when I was scouring the digital archives for information on anything that had to do with a 1989 Chevy IROC-Z Camaro or how to make a car run, trying for the life of me to figure out what parts I needed and how the hell I was going to re-build a vehicle, when my vast experience with cars consisted of pumping gas and washing windshields at the Pump and Go. The poster was a black-and-white photograph of a ripple on a pond. In white and red font above the waterline, the poster read, "If you are depressed, you are living in the past. If you are anxious, you are living in the future. If you are at peace, you are living in the present." I found myself standing in the middle of the hallway for God knows how long, just staring at it. Somehow it stuck with me, and I haven't been able to shake its influence since.

It is a harder practice to do than it seems, but every morning when I first wake up, regardless of if I still feel broken from losing Mom or if I am dreading the day ahead of me, I take a moment to lie in bed and just be. Trying to just resonate with the present. Trying to just find my peace.

It works about half the time.

With a final sigh, I crawl out of bed. Still in my black and red plaid pajama bottoms and black tank, my hair falling around my face and shoulders, from the loose knot that barely seems to be containing it after a night's sleep, I stumble toward the kitchen.

I catch my pops sitting outside in the morning stillness. He is rocking ever so slightly on the front porch swing, gaze cast out into the garden in front of him, thoughts far away. I make myself a quick cup of black tea and add a fair amount of honey to it. While I wait for the teabag to steep, I pour the last cup of coffee from the pot on the counter into one of the floral mugs Mom collected, leaving it black, just how Pops prefers it. "I don't need to start my day with frills," he used to say when I was little and asked him about it. Flipping open the lid of the yellow cardboard box I grabbed from Darla's a couple days ago, I shove an oatmeal cookie in my mouth. Trying to use the tip of my tongue and index finger to keep the crumbs from falling out of the corners of my mouth, I swing my favorite soft, black sweater around my shoulders, grab the mugs, and head out front.

"Morning," Pops says, slowly shifting over to make room for me to join him on the swing.

"Hey," I say as I hand him the white-and-lavender mug full of black coffee.

We sit in silence for a minute, lost in the crisp morning air. I wiggle my bare toes so they are tucked under the hem of my pajama pants, trying to keep them warm.

"So, what does the day have in store for you?" he asks without taking his eyes off the horizon.

"Just a regular Tuesday. I told Gary I would open at eight for him this morning. Apparently, he had a date last night with one of the waitresses at The Hitching Post. Once she got off her shift, that is, and he didn't think he'd be up and ready to open."

"Gary had a date? Wow. Times are changing... that or the gals in this town are starting to get desperate."

At this we both start to laugh. I bury my smile into the lip of my mug, taking a sip of hot tea.

Laughter still warming my lips and crinkling my eyes, I ask, "What about you? Are you going to work on that rocking chair commission that the Doyles keep trying to get you to do? They want a couple of them for the front of their shop, don't they?"

Robert and Kenny Doyle own and run the local hardware shop. It's a one-room building that doesn't look big enough to house all the nuts, bolts, and tools that it does. They seem to use every square inch of space available to showcase different items, with the overflow boxed up in plastic bins out back. But among all their inventory, they have always managed to display Pops' woodwork, with his furniture sitting proudly out front and several of his woodland animal carvings at the register.

At the mention of the Doyles, Pop's smile drops from his face.

It has been two years since Mom passed away, and he hasn't even stood in his woodworking shed, let alone placed his callused hands on a piece of pine. The Doyles are kind and loyal. They continue to hold out for Pops to make more creations for their shop, keeping business local. Besides, I know he misses it. He must miss it. I miss it. The smell and the feel of the wood, the joy of the accomplishment in creating something from nothing, the memories of happier times.

"I don't need or want the Doyles' charity," he says with finality, anger lacing his voice.

"That's not what they are trying to –"

His voice grows louder. "I don't care what they are or are not trying to do. It is not their or anyone else's business how I run my life." Then at almost a whisper, he adds, "That time is behind me... It died with her." At this he gets up, placing the mug on the wood railing of our porch, and walks back in the house, screen door clicking shut behind him.

I sit on the swing, absentmindedly rocking it back and forth with my toe, sipping my tea in silence. I wonder at how a mood can change so quickly, and I feel my father's absence in more ways than one.

A few minutes later, I prepare to head out after tossing on my favorite pair of faded blue jeans, which have a hole right above the right knee and a fringe starting along the hems. I don't care that they are threadbare and worn; I will never stop wearing them. They are one of those pairs of jeans that fit just right, hugging me around the hips and flaring out around my black-and-white Converse. I throw on a bra under my black tank, tying my sweater around my waist and readjusting my sloppy bun. I pin my employee name tag on and grab another cookie on my way out the door to work.

It is a calm drive this morning as I cruise down the main stretch of The Highway. No one seems to be out and about. The birds and bunnies are the only ones that appear to be ready to take on the golden and dusty Tuesday morning.

I begin shifting down Carly's gears as I prepare to pull off The Highway, taking a right into the big lot of the Pump and Go.

The Pump and Go is the only gas station in town and the only one for the next thirty miles. Like most of the places in South Brook, it is an original building, but it has been roughly remodeled and refurbished over the years, turning it into a more practical, modernish shop. It sits there, an old, white building with a red stripe running just below the flat roofline, with a single glass swinging front door and windows so small they must be what prison windows would look like. There is a large gravel lot off to the side that houses many of Gary's broken, rusted projects, and just to the left of the main building is a four-car garage where we have two cars sitting up on the lifts, waiting to be serviced.

I pull in and park just outside the glass front door, clicking the emergency brake into place. Shutting off the engine, I step out into the morning light.

The first thing I do is unlock the front door and prop it open; then I flip on the lights and ceiling fan, allowing for some fresh air to begin circulating. I hope it will knock back some of the grease and gasoline smell that is a permanent fixture at the shop. Next, I head over and flip on the activation switch for the gas pumps. We are one of the old-school, full-service stations that comes with the attendant pumping your gas for you and washing your windshield, so we shut off the pumps at night to avoid any kind of mishap.

As I walk across the gravel lot to open the garage doors—hoping to get some air moving in there, too—I spot Sally, our shop cat, lingering outside.

"Hi, girl! Thirsty?" I ask.

The black-and-gray tabby cat mews at me, rubbing up against my jeans, tail wrapping gently around my calf, as I unlock the padlock to the garage. I pull the chain loose and lift the large metal doors. They clank open as the chain rattles with the movement. Sliding the inner door's pulley chain onto a wall hook, I am able to secure the door open without it sliding back down to the ground. Heading inside I grab a discarded bowl from the workbench and start walking back to the office.

I fill up the bowl from the sink in the restroom and place it behind the counter at my feet. Sally comes over and starts lapping it up happily. Gary has made it a point that we are not to feed Sally, that she is a mouser, meaning that he has her wandering the garage area with the sole purpose of catching and eating the mice that would otherwise wreak havoc on the wiring of his project cars. That still doesn't stop me from "accidently" dropping some of the tuna from my sandwich from time to time.

I start to go through my checklist of making sure that everything is in the right order from the day before. Cash is in the register, lotto tickets and cigarettes are stocked, the fridge in the back of the shop is cold and running. I notice a black sedan pull up to one of the pumps. Grabbing my baseball hat from the hook behind the counter, I shove my bun through the opening in the back and head out front.

"Morning," I say as the driver begins to roll down his window. "Fill 'er up for you?"

The driver looking back at me through the halfway rolled-down window is terrifyingly handsome. His dark hair is trim along the sides, but long enough on top that I have to fight the thought of running my fingers through it. His eyes are as blue as the sky in the summer, with a hint of teal running through them; they have the essence of seeing more than the average person. I feel myself blush as he just nods at me, not saying a word, and looking at me with eyes that I feel can peer into my future.

Turning, I try to compose myself as I set the pump to work and go about scrubbing the bugs and dust off his windshield. After the pump clicks off, I place the nozzle back on the handle. As I pass the driver's side window, I tell the stranger, "That'll be twenty dollars, please."

With a look that feels like it is boring into me and a serious expression on his face, he hands me a crisp twenty-dollar bill and a five, "Keep the change," he says. Then promptly rolls up his window and starts his car. I don't even get the chance to say thank you as he pulls out and drives away, leaving a trail of dust that comes up from his tires as the car enters the main road.

I have the sense of being unsettled with a dash of butterflies in my stomach. I head inside to put the cash in the register, trying to shake the lingering feelings left behind from my brief encounter with the stranger.

The rest of the day passes without any more oddities. Because the day is slower than usual, which is saying something, I spend a few hours organizing Gary's tools, hoses, spark plugs, and other random items that litter the garage. It is amazing how he can even find anything in that pigsty.

Just as I finish coiling an extension cord, Gary walks in, looking content. The date must've gone well, I think.

"Hey, Gabriella. Everything go okay this morning?"

"Yup, nothing out of the ordinary," I tell him, mind flashing back to the stranger for a moment. "Couple sales, that's all, so I started tidying up a bit to stay busy."

"Good. Good. That is one of the many reasons I like you; you always have had a good work ethic. 'You've got time to lean, you've got time to clean,'" he states, then promptly cracks himself up with the deep, raspy laugh of someone who has been a smoker for more years than not.

"So, how was the big date?" I ask, surprising myself that I am even a bit curious. Not just at the fact that someone would want to date Gary—there is that—but also that I am fond of him and want him to be happy.

"Oh, it was good." He gives me a yellowed, toothy grin. "Had some beers and shared a plate of poppers. She said that she'd like to see me again next week." At this he wiggled his big, bushy eyebrows, and I can't help but smile and place my hands over my face.

"That's great, Gary. I'm happy for you, truly."

The rest of the day is slow, and I spend most of it staring out at the bus stop across the way and fantasizing about our family trip we had when I was about twelve to the beach. As much as Kasha dreams about running away from this small town, I just want to disappear to someplace beautiful, quiet and calm. The beach was that place when I was younger. I want to be brave enough to get on that bus and go where I can spend the rest of my days listening to the sounds of nature, riding horses again and enjoying the wind on my face. Hopefully, with a man that I am deeply in love with... Roughly pulling myself out of my daydream, I work for a few more hours before Gary tells me to call it a day.

"Go ahead and head home, Gabby. I've got it from here. You're young! Go get that blonde friend of yours and find some fun, maybe take a couple of guys dancing. You'd knock their socks off."

"When I meet a guy worth him losing his socks over, you'll be the first to know, Gary." I smirk at him as I pop open the car door, slide into the driver's seat, and start up and listen to the beautiful roar of my V8. Waving out the window, I pull out onto the highway, letting the wind jostle my hair.

I head to Darla's to go get Kasha from her shift. This time, I'm early, so I park Carly out front. I get out and plant myself at one of the splintering picnic tables, with the afternoon sun beating down through its faded yellow umbrella. Crossing my ankles under the table, my thoughts begin to wander... They are interrupted by Kasha standing next to me, hands on her hips and a smile on her lips.

"Welcome to Darla's, what can I get you?" The sarcasm is sparkling in her eyes.

"Just a tea and side of fries, please."

"No weird combo shake?"

"No, not today. I was thinking we could go walk down to the creek and put our toes in the icy water once you get off. There is something I want to talk to you about."

"Sure, but I don't get off for"—she checks her watch—"another twenty minutes."

"Hence, the order of fries," I say, propping my elbows on the table, chin in hands, giving her my best overexaggerated wink.

Laughing, she turns and heads inside to place my order. I sit there tipping my head back for a minute, allowing the heat of the afternoon sun to hit my face. I remember that I still have my Pump and Go name tag on, so I unpin it and toss it in my bag. I watch a couple of high school kids who look like they are having their first date a few tables down. They seem all giggles and nerves, and the sight makes me smile. The smile dissipates, though, when I think of my encounter today with the good-looking guy in the black sedan, contemplation now forming on my brow. We don't get many newcomers in South Brook, and I can't help wanting to know more about him. *Is he staying in town or just passing through? What is his name?* A sudden clench grips my stomach when I realize I'm hoping to see him again.

Kasha promptly drops my tea and fries off and then carries a couple of shakes over to the teenagers. I check my watch for the time and silently scold myself for being thrown out of orbit by a simple encounter with a good-looking man. Maybe Gary is right. I do need a date.

Chapter 5

The Stranger

I find myself in a dusty small town that reminds me of my home away from home, so many years ago now. It is amazing that I am still able to recall any nostalgia at all for that time in my life.

It is my second day in town and I am still early. I can feel the air is charged with impending change, a tragedy that I know will leave irreparable holes in the lives around me. But that is not my concern. I just go where and when the boss tells me to go. I know that my premature arrival is not a mistake. I am here for a reason. I'm early for a reason.

I am a seeker of sorts, someone who helps those that are lost find their way back, whether they want it or not. It's a decent job, one that feels intrinsically rewarding most days, but there are some days when the weight of it is almost too much to bear. I am constantly burdened by the tragedies and heartbreak of others. It seems so unfair or unjust, and no matter what I do, their pain lingers. It leeches and seeps from them, encompassing me. Their grief becoming contagious, taking a toll on my soul.

I allow myself to be seen when it suits me. When it suits the job. Otherwise, I am content on being invisible, sticking to the shadows. The elderly widow, Mrs. Carver, who runs the B&B I am staying at is blind and that suits me even better. She is kind and trusting, happy to have another soul under her roof. I do my best to be polite, even as I keep my distance.

It is a quaint little place, one of those old Victorian houses, with white shingles for the side paneling and a big wraparound porch. There are a couple handmade rocking chairs out front, branded with a JP on the back, and big wisteria flowers that drape the side of the house with their strong fragrance. A path made of paving stones curves along the side of the driveway. It is both decorative and functional, just how I prefer things. The path leads to a large sycamore tree in front of the house, providing some nice shade for the outdoor table. I think I would like to sit there with my coffee one morning while I am in town. It seems a peaceful place.

I was impressed that I was able to find lodging in such a small town but not surprised that I am the only patron at the moment. I believe that my presence brings Mrs. Carver much joy as I watch her bustle around the kitchen making sure I have fresh biscuits and sweets, trimming flowers from the garden to bring into the house. Her happy sense of purpose makes me feel a bit better about why I am here in South Brook.

As I get ready for the evening, I walk past the old-fashioned full-length mirror that rests in the corner of my room. I haven't been able to look upon myself in what feels like a century. I don't even bother lifting my eyes to where my reflection would be now either. Some things are better just left in the past. Walking to the edge of the frilly floral bed that matches the hanging purple flowers out front, I begin to put on the clothes that I've laid out for the night ahead of me.

Pulling the fitted, black T-shirt over my ruffled head of hair, I can't decide if I should tuck it into my faded blue jeans or leave it out. I opt for the latter. After all this time, it is still an odd feeling to go out dressed so casually. I find the strangeness of informality conflicts with the feeling of comfort and functionality, with comfort taking precedent over the need to always look your professional best. I find the whole thing a bit unnerving and something I don't imagine myself ever fully getting used to. Though I do have to admit not wearing constricting, high-collared shirts on the regular is nice.

As I run my fingers through my hair, my mind drifts back to the girl at the gas station. Gabriella. Her name tag glinted at me in the sun and had me wondering if that is the name that her friends and loved ones call her or if she cuts it down, making it more informal, much like our modern clothing. Gabriella means "God is my strength." The thought causes a shiver to run down my spine. I never allow myself to get attached, it would not be wise doing what I do. But there was something about that girl that has her lingering in my thoughts.

Sliding my feet into some flip-flops, I grab my room key off the end table and head out the door.

It is a nice day in South Brook, and I decide to walk to my destination. I have a few hours to spend before I plan on having dinner and a drink at The Hitching Post, so I take the opportunity to do some exploring. I head south, back toward the gas station, to the little diner that sits just off the main highway. Darla's, I believe it was called.

Strolling up to the entrance, I notice a handwritten chalk sign that says, "Best shakes in town. Will not disappoint." All right, let's see about that, I think to myself. Sitting down at one of the picnic tables out front, one that has seen better days, a young girl with blonde hair braided over the top and loose down her back and heavy black eyeliner approaches me.

Giving me the broadest of smiles, as if she already knows me, she says, "Hey, stranger. What can I get you?"

"I would like to try one of Darla's best shakes, please," I say as I nod toward the sign.

"Of course. You won't regret it. Which flavor, darling?"

Her outgoing persona makes the corner of my mouth lift into a slight smile. I love it when someone is confident in themselves. It is a trait that takes most people a lifetime to master, and others never master it at all. I can see why she is someone of importance. Just another reason why she has been placed in my path on this trip. I strongly believe in everything for a reason and there being no such thing as coincidence.

"Chocolate. Can I get an order of fries to go with it?"

I can't help the rumble in my stomach at the smell of fried food. I can't remember the last time I ate french fries from a diner. Now, I have had gourmet fries, sprinkled with ground rosemary seasoning, that are served with fancy burgers on white linen tablecloths back at the manor. But there is something devilishly decadent about eating greasy fried food.

"Sure thing. Anything else?"

"Nope, that'll do it for now. Thank you."

"Hmmm," she says, plopping down on the bench across from me and tossing her long hair dramatically over one shoulder.

Shocked, I just look at her for a moment. She confidently plops her hands on the table in front of her, interlocking her fingers and giving me what I think is her best serious look, but her eyes are dancing underneath her glare. This makes this situation all that more confusing.

Before I can say anything, she starts. "You may not know me..."

Oh, I know you. I think back on my research before coming here, but I don't say anything.

"But I know of you, and I want to know more," she continues.

I feel my eyebrows fly up. *Is she flirting with me?* I am too shocked to respond, though I suppose the way my mouth slackens slightly might be seen as its own reply.

She goes on. "This is a small town, and a stranger, especially one like you" — *What does that mean?* — "doesn't go unnoticed."

Yes, I think she is definitely flirting with me.

"Gabs told me all about a tall, dark stranger who rolled into town, although we didn't know you were tall, but I will be happy to confirm that information to her later."

Gabs. So that's what her friends call her. I can't help but to let out a laugh that rumbles in my throat. She's not flirting with me; she's collecting data for Gabriella. Somehow that thought makes my insides twist and my chest tighten.

"So, tell me, stranger, what brings you to town?"

"A job. Initially. But I may extend my stay – I like it here. It reminds me of another time in my life."

"Hmmm, mysterious."

I just look at her, forcing her to continue and guide the conversation. Allowing me control without her realizing it.

"A job, huh? And does this job have a name?" she asks, smirk on her lips.

Oh, she is entertaining herself.

"It does," I respond and let the silence stretch between us.

She looks at me for a long moment. Most people are intimidated by me and take my cold, short responses as a dismissal.

Not her. There is something in that that amuses me. I respect this girl's tenacity, but that doesn't mean I am about to sit here and offer up information that does not concern her. Not yet.

"Hmmm," she says again, giving me a quizzical look that has me believing she knows exactly what I am doing. "Okay, fine. But does this stranger at least have a name? As much fun as it is to have a tall, dark, and handsomely mysterious man waltz into our lives, I would much rather refer to you by a name other than 'the stranger.' That could make the situation sound more ominous than is strictly necessary. Wouldn't you agree?"

Raising one eyebrow she waits for me to speak, her eyes twinkling with mirth. I ponder this point for a second.

"John Finnley," I say, "but those who know me call me Jack."

Her mouth curves up into that full smile again, eyes lighting with some knowledge that has me wondering what exactly I have just walked into.

"All right, Jack," she says, letting a beat of silence sit after my name. "I'll be right out with your shake and fries."

With that she gives me a wink and jumps up to fill my order.

What was that? I am supposed to be the one gathering additional information, not the other way around. Surprising myself, though, I find that I am more amused than annoyed. That must stand for something.

I sit in the midday sun, enjoying my chocolate shake and fries. Both the sign and the nosy waitress were right. This is the best shake I've ever had, and it did not disappoint.

Polishing off my last crispy fry from the red plastic basket, I stand up, finding the need to walk again, especially with this added weight I now feel in my gut. Although delicious, the fries and shake sit heavy in my stomach. I am still too early to head further into town, so I decide that now is the perfect time to explore the trail that looks like it wraps around the back of Darla's.

I place a tip under the salt and pepper shakers on the table, crumple the checkered wax paper liner from the basket in my fist, and toss my trash in the covered bin next to the entrance. Taking in a deep breath, I glance up at the road, which looks like it curves up the side of the mountain behind the diner and start walking.

A third of the way up has me wondering at my decision to walk and not drive, but I silently scold myself for becoming lazy and push on. At a point I consider about halfway up the twisting road is a cliff that dangles just slightly over top of the road.

I need a moment to take in the sight and, if I am honest with myself, to catch my breath. The way the boulder hangs halfway over the road, right at a turn, makes for a unique image, one that I could see photographers gobbling up, especially when the sun begins to set to the right of the approaching curve in the road. Turning and taking a couple small steps to the side, I glance down the steep embankment to what looks like a creek down below. The slick decent to the creek is littered with loose, fist-sized rocks and a couple of beer cans. It has always bothered me when people don't care for the beauty around them, disgracing it with their selfishness and trash. I scowl back up to the overhang, and a thought clicks into place. Some local kids must use that overhang to party on, tossing their junk and stones off the side just to watch them fall.

I want to head back, but there is a nagging feeling in my core, telling me I need to keep going. So, with a grunt, that's what I do.

I walk up the continuously sloping road until I get to an interesting turnaround. If I were driving, I would think that the road just ended, but on foot, I notice that there is a narrow dirt road that juts off to the side, right where the cliff is. I walk up to it, and I see that it is wide enough to fit a car through—if the driver knows what they are doing and where the cliff's edge is. When I turn the corner, I can't help but gasp. It is heavenly, the way the steep, rocky incline at my back and the sheer expanse ahead of me offer a panoramic view of the valley. Nothing but rolling hills, dotted with sycamore and oak trees, bushes, and happy, black cattle grazing contently as far as the eye can see. The breathtaking view is silhouetted by an azure sky, so rich in color that the white, fluffy cumulus clouds look cartoonish in contrast.

Awed by the sight, it comes to me that this is God's work. This is peace and comfort that life's beauty is offering me in this moment. It is not just my job, but my duty to give a similar peace and comfort to those that I shepherd. I have been lost for a while now in my duty. I've been told that I am distant and cold when I need to be warmer and more welcoming to others. That advice just seemed to grieve me further. But here, standing on this overlook, I see it now. I feel it, my purpose returning, and the sense that this journey is not just about my future charges, but it is about my path as well.

Filled with a calm that I haven't felt in a long time, I start my trek back down the mountain. I need to get to The Hitching Post by six o'clock, so I can meet Jewel Pinkard.

A few hours later, I blend into the shadows as I sit at a small, wooden table along the back wall of The Hitching Post, sipping my beer, taking in the room. Tonight, I am here to observe, to listen, not to be seen. Even after my revelation earlier today up at the glorious overlook, tonight is about business.

The Hitching Post has been aptly named, having been an old saloon a century ago. It was a place for weary travelers to come water their horses and wet their lips, and it is still an old building made primarily of exposed wood paneling and smelling of pine and whiskey, an appropriate nod to its past.

Just as I begin to wonder if my timing has been miscalculated, Jewel saunters into the tavern. He sits down at an empty stool at the bar, sighing heavily, back hunched. The barkeep, whose name is Winnie, not a name you hear very often, pulls down a mug from a hanging rack above the bar and pours Jewel a beer. There is such familiarity in the action, him not having to order, her grabbing a mug from above the bar instead of one of the stacked pint glasses behind the counter, that it tells me this is a frequent occurrence.

I sit stone-still, ensconced in shadow, my eyes focused and ears trained on the conversation across the bar.

"I heard you had a big date with Gary the mechanic the other night," Pinkard says.

"I wouldn't call it a big date, but it was nice to have someone act like a gentleman for once," Winnie responds with a hint of humor on her face.

"Gabby tells me that he is looking forward to seeing you again. That he was even humming in the shop the other day. What are you doing to that man?"

Gabby... My thoughts begin to drift. They snap back into focus when Winnie lets out a cackle that draws the attention of a few other patrons at the bar.

"What am I doing to him?" Winnie crows, her sun-soaked weathered skin crinkling and strands of her long ash gray hair coming loose from her bun, with her howl. She places her hand on her narrow hips, thumbs hooked behind her rhinestone belt. "Everyone deserves a little love or lust in their lives, Jewel. It keeps us young. You know"—she leans in closer, dropping her voice— "it isn't too late for you to find love again either." At the look that Jewel Pinkard must have shot her way, she adds with a wink, blue eyes dancing, "Or lust."

With another small chuckle she walks away to pour another lager for a customer at the other end of the bar.

Jewel stares into his beer for a while before finishing it off and getting another. Then he has third and fourth, but I can see it does not bring him the joy or numbness he seeks. I can feel the sadness radiating off him. The despair. The heartache. Jewel Pinkard has been spiraling for a long time, but he hasn't hit bottom yet. He is fractured and lost, but not fully broken. Not yet anyway.

Even after my epiphany today, I can't help but think how cruel life can be. To see bad things, hard things, happen to decent people. I have come across life's suffering time and time again. It never gets easier. The injustice of it all makes me wonder where God's mercy is. Although I know deep in my soul my thoughts are unfair, blasphemous even, that His love and mercy show in ways that mortals cannot always see or are able to come to terms with, it is still difficult.

I finish my drink, having seen what I have come to see. Standing slowly and tucking my chair back under the table, I take one more look at my shadowed surroundings. Heart heavy and mind focused on the task I have ahead of me, I duck out the door and head home for the night. It is going to be a long road ahead.

Chapter 6

Gabriella - Darla's

It had been a few days since I spilled the beans to Kasha about the dreamy looking guy in the black sedan. Once she clocked out for the afternoon, we hiked down to the creek near the back entrance of Darla's and talked while wading in the icy water. That moment felt like it threw the next few days into motion. What is that old wives' tale about putting things out into the universe and having them actually manifest? Well, that is exactly how it felt like it happened.

As soon as I told Kasha about my heart skipping a beat when I met the blue-eyed stranger, that's when he started showing up. Everywhere. At least, it felt that way. I would spot him taking a walk through town, then at the hardware store, then at the minimart. It's not like I was looking for him, but he's kind of hard to miss.

Most people just pass through South Brook, with it not really being a destination or a vacation spot. But he seemed to linger.

It was another beautiful day; the sun was out, and the air was blissfully warm. I had the day off but was feeling unusually sluggish. Having a moment of self-pity, I couldn't help chastising myself about only ever dreaming about men and not actually being bold enough to let them know I was interested. I felt as if, at only twenty-five years old, I was destined to be alone for the rest of my life. A crazy cat lady, an old maid. Call it what you want, but that was the ugly idea that managed to worm its way inside my head.

Deciding it was too beautiful a day to mope around in my sweatpants, I knew I needed a pick-me-up. I figured I'd put on real pants and go get a shake. The sugar would give me the buzz I was hoping for and help snap me out of my mood. Besides, Darla's shakes were practically ice cream with a straw. *And the hell with it,* I tell myself, *I am a grown woman and if I want ice cream for breakfast, why not?*

I toss on a pair of jeans and run a brush through my long dark hair, but even that seems to annoy me today. So, I decide to twist it up in a sloppy top knot instead. Not in the mood to drive, I feel the need to walk off my mini storm cloud and begin the trek to the roadside cafe.

It is midmorning and there are only a few other folks already at Darla's, enjoying their diner style breakfasts. I trudge up to the line, not feeling like sitting and waiting for Kasha or Darla to come take my order. I needed my IV of frozen dessert, and I needed it now.

I barely notice the other people in line around me. Eyes pinned on the gravel at my feet, lost in thought, I shuffle forward in the line until it is my time to ask for my usual.

"Good morning, doll. What can I get for you?" Darla asks. Her sun-kissed skin, deeply lined with wrinkles, stands in sharp contrast to her overly done blue eyeshadow and bright red lipstick. Her long greying hair is braided and draped over her right shoulder, resting atop her black apron. My attention is snagged by the amount of jewelry she is wearing. Multiple silver necklaces hang around her neck, a dozen bracelets coat her arms, and nearly every finger is adorned with a ring.

"Chocolate-strawberry combo shake, please. Medium."

"You got it!" She tells me and disappears for a second to fill my cup from the machine.

I pull out a couple dollars and place them on the counter for her to grab when she returns. Handing me my shake, she swipes the money off the old, splintered counter and goes to hand me back my change. I just shake my head and wave my hand, motioning for her to keep it, already savoring the freezing milkshake in my mouth.

I take one step, still looking back at Darla and slam directly into a tall, solid form. My face and milkshake collide hard with the center of a man's chest, sending the shake splattering everywhere. I barely manage to swallow the milkshake that was in my mouth before either choking to death or spewing it all over this random guy.

No, not just any random guy – the guy from the black sedan at the Pump and Go the other day. The one with the dark hair and depthless blue eyes. He stands there now, a shocked look on his face, brown and pink milkshake now soaking his form-fitting white t-shirt.

Mortification envelopes me as I feel flames creeping up my throat to my face, cheeks igniting with a flush that I can feel in my bones. I want nothing more than to die, or at least be anywhere but right here. Right now.

To my utter surprise, his shock melts into amusement. His eyes twinkle, and he starts laughing. Like really laughing.

"Oh, my God," I exclaim, turning to grab some napkins from the counter. I awkwardly start wiping the shake off his shirt, only managing to make it look worse. "I am so sorry!"

He raises his hands up to stop my frantic - and if we are honest, too personal - cleaning frenzy. Still laughing he takes a step back to survey the damage.

"It is quite alright," he tells me.

"Alright?!" I protest, my voice as shaken as I feel. "I ruined your shirt, and now you are cold and covered in a sticky mess!"

"I never liked that shirt much, and honestly, a sticky mess is nothing a shower can't fix."

I feel my cheeks heat anew at his mention of a shower. *Oh, God, Gabby! Get ahold of yourself!*

Grinning like he knows exactly what he's doing, he leans in and says, "But hey, I do know a way for you to make it up to me."

"You do? Please, I am happy to help in anyway. I feel terrible."

Grin widening, he says, "Let me buy you another shake..."

"Wait, what?" I interrupt, dumbfounded.

"Let me buy you another shake. But you have to sit and drink it with me. I am new here and don't really know anyone yet. The company would be nice."

I have to remind myself to close my mouth, when I feel it hanging open in disbelief. I just stare at him, unable to fully grasp what's happening. I start to say something, but no words come out, and I snap my mouth again. Feeling like a fish out of water, gasping for air, I suck my lips in to stop myself from doing it again - thinking that this day absolutely couldn't get any worse.

"What are you drinking," he asks me, then promptly looks down at the mess on his shirt, "Chocolate and..." Here he trails off, noticing the two tones to my once delicious milkshake.

"Strawberry," I manage to say, embarrassment still tightly wrapped around me.

"Right, strawberry." His eyes flicker between mine before he continues, extending his hand. "I'm Jack."

"Gabriella," I reply, instantly aware of how large his hand is in my own. The heat of his skin and the rough callouses on his palm are strangely comforting against my skin, and I feel my face flush all over again.

Jack orders us two more shakes from Darla, who looks beyond amused by the situation unfolding in front of her. I can't help but notice that he orders himself one of my weird combo shakes, as well. When I ask him about it, he says he was here the other day and had the chocolate one—and that he couldn't get it out of his head. Apparently, it was one of the best shakes he's ever had. And the idea of combining two delicious flavors into one? That was just too intriguing to pass up.

As we move to sit down at the picnic table that is set off to the side, near the trailhead and drooping sycamores, I tell him that the reason why Darla's shakes are better than any others is because they're made with whole milk from the Garrison's cows. No added junk. No short cuts. I explain how the Garrison's have a big ranch just outside of South Brook and how they used to let me ride their big Appaloosa, Sundance, growing up. They've also got a small herd of cattle and sell both the milk and beef to town's folk for a steal - which is why Darla's shakes are so insanely good.

"Horses? Is that a passion of yours? Do you still ride?" Jack asks, as we both take another sip.

"I love horses," I tell him. "I feel so free when I ride, or if I am truthful, when I am even just near them. They make me feel both rooted and like I have wings at the same time. But to answer your question, no, I don't get the chance to ride as much anymore. Sundance is retired now. He is just a big, old puppy dog, but I still visit him and bring him a carrot from time to time. Someday, I would love to start riding again. I have always had a dream of riding on the coast... You know, with the sea breeze whipping against my face and the sound of waves crashing, blending with the pounding of hooves on the sand.

Kasha, my best friend, you might have seen her around. She works here. Long blonde hair–"

"And a lot of spice?" he asks.

I laugh, "That's her."

Smiling he says, "Yeah, I know exactly who you are talking about."

"So, Kasha, she dreams of 'dusting this dusty town off our boots and having an adventure.' Well, her aspirations have always been larger than my own. Don't get me wrong – I would love to move on, strike out on my own, so to say. But I hate big cities and crowded towns. I love the small-town feel, wide open spaces. They give me comfort. Peace. But I just want to be in a different small town. Not the one I grew up in, if that makes any sense."

Jack nods as he sucks in another sip of shake, his cheeks hollowing with the effort. My eyes are momentarily drawn to his lips as he licks the ice cream off of them. I take a gulp of air, before I continue. "When I was a young girl, around twelve, my parents took me to the coast. We went to Disneyland, but I just found it loud and too much... Well, anyway, on the way back home to South Brook, my pops decided to take the scenic route up the coast. That's what really stayed with me... not the rides or the crowds, but the ocean. It left such a deep impression on me that I know that is where I want to spend the rest of my life. It has been calling to me ever since. I am just not sure when I will ever get there."

"Yes," he says nodding thoughtfully. "I do know what you mean about the freedom horses can give you." I look at him quizzically, and he continues, "I actually have a bunch of horses on a ranch along the central coast. It is magical... and that dream of yours? You should absolutely pursue it. Riding wild and free with nothing but hills and sea around... it's like becoming part of something bigger. An extension of both mother nature and the animal beneath you. There is no feeling quite like it." Then he looks at me with a quiet curiosity, "But what do you mean that you are not sure when you will ever get there?"

After staring at this man who seems like he fell from Heaven or clawed his way directly out of one of my dreams, I can't help but wonder if fate is toying with me... or if this is somehow real. He seems too good to be true.

"My... my mom passed away not that long ago," I say softly, my voice catching. "And Pops is taking it really hard. I mean... of course he is, and I completely understand. But..." I hesitate, swallowing the lump in my throat. "I just feel like I can't leave him. Not yet, anyway. He still needs me..." I trail off for a second and feel flustered by my unusual openness with this man I just met. Trying to shift gears and have him take the wheel for a bit, I ask, "If you've got a ranch on the coast... what brings you to South Brook?"

"I came for work," he says. I intentionally remain quiet, forcing him to fill the silent void. "I sort of help lost things find their way home," he adds a little cryptically. "So, it takes me on the road sometimes. Anyway, that was what brought me here. But I found myself loving South Brook. It reminds me of another time. I love the small-town feel, too. Plus, these shakes?" He chuckles, lifting his cup. "They're killer." And we both start laughing. "But in all honesty, although work is what brought me here, I am thinking of sticking around a bit longer."

"Really? What about the ranch?"

"Oh, it will be fine for a while. Besides..." He flicks his eyes up to mine, his shy, charming smile making my insides twist. "I find myself enjoying the company."

He proceeds to tell me a bit about his ranch and giant Great Dane named Sam, who's blissfully unaware of his size. We fall into easy conversation, laughing and swapping stories like old friends – or maybe something more. There's a schoolyard quality to it, light and warm, full of teasing banter and shy glances.

Eventually, he asks if I am seeing anyone.

I snort. "Nope. I've officially sworn off local men."

He raises an eyebrow, clearly amused. "Oh yeah?"

"Yeah. After a string of terrible experiences – from dirt-caked fingernails on a first date to guys who chew with their mouths open – I decided I'd rather do life with Kasha than suffer through that again."

He laughs, a low, genuine sound. "Honestly? I don't blame you."

We sit in the sun on the worn wooden bench, not bothering to raise the yellow umbrella when the sun is at its peak. I welcome the warmth on my face and shoulders, marveling at how my day has taken a complete one-eighty-degree turn.

At some point, I realize our milkshakes have been gone for a while... but I don't want this to be the end. I find myself wanting to see him again. The thought alone has my heart racing, pounding so hard in my chest I wonder if he can hear it's thump-thump-thump echoing between us. *Just say something, Gabby. Isn't this exactly what you were bitching about earlier? Never being bold enough to say what you want.*

"So…" I begin, my nerves swelling in my throat, threatening to choke off my words before they can leave my mouth. "There is this little joint up the road called Annie's. They serve wine and flatbread pizza, and they host live music every Saturday night. Anyway, Kasha and I usually go dancing. If you would like to come… it is usually a good time."

"I would love that," he says, his eyes gleaming with quiet amusement – probably at how obviously nervous I am. "What time should I be there?"

"Band starts at seven."

"Great. See you tomorrow."

"See you tomorrow… and thanks for the shake."

I can't help the smile, or blush, that spreads across my face as I stand and head home. At the edge of the lot, I glance back to find Jack still watching me. I give him a small, awkward wave, then spin back around quickly – only to nearly trip over my own two feet, a full, stupid grin now stretched across my face.

Chapter 7

Annie's Place

Annie's is a small contemporary pizza and wine house that makes decadent, wood-fire grilled pizzas, using high quality ingredients, and serves the best, local California wines. And every Saturday night, Annie's has a live band come in and play. Most often the band is a local one, made up of either high school kids trying to make it big, using the small stage as practice and to get noticed, or dusty regulars who have been playing at Annie's since they, too, were in high school. On the rare occasion, an out-of-town group will ramble in, on their way through town to a bigger, more promising gig either south in L.A. or north in San Francisco. The regulars have taken to calling those nights "pop-up nights" because you never know what type of music will pop up. The groups that come in and perform for free drinks, tips, exposure, or just for the fun of it.

Kasha and I have made it a habit to attend pop-up nights, and we haven't missed a Saturday evening if it could be helped. Tonight is no exception.

Located on the far end of town, out past the hospital, Annie's is where South Brook's younger crowd hangs out. It is a small, brick building with red clay roofing shingles and a solid oak door with matching shutters that hang next to the tiny arched windows. The building is covered in white, smoothed-out stucco that is cracking and flaking in chunks, exposing some of the red bricks and adding to its classic Californian Mission vibe. Annie even has an old, tarnished mission bell hanging inside its campanile, that she had custom built when she bought the joint.

Inside, it utilizes its small space well. The walls are made of fully exposed bricks, the original structure of the building, with dark-stained oak furniture. As you enter, the bar sits to your right. The bar top is a pewter counter that looks like it has been beaten with a ball peen hammer in random places. It has big rivets along the edge, and no one seems to know if they are functional, holding the bar in place, or if they are purely decorative. Built into the brick wall, behind the bar, is the enclave for the woodfire brick pizza oven. Having the oven so close to the front of the building only adds to the permanent smell of pizza cooking that lofts from Annie's and into the parking lot on a regular basis. The rest of the small space is filled with oak tables and chairs and a dainty stage up against the far back wall.

Annie's is owned by a couple of our locals, Annie Howard and her husband, James. The Howards are obsessed with everything western and have fully embraced living in a small town, bringing their love for the Wild West with them. They have incorporated their passion into the décor and ambiance of Annie's, covering the bar in Annie Oakley and Jesse James memorabilia, from the posters of the outlaws, horses, and steam engine trains to stiff lassos hanging from the walls to the 1873 Winchester full-lever action rifle that hangs above the stage. Every time Kasha and I plan on going to Annie's, we can't help the image that comes into our thoughts of Annie Oakley shooting her gun off the back of a horse. Annie Howard and Annie Oakley have begun to blur together, and that is something I don't think the modern Annie minds one bit.

I stand in my tiny room trying to decide what to wear for the night. I check my thin, silver watch for the time. I have thirty minutes to figure it out and get over to Kasha's to pick her up. The bands usually start at seven, and if you aren't there promptly, it's tough to get in.

South Brook may be a small town, but when there's something to do, it seems like the whole place shows up. There is extra anticipation for tonight, as Annie's has a pop-up band called The Haunting slotted to play this evening. Apparently, they are on their way up the coast to San Jose, planning on opening for one of those large music festivals where there are multiple stages and shows all going on at the same time. Word has it that they are primarily playing classic rock covers, with a few originals thrown in there for exposure. The night is always extra fun when the band isn't our usual fare.

I opt for my go to form fitting bootcut jeans, leather boots, and a black tube top. I quickly latch my silver chain choker around my throat, feeling like it gives me an edge, and the added confidence helps. I run a brush through my long, dark hair, deciding to wear it down and free tonight.

As I check and touch up my eyeliner in my antique vanity mirror, I still can't manage to get the guy from the black sedan out of my head. Jack. His twinkling sea blue eyes, broad shoulders and calm demeaner. I've never met a man who can send butterflies to my stomach and make my heart race with just a look. Of course he is probably the most beautiful man I have seen, but it – he – seems so much more than that. His sense of humor is so much like my own and his presence gives me such peace, that I feel enveloped in a warm, calm blanket whenever I am with him. Our time at Darla's went by in a blink of an eye and I felt like I could spend forever with him. Like he is the only person, other than Kasha, that truly seems to get me. I shake my head, wondering at how it is possible that I am tumbling so hard, so fast.

Kasha told me how he came into the diner the other day, and how Kasha, being Kasha, grilled him.

The warm glow of memory washes over me, transporting me to that moment:

"It's on your behalf," she claimed.

I just sat there with my toes in the icy creek and rolled my eyes at her.

"Please tell me how you digging for details on him was for me and not just for your own nosy benefit?" I asked.

"Because, girl, friends are all about helping the other one get what they need." I shot her a look out of the corner of my eye as she continued. "Not what they want, although that wouldn't hurt. But, yes, I said what they need. You need a man like I need to get away."

Laughing and using my toes to splash her with some of the chilly water, I can't help but say, "I promised you already that we'll take our drive to the coast next summer. I just need to save a bit more before we can go. We'll even drive past that creepy abandoned cliff mansion that you haven't stopped gabbing about for the last couple years, the one that sits on the coastal overhang with the lighthouse."

Squeals and clapping erupted from Kasha, and I found myself both cringing and smiling at her overexcitement.

"I know, I know," she said after spotting my reaction. "I am stupid excited about it; in case you couldn't tell. But that is exactly why I now must find you a man. Even if it's just one date or one evening, a deal is a deal. And the clock has started ticking with our impending trip. Girl, you are pickier than a vegetarian cat."

I snort at this because Kasha's terrible analogies will never cease to surprise me.

"I mean, you won't go near any of the local guys—for which I don't blame you," she adds quickly, "so when you told me about this mysterious guy who pulled into the gas station, the one you couldn't shake thoughts of, did you seriously expect me to not investigate? Because that would hurt my feelings if it was the case." As Kasha says this, she clutches her heart in a dramatic display, pulling a smile from my lips as I feel my heart start to pound just thinking about him again.

She went on to tell me about their encounter. How she invited herself to sit down and began to question him like the detective she has always wanted to be in one of those crime shows she loves.

"He told me that his name is John Finnley, but those who know him call him Jack. He is staying at Mrs. Carver's until the job he is on calls him home. But man, Gabs, this guy is as equally good-looking as he is tight-lipped. And he is tight-lipped as a stone. Although I did notice the two of you seemed to really get on the other day at Darla's. I have never seen you sit and talk to someone for so long, let alone laugh. He actually had you laughing, girl. That has to count for something."

I sat there for a second trying to imagine a tight-lipped stone, and feeling my cheeks heat recalling our afternoon together, before she went on. "What could it hurt? I look at the situation resulting in a few different outcomes." At this she started ticking off her fingers. "One, absolutely nothing comes from it other than some eye candy for a bit while he's in town. Two, you get a hot date out of it, and I have fulfilled my end of the friendship bargain, even in the most minute of ways. Or three—and definitely my favorite that I am secretly crossing all my fingers and toes for—is that you two fall madly in love, and he becomes our ticket out of this small, dusty town. You were the one that told me he has a house near the coast. I mean, seriously. This has to be kismet."

"Okay, I surrender," I said, tossing my hands up in the air, "but I am not seeking a date with him. Whatever is meant to be will be. Okay?" As I said it, I tried to force her to make eye contact with me, though she avoided it rather successfully.

"Okay, okay! No forcing." At a near mumble she added, "Maybe just some appropriately timed nudging."

I splashed her more forcefully this time, and we both burst into laughter with the feeling of giddiness and possibilities.

Back in my room, I smile at the recent memory. I shove my driver's license and some cash into the back pocket of my jeans. The last thing I want to be thinking of tonight is dancing with my purse or worrying about some ass stealing it. Then I head out the door.

We pull into Annie's at twenty to seven, and the parking lot is already pretty full. I shut off the ignition and clip my car key onto one of my beltloops, shoving the tip of the key into my pocket to keep it from swinging around when I dance.

Kasha and I stride up to the front door like we are Romy and Michele heading to our high school reunion. I toss my long hair over my shoulder, owning every step I take. Tonight is going to be memorable. You can feel the buzz in the air already.

Walking right up to the bar, Kasha orders us each a glass of wine and a couple of over sliced pizzas as I find us a table off to the side. She comes over, two chilled glasses of white wine in her hands that seem fuller than even a nine-ounce pour.

"Thanks," I say before taking a long, delicious sip. We will need both the buzz from the wine and energy from the food if we plan on dancing as much as I think we will tonight.

We sit at our little table enjoying our wine and snacks, watching others stroll around the bar and the band set up on the little stage that sits against the back wall of the joint.

The stage is just big enough to be considered a stage. It is only six inches off the ground and wide enough to hold a drum set and maybe three people. They are running cords, adjusting the microphone stand, and checking the settings on the amps and the sound system.

The light starts to ebb outside as dusk sets in, casting the interior of Annie's in more of a shadowed appearance than usual. The only light inside is dim and is coming from some yellow, low-hanging fixtures throughout the bar. Kasha and I finish our wine and pizza just as the band opens with their first song of the evening.

We keep to ourselves, moving in and around the crowd until we find a little space on the dance floor. Annie has moved the tables and chairs into the main room, making seating tighter in there but allowing space for people to dance the night away near the stage.

After a few good classic covers that get the audience loosened up, The Haunting launches into one of my favorites, "Black Velvet" by Alannah Myles. Her sexy, raspy voice never fails to get me moving, and the front woman with the black, punk-style bob haircut is nailing it.

Closing my eyes, I let the music fully take over, feeling every beat and riff in my core. In that moment there is no one else in the bar, just me, Kasha, and the music. I don't need to see her to know she is moving wildly next to me on the dance floor.

My feet and hips move of their own accord, following the rhythm of the band. My hair swings loose and free down the center of my back, countering the movement of my waist. I twist and raise my hands above my head, weaving my body back and forth, embracing the freedom that the night has offered me into my heart. I open my chest and soul to the magic of the music, feeling like I can take on anything. Be anything. Go anywhere.

With the smell of sweat, alcohol, and pizza, the air sits heavy inside Annie's. It has the sense of too many bodies moving in an enclosed space, and the tiny windows and open front door don't offer the fresh air movement needed to take a full deep breath. But it is the music and the drinks and the thick air that leads to the drugged state that the evening has begun to possess. Even with all the energy circulating throughout the small room, it is one of those moments that you feel deep in your bones. A moment that, even if you grow old and forgetful, stays with you—because it's not just a memory, but a feeling that lingers beyond a lifetime.

As I spin, swinging my hips in a low, slow sway that matches the crescendo, I feel the presence of eyes on me. Opening my eyes and turning to the sense of a supernatural pull, I lock eyes with Jack as he walks in the door. He has stopped mid-step, at the entrance of Annie's. My heart seizes for a split second, stomach tightening, and my hands suddenly feel both jittery and sweaty.

Jack's devilishly handsome blue eyes are boring into mine, as if he can see things that no one else can. His shoulders are broad and solid under his sculpted black tee. His chest is well formed, and my eyes skim down his torso to his flat stomach, which disappears into the top of his very well-fitting jeans. A gasp gets stuck in my throat, and I feel my cheeks flame as I realize that I've been staring.

Spinning around I head over to Kasha, who is moving freely on the dance floor. Grabbing her elbow, I whisper in her ear, "Jack just walked in."

"What?!" she exclaims and immediately starts looking around.

"Be cool, Kash. I'm going to go get some water."

Feeling my heart pound and knowing it is not from the dancing, I head up to the bar to get a glass of water.

Annie hands me two glasses of water. I thank her just as Jack appears at my side.

"Hey. Gabriella." he says in such a nonchalant way that still seems to make my stomach flip.

"Hey," I manage to get out. My voice barely above the sound of the music.

Jack reaches a hand forward in invitation and I instinctively set the waters back down on the bar, placing my hand in his large, callused palm.

He pulls me in close, his eyes never leaving mine, as we sway and move to the music, as one. Our bodies are pressed together so tightly that I can feel his warmth radiating off of him, his chest falling and rising with his breathing. Neither of us saying a word and holding each other's gaze, it feels like we have lived a century in each other's arms.

Once the song stops, his arms hesitantly drop away from me and he takes a respectful step back, looking just as thrown by our connection as I am.

"So, Kasha told me you spoke at Darla's. More officially this time, if you can call it that," I awkwardly try to fill the silent void building between us, now that we stopped dancing.

"Ha. You can say that. She's a force to be reckoned with, that one," he says with the slightest hint of humor behind his eyes.

"That she is," I say and can't help my smile. "We... Kasha and I that is..." I stammer, nerves are beginning to take over. "Well, we usually head up to The Hook after Annie's on Saturday night."

At Jack's blank look, I try to clarify, my heart beginning to race. "It has always been kind of our secret hang out. It is a tiny dirt turn off at the top of Hill Canyon. It has incredible panoramic views of the valley below and it is just beautiful at night with all the stars and not a manmade light to be seen. Not many people go up there as it is hard to get to. Most folks that want a secluded spot usually stop just before it at a place we call The Bird's Nest. That's a big rock overhang..." Feeling like I am rambling, my mouth going dry I flush and try to recover. "Anyway... It would be cool if you wanted to follow us up there after. It would be a proper introduction to our little town."

"That does sound beautiful." Then after a beat, he continues, "I would love that. Thank you, Gabriella."

I love the sound of my name on his lips. The silence stretches between us for a moment, and I chew on my bottom lip before saying, "Well, I should probably get back to Kash..."

"Yeah, maybe save another dance for me, though" he says, "if your dance card isn't too full yet."

Save another dance? My dance card? This guy seems as old-fashioned as he is good-looking.

"Sure." I manage to get out as I turn and head back toward Kasha, heart pounding, cheeks flushing.

Walking back to the dance floor I can't help myself, the giddiness in my center is too strong and it forces a smile onto my lips, as I take one more look over my right shoulder at Jack.

I suddenly have the twin urges to have another glass of wine and the need to sober up all at once.

Kasha and I have another glass of wine each and dance the night away. I am constantly glancing around for Jack but haven't spotted him since we shared our dance. I am a mess of nerves and annoyance.

"You sure you saw him and didn't just imagine him?" Kasha asks when my distracted state is too much to ignore.

"Yes, we danced. God, that was hot. Then we talked and I told him about The Hook. He asked me to hold another dance for him, like he was some dude from a century ago and we were at a ball. He said he'll follow us up there tonight to check it out. But I haven't seen him since."

"And you're really looking, too," Kasha remarks, and I gently slug her on the shoulder. "Maybe he had to step out early for a work thing or wanted to get a head start on the way up to The Hook? He did promise that we would all meet up there."

"He said he'd follow us," I correct her.

"Whatever. It was a fun night regardless. You want to get out of here? I'm not quite ready to go home yet, though."

"Yeah, okay. Neither am I. Let's just go up and chill at The Hook for a bit, like we planned. Who knows, you may be right, and he will be waiting for us."

We down the rest of our wine and grab our sweaters off the backs of the chairs at our table and head out the door. I am determined not to let Jack's disappearance ruin my night. The Haunting were a great cover band, dancing was freeing, and the evening was a lot of fun. Some dude's brooding manner and lack of presence have no place in my head tonight. None. As much as I try not to admit the effect this guy is having on me, I can't shake the feeling that we're on the cusp of something big... that he's at the center of it.

Chapter 8

Hill Canyon

Kasha and I pull out onto the highway, windows ajar and music up. We are determined not to allow the euphoria of the night to escape, and we grasp on to the ecstasy that the music gives us. I will not allow some random guy to throw off my equilibrium, no matter how good-looking he may be. No matter how much of a magnetic connection I feel when I am around him. No matter how desperate I may be for love. For a distraction.

I make the left turn off the highway, followed by an immediate right wrapping us around the back of Darla's as we begin the climb up Hill Canyon. The night is clear, with the stars sparkling and the moon large and full, illuminating the road ahead of us. The air is crisp and cool on our faces through the cracked windows. It is refreshing after dancing in the stuffy back room of Annie's.

I feel like an extension of the car, hands tight on the wheel, shifting and pumping the clutch seamlessly as I hug the corners of the road. Climbing and turning. Feeling free and alive. Using the hand crank on the door, Kasha rolls down her window further and leans her torso through it. She sticks her head and arms out, wind whipping her hair back, eyes closed, as she hoots at the night. Laughing at her, I punch the accelerator coming out of another turn.

I slow the car just slightly as we approach The Birds' Nest. When I do, time seems to slow down, everything becoming hyper-focused. I hear the Red Hot Chili Peppers singing their new hit, "Californication," on the stereo. I see Kasha embracing the night through the open window, hair slashing across her smiling face. I feel the sweat bead between my palms and the steering wheel, making things slick.

As if in slow motion, my gaze lifts up and to the left, and I make eye contact with a teenage boy on the cliff above us. His eyes are wide in shock, mouth open as if in mid-yell, hand reaching forward. I notice the beer bottle flying through the night sky, and that's when everything speeds up. There is a loud crash as the bottle shatters my windshield. I jump, heart racing, hands and feet tingling from the rush of fear and adrenaline. I hear Kasha scream. There is a big spiderweb in the glass from where the bottle made contact, and thick, foaming beer is now coating the windshield. I can't see anything. I'm shaking too hard to hit the wipers, my hands not wanting to respond to the simple request. Screeching on the brakes, I desperately try to stop the car. I know there is a corner coming up that leads to a drop-off, but I can't see it. I frantically jerk the wheel to the left, trying to avoid the edge.

I feel it first. The car tips forward, and there is a sense of empty space below me. My seat belt locks forcefully against my stomach and collarbone as we hit hard, and I get the feeling of us rolling forward. We flip over and over. There is a mess of dirt, sticks, stones, and broken glass flying throughout the cab. I close my eyes against the debris. I can't tell if I'm screaming or even holding onto the wheel. All I feel is the lump in my throat and the pounding in my chest. My body violently tries to slide around the car, and my seat belt is digging into my skin.

This can't be happening. This is just a dream. I will wake up. I need to wake up. *Wake up!* I can't tell where the car is, what is happening. I am completely disoriented.

There is a final, hard impact as the car slams into one of the oak trees at the bottom of the ravine. I fly forward and feel my head collide hard with the steering wheel, then violently slam back into my seat.

We've stopped. I think we've stopped, but I feel spun and confused. My neck and head hurt.

My vision starts flickering in and out. Faded edges of my sight are narrowing and expanding. Narrowing and expanding. I feel sick to my stomach. My head feels hot and wet. It feels like there is water running down my face. *Why is there water?*

I see Kasha next to me in the passenger seat. *What is that added darkness coating everything? Is that blood?* There is so much of it. Everywhere. Kasha's eyes are closed, and there are dark splotches across her face and neck. Her hair is matted and stuck to the side of her face. Her head rests on her shoulder, facing me. She looks asleep. Peaceful. Face and limbs relaxed.

I try to reach for her but moving feels hard and sluggish. *Why is there blood? No, it must be water from the creek. That's why I'm wet. Why are we at the creek?* I have the vague recollection of crashing. *I think we crashed... I don't understand.*

It is so dark. I feel like I can't see anything. Everything keeps going black. There are no streetlights on Hill Canyon. I glance up through the shattered window, and the motion makes my eyes hurt. Now the moon is bright, making the night too bright as well. *Why is it so bright?* It hurts my eyes, so I try to squint and see that there is dirt covering the dash. *Why is there dirt in the car? We have to get out of the car. Get out. Get out!*

"Kasha! Kasha!" I try to shout. But it only sounds like a rasp to my own ears, like I am underwater and there is a slight, constant ringing sound. She doesn't respond. I try to reach for her, to shake her. To wake her. I touch the sleeve of her shirt, but I feel so weak. Moving is hard. She doesn't wake up. *Why is moving so difficult?* I am so tired. I just want to go to sleep.

When my vision comes to me again, it has blurry, wobbling edges. I have the sense of moving and being still at the same time, like sitting on a ship in the sea. I feel sick and can't seem to remember where I am. I spot Kasha and Jack standing in the clearing next to the creek. They look like they are talking, but when they notice that I'm looking at them, they stop and begin to come toward me. The pounding in my head makes it hard to focus. *I thought Kasha was in the car... What is Jack doing here? Annie's... Dancing... We drove to The Hook.* Things are coming back to me in snippets, but it is difficult to focus.

I hear sirens, and there are red and blue flashing lights reflecting off the trees. The light and sound make my head hurt worse. I can still see the light pricks and pulsing behind my closed eyelids. *Please stop*, I think. I just want it to stop. *Make it stop!*

Someone is talking. I think they are asking me questions, but I can't understand what they are saying. My fluttering eyelids are pried open one at a time, and the light makes everything worse. I want to scream, but I can't seem to make my voice work. I feel a solid object shoved down my throat, and I want to gag. There is more talking. I don't understand. *Why can't I understand what they are saying?* Then a hard collar is strapped around my neck, and I can't turn to look at Kasha. *Where's Kasha? She was in the car with me. No, she was outside with Jack. I am so confused.* I want to vomit, but I have this thing shoved down my throat.

I have the sense of being lifted up. I hear doors slamming, but the sound feels far away.

Then the world goes blissfully dark again. Silence. Peace. Calm envelopes me.

The next thing I know, I am standing outside the car. I don't know how I got here. *Is this a dream?* The edges of the forest around me are fuzzy. *This must be a dream,* I think, but it feels so real. My boots are standing in the foliage that grows along the stones in the trickling water. It is a clear night, and I can see some stars winking through the branches of the trees above our heads. The night sounds seem loud, in stereo within my head. I hear the swaying grass, the bubbling stream, crickets and owls chirping and hooting far off in the night. There is the slight sound of sirens pulling away in the distance. *Why are there sirens?*

But in an instant, I forget the sirens and all my questions. All I feel is confusion and anger. The night is cold and dark and noisy. I am consumed by the cold and the dark, the noise overwhelming me. I feel dizzy. *Why am I dizzy?* I grab the side of my head to try to make the world stop spinning.

I see my car crumpled and resting up against a tree, reflective markers around it and tracing the way up the hill, but the scene doesn't seem to register. All I can feel is cold rage and frustration. I have the strong urge to boil over. I need to release this steam.

Ignoring the shocked and sorrowful look on Kasha's face, I storm up to Jack. One mission is on my mind, and vexation seems to consume me in a way I don't fully comprehend.

"You just fucking disappeared!" I shout at him, shoving him in the chest. "No goodbye, no note with Annie. Just gone, so what was I supposed to think?"

"I would never intentionally hurt you, and I didn't mean to make you feel abandoned. It was work-related, and I didn't have a choice. When I am called, I have to go. Sometimes suddenly and without warning."

"So suddenly that you just vanish?" I ask, incredulously. "We were dancing, having a good time. We were supposed to meet... I don't... I don't understand..." I trail off, emotion welling up and lodging in my throat.

Jack just looks at me with those teal blue eyes that seem to bore into my soul, but this time all I see in them is hurt. I will not be thought of with pity, and as I feel the storm continue to rise in me, I turn and stalk away.

After a few steps I start to feel the shame of my angry outburst. Shame, not just for being abandoned when Jack seems to have made it clear that he did not have much of a say in the matter, but also for my instant fury. I don't want to be my father, so lost in myself that I lash out at those trying to offer me a lifeline, showing wrath over something as simple as an early and unexpected departure. *Why am I so incensed? This is not like me.*

My pace slows for just a second, and that is when I feel his hand firmly grasp my wrist. He must have launched into stride immediately after I started walking away from him.

Taking advantage of my shock he spins me toward him with ease, and I find myself encased in his strong arms. Before I even fully register what is happening, he pulls my hand up to his mouth. His lips press delicately to the inside of my wrist, where it meets the palm of my hand. For one beat. Two beats. I can feel his desperation in the kiss, the closeness of our bodies, his eagerness to never let go. I find myself melting into it, anger and hurt vanishing with every passing heartbeat.

"Where did you possibly need to be that was more important?" I ask at a near whisper.

His words come light against my skin, "Here. With you."

Chapter 9

The Aftermath

I awaken in a hospital bed. The world is fuzzy, as if I'm in a hazy dream. All my senses are glazed over and muffled. I try to move, to look around, but my body is unable to respond to my thoughts. I feel like my head is going to split in two, and it takes nearly all my effort, but I manage to successfully open one of my eyes a crack. There is a big, tightly wrapped cotton bandage that covers my head and is secured under my chin, pressing my left eyelid down, limiting its mobility even more.

Everything feels tight and swollen. I find my head wedged into the center of a fluffy pillow, and the hospital blankets are tucked snugly around my body. It is hard to breathe, and I am unable to move my neck or turn my head.

I try my best to glance around, taking in my surroundings. There are computer screens with wires coming out of them next to my bed. Moving lines and flashing lights dance across the screens, waving as much as Kasha and I had done on Annie's dance floor. I hear slight beeps and pulses in the background. I see my pops asleep in the low chair next to me. He is leaning to one side, slumped in the chair, head resting in his big hand. His clothes are rumpled, and his hair is disheveled, going up and out in all directions. There is a hint of whiskers on his face, like he hasn't shaved in days, and dark shadows under his closed eyes. I notice that he looks sober, even in his distressed state. I try to call to him, to tell him I am sorry, but there is something over my mouth and nose, emitting cool air every time I take a breath. Even still, under the contraption, my mouth and throat won't form the sounds I am trying to make.

I feel so heavy and so very tired. I just want to sleep. Slowly and gently, my eyelids begin to fall, and I allow the serenity of unconsciousness to take me away. My pops draped across the chair is the last thing I see before the darkness envelops me.

Not knowing how long I was asleep, I delicately peel open my one uncovered eye again, to the sounds of people talking.

"Oh good, she is awake. Thank God! Gabby, can you hear me?"

I try to focus. My pops is there talking to Gary. Upon seeing my eye flutter open, they both quickly rush to the side of my bed. My pops grasping my bandaged hand so tightly, I can feel the needles from the IV pressing further into the back of my hand.

I try to make a sound, but nothing comes out other than a gurgle rasp that is muffled from the tube in my throat. Alarms start beeping and before I know it Pops and Gary are no longer in my line of vision. I am surrounded by nurses and doctors in teal scrubs, calmly but rapidly pushing buttons, checking my vitals and slowly removing the uncomfortable piece of plastic from my mouth. I gag as it is pulled up and out of my throat, followed by a gasp of air as a nurse places a mask over my nose and mouth. I take another deep breath, easier this time.

The nurses step away, telling my pops that I am stable for the time being, but that I may be exhausted and fall back to sleep. Don't be surprised—just enjoy this huge win.

I glance over and both Gary and my pops have tears streaming down their whiskered faces. As I continue to struggle taking in breath, drawing my attention to how much my throat hurts.

No one says anything for a moment, my pops appearing to be too choked up to speak. Gary seems to notice the new swell of emotion from Pops and takes the lead.

"Gabby, darling. We are so grateful and relieved to see you awake. Your pops here has been keeping me updated on your condition and hasn't left your side... your side since..." here he chokes down a silent sob and quickly clears his throat and changes the direction of the conversation. "Well, that is – I was just telling your pops here, that you will always have a place at The Pump and Go. Please take as long as you need to recover. Absolutely no rush, my dear. If you need an advance, I am happy to do that. We all – I – just want to see you back up on your feet again. The station will be there for when you are ready."

I try to nod, my throat feeling too raw to speak, but only manage a blink. Thankful for Gary's love and patience.

"Well, I should get going and let you visit with your pops and get some rest. It was, it was good seeing you, Gabby. You take care now," Gary says, clearing his throat a final time before striding out of the room.

I want to tell my pops that I am sorry, again... but I am suddenly so tired. He must sense what I want to convey, because he tells me it is ok. That everything is ok. I give a slight nod as I feel my head drift to the side and my hand slip from the oxygen mask, eyelids growing heavy. I try to fight it, but the sleep that comes is too strong.

I'm back at home, lying in my bed, sunlight pouring in through my windows. I roll over, letting it wash me in its warmth and light. Finally, though, I groan and drag myself out from under my comfortable covers to get dressed for the day. It's Thursday, and I need to be at work in a couple hours, but it takes me longer to get there now that I don't have Carly.

There are many memories and chunks of time that seem to be missing, but I am hopeful that it will get better with time. I barley recall the accident, and everything after is pretty much an open void. I can't recall how long it has been since I was in the hospital or even being discharged afterwards. It is like a giant time hop that leaves me disoriented and scared. I read once, though, that amnesia can be temporary after head trauma, so I am trying to focus on that and not on the fact that I have these large black holes in my memory. Even with all that,

I find it important to get back to my routine. That much seems right.

I kick my legs through my jeans and wiggle them up and over my hips. Then I grab one of my old band T-shirts and slide it over my bra and wrap my long hair into a messy knot at the back of my head. I haven't been able to look at myself in the mirror since my accident. I don't want to see the puckered, pink scar that runs across my brow, forcing my left eyelid to droop. Reaching my fingers up to delicately touch it, my heart sinks slightly. I pop my baseball cap on, pulling my knot through the back, and head out into the kitchen.

I start the water to boil on the stove for tea and rummage through the cupboards to find something to eat. *When did we stop stocking food? I should really go shopping.* The teapot begins to whistle, and I pull it off the burner and fill my cup, letting the boiling water soak the tea bag on the bottom, causing the liquid to turn a honeyed brown. Sliding the coffee pot off the maker, I pour the last cup of coffee into a mug for Pops. Two mugs in hand, I bump the screen door with my backside and head out onto the porch.

Pops is sitting on the swing, gaze straight ahead.

"Morning, I grabbed the last cup of coffee for you," I say, handing him the mug.

But he doesn't take it or respond. Just continues to stare ahead, off into space. His only acknowledgement was the slight turning of his head toward the sound the screen made when it clicked closed behind me.

"Okay..." I say, allowing for a long pause to stretch between phrases. "I'll just leave this here for when you want it." I place the steaming mug of coffee on the railing. Reflecting on how he must have started drinking again.

As the silence continues to grow, awkwardness stretching between us, I feel my temper rise but try to stuff it down.

"Welp, good chat. I'm headed in to work. Hope you have a nice day." Taking a deep breath, I stomp off in the direction of the Pump and Go, leaving my own drink to sit and get cold on the railing as well.

It's about a mile and a half to the service station, and it takes me approximately half an hour to walk to work. I stay to the side of the highway, on a narrow walking path, allowing my thoughts to wander and my feelings to simmer. I manage to make it a little faster today, having unintentionally quickened my pace due to my frustration with my pops' cold shoulder.

I find Gary in the garage, bent over a carburetor that he's disassembled on the workbench in front of him. The float, jets, gaskets, and O rings are precisely placed on the faded red garage rag. His coveralls are tied around his waist, and his white tank is marred with grease stains. His shoulders seem to have a new hunch to them that I don't remember being there before.

"Hey, Gary. You know, the coveralls are there to protect your clothes from the grease stains, right?"

He lifts his head just slightly, like he thought of something or heard a noise off in the distance he didn't recognize, but he doesn't respond to my playful dig. He starts mumbling about the amount of work that needs to be done and goes back to his task at hand.

"Well, I can help with that. Want me to work the counter and pumps today or tidy the back?" I ask. "I think our order of snacks and cigarettes arrived the other day."

He merely grunts again, not lifting his head from the assortment of carburetor parts laid out on the rag under his round nose or the wire cleaning brush in his hand.

Wow, everyone is in a super nasty mood today.

I head inside and start organizing the shelves behind the counter when I notice a navy-blue SUV pull up to the pump with a load full of kids in the back seat. I head out front to ask if they want it filled all the way up, but the parents in the front seat can't seem to hear me over the din their children are making.

Before I realize it, Gary is at my side and already has the nozzle in their car and is wiping down their windshield.

Fine. Just freaking fine. I can take a hint, I think to myself, though I feel the hurt and frustration sit in my stomach like a stone. I turn and walk away to go back to my tidying. I can tell when I am not wanted somewhere.

Obviously, any sympathy I had after the accident is gone. Not that I need or want any. But I can't help the inkling of self-pity welling up inside me. The tears feel hot in my eyes and threaten to fall. I push it all down deep inside. Nope, I am not going to do this. I am stronger than that, I think to myself, transforming my grief into something sharper.

I set my lips into a thin line and continue across the gravel lot, pulling my cap farther down over my scar, and adjusting my shoulders.

Jack is sitting off to the side of the garage on a spare tire, running his hand across Sally's back and up her tail as she rubs and purrs up against his shins.

He glances up when he sees me coming. I have a slight pause in my step when I notice him but quickly try to hide it as I continue walking at a slower pace in his direction, readjusting my hat to hide my scar.

"What are you doing here?" I ask, hearing and cringing at the disdain in my own question.

Jack doesn't seem to notice or care about my foul mood when he responds. "I wanted to see how you were doing."

I find myself sliding down the side of the garage to sit next to him, back resting against the wall, and I pull my knees up to my chest. I close my eyes and take a few deep breaths, counting out slowly in my head as I release them. His kindness is gently disarming my mounting frustration. As I sit there for a moment, I can't help but notice that every time I am around him, he seems to calm my raging sea of emotions.

"Things just haven't been the same since the accident," I find myself telling him. "I mean, that's obvious, and I didn't fully expect to go back to normal, but I also didn't expect all of this. Plus, there are big missing parts in my memory. I can't seem to really grasp anything that has happened since that night, you know?"

Jack looks at me for a moment, our eyes connecting, before he continues to give Sally the attention she seems to be demanding of him.

"And," I continue, "it's just that I feel like I'm being ignored everywhere I go. Apparently, no one wants to look at me directly. They just stare through me or past me. Even with

TES

Gary and my pops, the two people I am closest to other than Kasha. All I ever seem to get is grunts or sighs and their turned backs. I suppose I can sort of understand the others, strangers or random folks from town not being able to look directly at Kash or me. I have this disgusting scar, and Kasha has such an obvious limp; we're a constant reminder of the accident to them. A reminder of the horrors of what can happen at any moment... I can't even look at myself, so how do I expect others to?" A bitter laugh escapes my throat at the thought.

I allow a pause to follow my outburst, but Jack doesn't try to fill the void before I continue. "But with Pops and Gary... that I just don't understand. Isn't your family supposed to be the ones who are there for you after things go awry? It hurts more than I want to admit. Do they blame me? Did I take too long for Gary and now he is frustrated and behind in work. Do you think he regrets keeping me on? I don't know, and I cannot bring myself to ask him. And my pops – well I think he is drinking again..." Here I pause for a moment before continuing. "In fact, I'm not even sure why I'm telling you all of this. Why would you even care about my problems?"

I lean my head back against the wall of the garage and close my eyes while Jack continues to quietly and calmly stroke Sally's back.

"I just feel like you and Kasha are the only two people in this dusty old town that truly see or hear me anymore."

"I do understand, Gabriella," Jack says, and I notice how much I love the sound of my name on his lips. "In fact, you would be surprised by how many people have similar experiences and feelings after such a life-altering event."

"Really. And what makes you say that?"

"I have seen it time and time again. It's a part of what I do. I help people with their transition after a tragedy, to find where they need to go. What they need to do. Sometimes it's as simple as listening to their story; sometimes I'm not needed at all; and others..." He trails off.

"Others?" I ask, feeling curious and not wanting him to stop talking. It feels like it has been so long since I have had a deep conversation with someone.

"Others need more guidance," he concludes. "Everyone is a little different, even in all of their similarities."

His pacifying words ground me and give me a sense of not being as isolated as I thought. A new calm begins to wash over me.

"Kasha told me about the trip that you wanted to take to the coast," Jack says. "I think it's a good idea." He looks up at me, and our eyes lock. "You guys can still go. I can even help if you want. As I mentioned before, I'm from that area and was telling Kasha that I'm on good terms with the crew that cares for the old Coastline Mansion."

"Oh, Jack, I don't know. A getaway sounds really amazing, and Kasha and I were saving up to go next summer. I just don't know if it's a good time. Carly is going to cost me, and we won't have her to get us there. My pops is even more withdrawn than usual. Everything seems wonky, and I can't imagine leaving just now." Even as I say it, I hear the invalid excuses. *Wasn't I just complaining about everyone not caring for me? Maybe this is what I need right now.* Then I start to question, what does a handsome, smart and well-off man want with two small town girls? He did just fall into our lives in a time of turmoil. *There are no such thing as coincidences, Gabriella.* I chide myself. Besides, why is he interested? As much as I want to believe in love at first sight, I feel dubious. It doesn't make sense; this isn't a hallmark movie. That is not how life really works.

"Okay, no biggie. Just thought it would be a good idea. Help recenter you and Kasha after the accident. The offer stands, no matter how long you need. Please think about it."

I blink, trying to pull myself out of my wayward negative thoughts. *What am I doing?* Jack has been nothing but kind.

Stop it, Gabriella. Stop it. You don't need to make problems where there aren't any. "Thanks, Jack. I do appreciate it." Pushing myself up and off the wall to stand, I dust my hands on the thighs of my jeans and look out onto the golden field of grass across the way. Dust particles float solemnly in the air. "I think I'm going to punch out early. Gary doesn't appear to really need me today, and I can go see Kasha at the diner. I could use a shake and fries, anyway." After a pause I turn to him and add, "Want to come?"

After a slight beat he says, "I'd love to," a smile cresting the corners of his lips.

Chapter 10

The Hitching Post

Things haven't changed much in the few weeks following the accident and my talk with Jack. There is still the continuous feeling of being ignored and outcast at home and in our tiny community. It is all starting to wear on me, the isolation, the shunning. At first, I thought it was due to my hideous scar and how three lives were seriously altered in South Brook that night. The kid who threw the beer bottle was arrested and charged with a misdemeanor, but because he was a minor, his wrist was slapped with probation, community service, and a fine his parents paid for him. Although he appeared to get off light for the offense of causing the accident, a small town doesn't forget easily. Even though I don't ever see him, I hear that he is struggling with his own demons over that night, too. If I'm honest with myself, I'm struggling to find the energy to care or to try to figure it out anymore.

Depression sits heavily on my soul. Every action and thought feels like it consumes more energy than it should. I don't want to do anything or talk to anyone, but I force myself through my daily tasks and routine. I force myself to care.

I sit on the couch, my legs folded underneath me, a cup of steaming tea in my hand trying to enjoy the lazy morning of my day off. I watch my pops nervously bustle around putting on his best and only suit, combing his hair, to only run his hands through it and have to comb it again.

"What are you getting all spruced up for?" I ask, noticing him dragging his socked feet over our old, faded carpet like a petulant child.

"I need my tie. I can't find my tie."

"It is on the armrest of your chair. So... Do you have a hot date?"

"Not the red one. I need the blue one. Where on earth is my god darn blue tie. I swear I just had it a minute ago," he says now visibly steaming, big mitten hands folded on his hips.

TES

"Still on the arm of your chair," I tell him as I take another sip of tea.

"Ha. There it is," he mutters, glowering at the tie like it got up and hid itself on purpose just to make him mad. He snatches it up, stomps into the other room, and grumbles, "I don't know why I have to do this anyway."

Before I have a chance to question what it is exactly that he 'has to do', the screen door opens and Gary and Winnie come right inside, followed by Kasha pushing her way in underneath Gary's thick arm and past his wide stomach.

"Oh, please, come right in," I say sarcastically as I now have a house of self-invited guests in my living room. Noticing that both Gary and Winnie are dressed in their Sunday best, as well, my brow wrinkles with contemplation.

"Wow, you have quite the commotion happening this morning. It is busier than a herd of goats at feeding time in here," Kasha remarks, as she plops herself down on the couch next to me to watch the scene unfolding in front of us.

"My shoes. I can't find my shoes. I swear someone has it out for me and is constantly moving my stuff. Why can't it just stay where I put it?" my pops sputters from the next room.

Gary waddles down our narrow hallway to help Pops find his shoes. "They're here, Jewel," he shouts.

"Now why on God's green earth would they be in the hall closet and not my closet?"

"Well, that I couldn't tell you," Gary responds.

"Come on out here, Jewel, and let me help you with those. Those laces only get harder with age."

"I don't need hel..."

"It wasn't a suggestion. Now come here and sit down," Winnie demands and surprisingly enough my pops listens.

"Maybe I should try that," I mumble under my breath to Kasha. She quickly pretends to rub her nose, trying to suppress a smile.

"Do you know what the three of them are going on about," she asks me, and I can't help but notice the dark circles under her eyes.

"Not a clue, it has been a bit of a whirlwind all morning."

"I don't know why I have to do this. I don't want to do this," my pops says to Winnie as she in kneeling in front of him, lacing up and tying his shoes for him.

"It will be over in no time," Gary tries to reassure him, arms folded over his bulging belly.

Winnie shoots him a glare, that has my eyebrows flying up and a spark of joy forming at the thought of her keeping him in his place. "Honey, it is important to move on. This will help you move on."

"I don't want to move on," Pops says, dragging out the word *move* like it tastes sour in his mouth.

"Okay," Kasha says suddenly and pulls me up by my arm. "It is time we go, too."

"What?" I ask, as I try to keep my balance from rapidly unraveling my feet. Kasha takes the mug from my hands and places it on the coffee table, never letting go of my hand, quite literally dragging me out the front door.

"Bye Mr. Pickard, Gary! Winnie!" she shouts as we stumble outside into the midmorning light, the screen banging shut behind us.

"What was that about? And where do we have to go?" I ask incredulously. "Things were just getting interesting in there, and I never found out why everyone was all dressed to the nines and in a tizzy."

"Oh, Gabs, isn't it obvious?" When I just raise my eyebrows at her and give a small shake of my head she clarifies, "Gary and Winnie are finally dragging your pops out on a double date. Duh." At my slacked jaw response, Kasha has no problem filling the silence. "Besides," she goes on, "Jack mentioned wanting to see the waterfall down by the creek. It is such a gorgeous day and there is no time like the present. So there you are. I am officially kidnapping you."

"You are what?"

"I am kidnapping you. We are going to get burgers and fries to go from Darla's and take the hunk on a hike to the waterfall. And before you try to say anything else... no, you don't have a choice in the matter."

I gape at my best friend as she successfully avoids my eye and I let her drag me along and in the direction of Darla's. I can't help but notice she has a new pallor to her skin that wasn't there a second ago. But I think she is right. The hike, food and sunshine will do us all some good right now. We both seem to just be hanging on at the moment.

Later that evening, after a fun day of laughing and splashing in the icy water, basking for hours on a large sun-soaked boulder and enjoying the rush of the falls, I make my way to the Hitching Post, our small town's dive bar, and try to coax my intoxicated father home safely. Again.

The Hitching Post is one of those buildings that has been around for a hundred and fifty years, with the only major changes being the décor and the fact that they added electricity

and running water. It is the same splintering deep-oak paneling that covers both the inside and outside walls, tiny paned
windows that don't ever let enough light or air movement
in, and a fine layer of sawdust on the flooring. They say that
the sawdust coating the floors was originally intended to soak
up the tobacco spit, beer spills, and, well, blood from brawls
back in the 1800s. Why it still coats the floor today, I don't
know. Authenticity, they tell me, but I just find it unsanitary.
I mean, can you honestly imagine them sweeping up the sawdust, mopping the floors, and then applying a new, fine layer?
Of course not. Especially not when wiping down the counter
and tables seem to be a challenge, considering the mysterious
stickiness that permanently coats their surfaces.

The sawdust does, however, give the place a dusty pine smell
that I do find nostalgic. As odd as it may seem, pine dust is one
of my favorite smells. It takes me back to when Pops would
tinker in the outdoor shed making rocking chairs, little tables
and stools, and all my little horse figurines. Our home always
smelled of pine from his creations. Mom would go out to her
garden whenever he was outside working, just to be near him.
Their love was like that. Close. Genuine. There would be dirty
knee prints on her jeans, trowel in her hand. She would weed
around all her beets and carrots, cursing at the bunnies for

eating her lettuce, even though we all knew she found them adorable and could never really be that mad at them. All the while I would be playing in the grass, in some imaginary land with my horses, having them stomp in the mud puddle river I created using the garden hose.

No. Push that memory down, Gabby, and move on. Nothing but tears come from those memories. Tears and regret for not being able to care for him the way she did. For not being able to stop him from falling into the bottle after her passing. For time lost. For apparently making things worse after my accident. Reminding him how fragile life can be, even if I am still right here with him. The guilt sits heavily on my chest, making my depression feel even darker. Stormier.

As I walk through the heavy oak door of the bar—the bell refusing to jingle above my head, most likely from years of corrosion—the staff and patrons of the Hitching Post don't even bother looking in my direction. It must've been bad this time. As I stand in the entry of the dimly lit space, scanning the stools and billiard tables for Pops, the smell of whiskey and cigarette smoke assail my senses.

My eyes slowly adjust to the bleary lighting, and I spot him in the back corner of the room. He's standing over a pool game he must have just lost, judging by the confrontation glaring from his eyes and his rigid back. He still wears his suit from earlier, but his tie and coat are discarded on the back of a nearby chair. His shirt is unbuttoned at the collar and is halfway pulled out of his rumpled pants.

Taking a deep inhale to help settle myself, I gently place my hand on his shoulder. "Pops, I think it is about time we head home and have some dinner."

He goes still as stone, whatever injustices he felt dying on his tongue. He turns and looks in my direction, eyes bloodshot and dilated, then looks down at his shoulder and stalks out of the bar without a word, leaving his opponent's cash winnings in a messy pile on the pool table behind him.

As soon as we walk in the front door of our home and the front screen door clicks shut behind us, his emotions boil over. He spins, red-faced, hair askew, spittle flying from his alcohol-poisoned lips.

"Leave me alone! You're just like your fucking mother!" he bellows at me, reaching for one of his many empty beer bottles. I see it flying across the room moments before it shatters on the far wall, glass shards and stale beer coating the wall and floor. I flinch, reflexively throwing my arms in front of my face like a shield.

Pops was never violent toward me or my mother. His rage always simmered under the surface, where you could see the storm in his eyes, but he was our protector, not our tyrant. Things changed after Mom... after my accident.

"All you ever care about is yourself and not about the people you're supposed to care about," he bellows into the room. "The people you're supposed to be there for. The ones you say you love." A sudden, exhausted sob racks his chest, and it about breaks mine wide open. "You're a selfish little bitch, just like her," he whispers. "We used to have everything... Now I am alone... So just leave me alone."

I watch him collapse into his chair, face buried in his large hands, back slouched forward, elbows on his knees. Deflated.

I find myself unable to move.

To speak.

I am rooted there in the middle of our stuffy living room with the wallpaper that has begun peeling along the seams, beer bottles and newspapers littering the end tables and floor next to the couch. The smell of old beer permeates the house. I look down at the faded carpet, the one I used to sit on, legs outstretched while Pops watched the game, trying to understand all the rules and play, the smell of warm beef stew in the Crock-Pot.

When did things turn so sour?

How did we slip so far?

Things got rough after Mom, but life seemed to end for us this last month, with everything slowly fraying at the seams. It feels as if an irreparable cleft now opened up between us.

I find myself unable to comfort him. His words sting. I know they come from a place of anger and hurt and liquor. From the tragic feeling of injustice. I feel his pain, too, deep in my center. He is not alone in this. But this time, I am unable to help piece things back together. They never seem to stick anymore. *I can't do this anymore.*

Without a sound, I lift my stiff, army-green shoulder bag off the edge of the couch, where I dropped it, and drape it over my shoulders. I turn and head toward the door.

Hand on the doorknob, I hesitate for a moment to say in a low, quiet voice, "I am so sorry, Pops. I tried."

A weight on my chest, cheeks flaming, and tears piercing the backs of my eyes, I don't wait for his response, as I let the door click shut behind me.

Carly still sits on the dirt path where she was towed and dumped after our crash. I take a moment to look upon her crumpled shell. My heart drops farther into my stomach, not fully knowing how this is possible. Her bumper is forced into a downward position that is impaling the dirt where she sits. The brick-red fenders are bunched and wrinkled like they are made of paper and not sheet metal; the hood is folded nearly in half, sitting on and blocking the smashed windshield. The roof is caved in, making my girl look more like a discarded toy than an actual vehicle. I can't bring myself to look inside at the blood that still coats both of the front cloth seats, staining them in a dark brown pattern. It is amazing that Kasha and I walked away.

It is just over a mile to Kasha's house, but I need her. I need to talk, to cry, to yell this out. It doesn't matter that it is close to midnight or that I saw her a few hours ago. It doesn't matter that I didn't call before I left the house to give her a heads-up that I am coming over or that I will be walking the whole way there. She will be there for me. Like always. Like I am always there for her. We are the only two people who matter now.

I head down the dirt drive and turn left on the small trail that runs parallel to the highway.

It is a moonless night, making the shadows darker, the trees more ominous. I feel like it fits my dark mood perfectly, and I wonder to myself if I am matching the night or if the night is mirroring me. I can only see a few feet in front of me, kicking dust and pebbles up as I go, adding a fine layer of silt to my Converse and the bottom hem of my jeans. The night is alive with the sounds of nocturnal animals that call the valley home. A cool, slow breeze rustles the leaves in the trees, crickets chirp loudly in the grass off to my side, and an owl is hooting in the distance. I wonder if he is calling to someone or if he is proud of the midnight snack he just caught. Poor little vole, but someone needs to be the vole sometimes, I suppose. Tonight, I feel like the vole. I want to feel the freedom and strength of the owl again, but I don't know how to get there.

Lost in my own heartache, I trudge down the dirt path, reflecting on my life here in South Brook. As much as I like the small town, cities have always overwhelmed me. *But what does South Brook have to offer me anymore? What did it ever have to offer me? I have a good, steady job, but it merely fills the days; it does not fulfill me. Do I really want to be working in a garage and gas station for the rest of my existence? I love tinkering with cars, but do I love it that much? I will never meet a man unless he is some stranger who rolls into town and doesn't mind staying and living humbly.* After my failed dating attempts with the local men, I would rather stay single than settle. It all seems like a far-fetched dream, even with the coincidence of Jack lurking in the back of my mind. I reflect on how Kasha and I have our routines, hangouts, and places that help us escape the mundane and bring us some joy, but it all feels so worn down and old. *Do I really want that to be my life for the next fifty years?* Nothing seems to hold the luster and joy that it once did. Life around me is decaying, rusting away and transforming into something that doesn't seem to have a place for me anymore.

I come to the realization that I think I am finally ready to leave. To move on. I want more. I need more. Freedom, peace, happiness. To be the owl. Maybe I can even start riding horses again. Taking care of myself for a change.

When I arrive at Kasha's, she and Jack are there, sitting outside around a dying campfire. The embers in the stone firepit send up a molten glow that reflects off their faces. I find myself wondering for a moment what he is doing here. It feels like he has infiltrated our duo, but I can't seem to bring myself to mind all that much.

Kasha has been more withdrawn and less eccentric in the past month. She seems tired and her braids are frayed, and eyeliner is smudged more times than not. The last month has been hard on everyone. But as I stand there in the shadows and watch her and Jack sitting around the smoldering embers of what was once the fire, and I notice she appears to have more life in her.

Doubt and jealousy itch at the back of my mind, spinning, spinning. Building a web of suspicion in my mind. *Is Kasha keeping something from me? Could she keep something from me? Is that why she has been so withdrawn and less animated? And why is Jack here, really. Sure, we three have become close, but I thought he and I were at the start of something. And wasn't he just here for a job... but that was over a month ago now.* I lurk there in the shadows, face scrunching with the dark thoughts emanating from my already dark mood. *Why is he alone with Kasha at her house? Could there be something between them, could I seriously be that blind?* Kasha has never expressed interest in men past our senior prom, when that night ended with streaked mascara, a broken heel and a torn dress. She has always been strong in her relationship with independence. But maybe she feels the calm and the magnetic pull to Jack that I feel too and is just too ashamed to tell me, knowing that I am falling also.

Stop it, Gabriella, I chide myself. *She is your best friend. Just because of what happened tonight with Pops does not give you the right to take your hurt out on others. Others that love you. Don't. Be. Him.* Closing my eyes and taking a deep and slow inhale of the crisp night air, I emerge from the gloom of the trees and my mood, then start my way towards my two friends.

The two of them are hunched forward in a quiet conversation over the glowing coals, and they don't notice my approach at first. When they do glance up, Kasha's face breaks out into a grin, and she quickly stands up to embrace me. Jack gives me a nod, eyes seeming to twinkle even in the dim light of the night.

"Look at you! Did you walk over? I'm so glad you came by!" she says, genuinely glad to see me as she squeezes me tight, and I further chastise myself for my earlier episode. "Sleep seems to be eluding me lately, and I thought I would try to enjoy the nice night when I noticed Jack walking by. We started chatting, and he was telling me all about what he does and where he's from. The next thing I know, the fire has burned down, but now that you're here, too, I'll grab another log. Want something to drink?"

"Just a water is fine. Thanks, Kash," I say.

She darts off into the dark to grab a glass from the kitchen and another log from behind the shed.

I turn to Jack. "Hey. Funny bumping into you here. Couldn't sleep either?" Unable to keep the speculation from my tone.

"Just out for a night walk, enjoying the quiet and serenity of the evening, when I saw the flames from the path. I thought I would investigate, as the brush around here seems like a tinderbox waiting to ignite. Turns out it was just Kasha," he says with a small smile.

Kasha returns, handing me a glass of water from the tap, and plops the log on the dying embers, sending little sparks up into the air. She stirs the burnt bits and fresh log around until she has it situated just how she wants it, then sets down the poker and looks at me. It is the look of a friend who knows you better than you know yourself. A look that I know will come with questions. I take a sip of my water and brace myself for them.

"What's up, girl?" she asks. "And don't give me, 'I couldn't sleep,' or, 'I was just out for a night walk,' because both of those cards have been played already." There is humor in her eyes and tone, but there is an underlying hint of seriousness coating the question.

I don't even try to deflect. "I had to get Pops from The Hitching Post again tonight. It was ugly and only got worse once we got home. I just needed to leave, clear my head and find space to breathe. You are just my homing beacon," I say, trying my best to smile.

"That rough, huh?" she asks.

"Yeah, this was the worst one yet. His temper and drinking are only spiraling, and he acts like I am dead to him. Like I don't even exist anymore. I'm not sure what to do. I am so tired. I just don't know how much more I can take. I feel like I am getting ready to snap, myself."

Kasha's eyes have a somber look in them as she weaves her fingers through mine, taking my hand. "You can't save him, Gabs. There are only two things in this world that can save someone: themselves and God. You are neither," she says. The sad curve of her mouth tries to climb up into the semblance of a smile. "His struggles are not your struggles. You need to take care of yourself. His time will come all on its own."

I take in what she has just said to me. I feel it in my center that she is right, but it still feels like a monumental task. Jack is as silent as a crypt as he stares into the flames of the firepit. Somehow it doesn't bother me that he is witness to my sorrows. We seem to have made a connection, and I feel nothing but a secure, understanding presence from him. I find it funny how people can bond so quickly. It's like he has been a part of our group forever. Even with my previous doubts, I don't know why I stress over things I don't need to. I need to learn to embrace the good.

After a few minutes of letting words and feelings settle, Kasha continues. "We can go anywhere. It's not like we're tethered here." We lock eyes as she says this to me, and I know deep in my soul that this is exactly why I came here tonight. This is the first step in finding what I need.

I break Kasha's stare to glance over to Jack. A heartbeat passes. I turn back to Kasha's awaiting expression, then find myself saying, "I'm ready. I think I need to move on, to move forward. I believe a change will do us some good. What do you think?"

A smile starts to spread across Kasha's face, lighting up her eyes with merriment.

I turn to Jack. "Tell us about this manor of yours on the coast."

We sit around the campfire for what feels like hours, talking and planning. Kasha keeps adding logs to the fire, and we have switched from water to wine. There is still a lump of sadness lodged in my chest, but I find myself embracing the change in mood, from misery and darkness to hope and excitement for what lies ahead.

I explain that even with Carly being out of commission, I am not sure I am comfortable getting back into a car for a while. Kasha hurriedly agrees with me, nodding in serious enthusiasm. The rawness of the trauma from the accident is still too fresh to come to terms with just yet. Jack is understanding and explains that neither his car nor his job will be an issue. That the car can be delivered back home anytime, and he is recently on leave, having simply wanted to extend his stay in South Brook. We discuss our other transportation options to the coast, through buses and trains. The idea of riding in a train car excites me. I have always loved trains, especially the old steam engine locomotives, with their smoke billowing out the top of their stacks, chugging along on their old iron rails.

Jack tells us about the rocky beaches and jagged shoreline of his home. He describes the big Victorian house that sits on a cliff, with its turrets scraping the low-hanging coastal clouds. He continues with how it has tales of hauntings and classic grand balls. Of huge fields filled with horses and a traditional barn that houses them, though they often choose to spend their time outside in the thick, salt-laden air. There's a big, goofy, gray dog named Sam, whose drool can melt both the floorboards and your heart. There is an old lighthouse that peers out into the sea nearby. It stands tall on its rocky island, and you can hear it bellowing its warning to approaching ships in the distance on foggy mornings. He paints the picture for us of a place of dreams and peace and change.

Feeling the warmth of the fire on my face and shins, I shift forward on the stump, which acts as my chair, and set my empty wineglass on the ground, allowing the heat to hit my hands as I hold them out toward the flames. Smoke circles on the air around us, caught in the gentle night breeze. My hair will smell like ash in the morning, but I can't seem to care. For the first time in what feels like a long time, I am looking forward to something. The clouds of darkness parting slightly in my mind, I can't help feeling that what we are doing is fundamental and good. That this is the right decision, even though I have a slight tug of apprehension flickering deep in my core.

Chapter 11

Doubts

The next day, I awake to a storm of emotions. Though excited about our upcoming trip and desperate for an escape, I still can't shake the feeling of apprehension. *I mean, seriously - why on earth would some rich, good-looking man want to whisk Kasha and me away to his private coastline manor? He just happened to fall into our lives at the time we were most vulnerable? It is not adding up no matter how much I want, I need, it to be real.*

The sun is already warm with the approach of summer, and I know I need to clear my head. So, I head out to the one place

I know I can find peace and be alone: the Garrison's ranch. It's a long walk, but it gives me time to think.

By the time I arrive, the sun is high in the sky, beating down on my skin and warming me to my core. Sundance has his head bent low, happily grazing, nosing through the grass for the greenest sprouts. When he sees me, he lifts his head and trots over, on his old arthritic legs, letting out a soft knicker that ruffles his velvety nostrils. Even at the ripe age of twenty-seven, he's still full of life – and love.

"Hi, boy," I say, running my hand down the length of his face and toying with his fuzzy top lip. "Sorry it has been a while. But I brought you something."

As I softly speak to this beautiful creature – the one who got me though the trials and tribulations of high school – I pull a carrot from my back pocket. He wraps his lips around it and sucks it straight into his large mouth. Then suddenly, with a loud crack, he snaps it in half with his oversized teeth, the bottom half of the carrot plummeting out of his mouth. Somehow, I manage to catch the grass and drool covered vegetable before it hits the dirt. Laughing at the nastiness and how much it oddly makes me happy, I feed him the remaining carrot and wipe my hand on the back of my jeans.

Sundance gives an abrupt snort and a toss of his head, then turns and begins grazing again. *Typical man*, I think. *Only thinking about your stomach.*

Laughing to myself, I climb the rust-covered fence and perch on the top rail, watching as Sundance grazes, his tail swishing in quiet contentment. My thoughts begin to wander back to my inner conflict. I need to get this sorted out – and I need to get this sorted out today.

I decide the best approach is to tick off all the points of everything that's bothering me – to lay it all out and hopefully get a clearer picture.

Ok, Gabs, I tell myself. *Let's start with the negative and see where that gets us. Might as well just rip the Band-Aid right off.*

One: I touch my thumb to my index finger. *A random, rich, good-looking guy waltzes into town right when I'm at a major turning point in my life. He just happens to show up every time I start to spiral. He also just happens to have a big beachside manor with horses – and he invites us there? Really? That alone is suspicious, considering it's been Kasha's and my dream for years. What is in it for him? Could he have dark intentions, I've seen Dateline. Or is he telling the truth – maybe he really does just enjoy our company? And wasn't he only supposed to be here for a job? It has been... what, a month? Or...* I frown, struggling to recall the exact timeline of the last few weeks before moving on.

However... I counter, *he did give you a legitimate explanation about loving it here in South Brook and wanting to extend his trip. And maybe meeting people is hard for him. He's always on the move, and he hates crowded places – just like I do. And... he does seem genuine every time we talk. Plus, Kasha seems to trust him, and she is not someone who lets her guard down easily.*

Watching Sundance nip at a pesky fly buzzing his flank, I tap my thumb onto another finger, brow furrowing as I inwardly think about my second point.

Two: Can I still trust Kasha? She has changed since the accident. It is like she's keeping something from me – and I hate it. But I am not ready to ask. Not yet. Asking makes it too real. We've never had secrets before, so why can't I shake the feeling that she's hiding something now?

But... I think, raising my eyebrows at my thought, *why would Kasha hurt me? Why would she do anything that would cause a rift in our relationship? We are each other's ride-or-die, best friends for life, soul sisters, the 'do anything for each other' kind of friends. It doesn't make sense. Could she also be falling for Jack and feels too guilty to say something? He doesn't really seem her type, but they were hanging out last night before I got there.*

What if she blames me for the accident? What if that's the crack I'm starting to feel forming between us?

I grasp the metal fencing on either side of my body and start rocking gently back and forth, lost in thought. The old rail is rough under my palms, but I embrace the feeling of being on a ranch again. The smell of dust and horse centering me. Sundance begins to twist and turn back and forth in small, slow circles, knees bending as he searches for the perfect spot to drop and roll. Once he's satisfied, he lets his knees buckle and he hits the ground with a dusty plop. I smile as he kicks his legs out, trying to build the momentum to roll over. After a good, satisfying dust bath, he stands and give a big shake, sending a tan cloud of silt puffing up from his coat. The dust blends easily into his red roan fur, merely giving it a slightly duller hue. *Just one of the many reasons never to own a white horse,* I laugh to myself. *Keeping these beasts clean in impossible.*

Feeling calmer now – horses have always anchored me – I let myself reflect again.

What if Kasha is just using Jack as our ticket out of South Brook? That makes more sense than some dramatic love triangle or her secret resentment. I shouldn't create problems that don't exist. And besides, I should trust in Kasha's judgement – it feels safe to trust Jack, and she clearly believes it is. I need to have faith in her, in our plan. I can't stay – not right now. That much is for certain. Like Kasha said, "Sometimes a little break from a situation is what the situation needs most in order to heal."

Still, I'll just need to take precautions. There's time before we leave – time to put a few things in place.

Yes, I tell myself. *This is the right choice. Have faith, Gabriella. But also... a Girl Scout is always prepared. So, be prepared. I need to be ready for anything.*

Chapter 12

Preparations

It has been two weeks since the incident with my pops, and we have successfully managed to avoid each other like the plague since then. I still feel resolute – even if a bit nervous – in my decision to move on with Kasha and Jack, especially after my deliberation at the Garrison's. To have a fresh start somewhere—or a reprieve, at least for a little while.

Even with my newfound confidence, I still decide to sneak Pop's old hunting knife and its caramel-colored leather sheath along on my trip. I doubt he will even notice it missing. After I run a couple of extra straps through the sheath's loops on the back and secure the knife to the side of my calf, I shake my leg and give it a tug, making sure that it won't slip. Then I pull the hem of my jeans down over it, hiding it fully from view. There is still something that Jack is keeping from me, I sense it deep in my bones, regardless of how much Kasha is pushing me to trust him. *Again, preparation is key,* I tell myself.

I stand in the middle of my room, hands on my hips, surveying the small, messy space I call my own. As I look around the cluttered bedroom, I try to decide what I can pack and take with me on our trip. *What will I need? What will I wish I had brought with me?* Jack said to pack light; that we can get provisions and necessities along the way; that the mansion will have an abundance of clothes, food, and things that will suit our basic needs. Convenient, I think to myself. There will be little space on the buses and trains, and because we will not be driving at all, there is a seven-mile stretch of road we will need to backpack. Kasha and I assured Jack that we were up to the challenge, but now that I stand here with my backpack open on my bed in front of me, I am wondering just how I will manage.

My light blue Jansport sits open on my bed, waiting. It's funny that my backpack is a sky-blue color, such a happy and uplifting color. Not my usual flair. I normally would have much preferred a midnight blue or black backpack. Honestly,

I would have even chosen a forest green or brick red color, something darker in tone, but beggars can't be choosers, I suppose.

I plop down on my vanity's vintage bench, leaning my back up against the old dressing table and resting my elbows on the edge. I have always loved old, solid and ornate furniture from the early turn of the century. I find its history both comforting and alluring, and I never miss an opportunity to stop at an antique shop.

With a heavy sigh, I find myself reflecting on the summer before I started high school, when Mom took me school shopping in the city. It was a special occasion because we usually didn't have the money to buy new things. We'd make do with what we had around the house, hand-me-downs from friends, or things from the local thrift shop. We drove all the way into Merced, though, to go to one of their strip malls. I remember being so overwhelmed by all the noise and traffic there. All the lights and people made me feel claustrophobic, panicked, like I didn't know where to look and when, but I pushed down the feelings and tried to enjoy the day with Mom.

The store that we went to only had a few backpacks left, as most everything was picked through and previously purchased by other anticipatory students. I had the choice of white, pink, or baby blue. They weren't good options, and I recall feeling the disappointment sit like a stone in my stomach. Mom had such a happy look on her face, fussing over all the things on the display shelf, while she awaited my choice. Not wanting the trip to be wasted or to have her disappointed in me because I was 'picky,' I opted for the light blue one.

Before heading home, we stopped and ate burgers and fries. The fries were covered in some mystery orange sauce mixed with relish and tasted absolutely heavenly. As we sat in one of the hard plastic booths, chatting and laughing together, watching the juices and condiments shoot out of the ends of our burgers, I couldn't help but think to myself that there are worse problems to have than to own a backpack of a color you are not a fan of.

To this day, I can't find the nerve to get rid of that backpack or buy one in the color of my choosing. The memory that was built purchasing the ugly thing is what makes it beautiful, and I will carry it until the seams pop.

Standing up I decide to keep my packing basic. I toss in an extra pair of jeans, a couple shirts, socks, and underwear. I grab my hairbrush and toiletries from the adjoining bathroom. I figure I will wear my black sweater and I'll attach my baseball cap to the loop on my backpack, so it's both easily accessed and won't get squished.

Stuffing my belongings in and zipping up my pack, I hoist it onto my shoulders and head into work. I owe Gary my notice, even if it will be short, or at least an explanation of the trip. I can't bring myself to talk to Pops, afraid I will lose my nerve. But I am sure he and Gary will chat. Over beers. At the Post.

The night after our big fight, I poured the remainder of Pop's bottles down the kitchen sink. I felt the liquid chug out of the necks of the bottles and down the drain, the aroma of liquor accosting my senses. There was a part of me that felt guilty, but I was overwhelmed with a stronger feeling of disgust. It was for the best. Leaving the empty bottles lying in the basin, I leaned forward, resting my elbows on the edge of sink. I caught my breath as I tried my best to gather my mounting emotions.

The hurt and heartache are still raw as I stand in the kitchen now. Both Pops and the bottles are gone, and I can't bring myself to see if he has replaced them already. A part of me doesn't want to know. I take a paper and pen from the shelf, and leaning over the pocked kitchen table, I write Pops a note:

*I am sorry for how things turned out, but I need a break. Kasha
and I have decided to take that trip I told you about, earlier than
we planned. Please don't worry, but I don't know when I will be
back, and I will call if I can. I will be fine, try not to worry. Please
take care of yourself. I love you, Pops.*
~Gabby xoxo

Feeling a lump rise in my throat and hot tears prick the backs
of my eyes, I leave the note on the table, not bothering to put
away the pen. I'm glad he wasn't here. It makes things easier.
Even with our blowout a couple of weeks ago, I don't know if
I would have the strength to leave if I had to face him. To look
upon his face. Even with me knowing that he is the only one
who can help himself, I still feel like I've failed him. Like I am
giving up somehow.

I take a moment to stand on the porch and gather myself.
I survey the swing and have a flash of memories: sitting on it
with Pops in the morning, drinking our tea and coffee before
the start of the day; having Kasha hold me after Mom's funeral;
and my solitary midnight rocking, embracing the chilled night
air and staring up at the endless stars.

Glancing over to my right, I look upon the shed. The weeds
have grown up its sides and have begun lingering under the

lean-to. Between the weeds and dust, it looks fully abandoned. I wonder if it will ever see life again or if its days are behind it.

Carly is still a crumpled heap parked next to the shed, where the tow truck driver dropped her off. There is a car cover fastened over her to help keep the weather out and hide the memories of that night. I wonder if her days are behind her, too, but I am grateful that we hadn't had her hauled to the scrapyard. I still see myself in that car, and some irrational part of me feels that if her life were to be over after the accident, then why shouldn't mine be as well?

I remove my hat from the strap on the backpack, twist my hair back, and shove it under the ballcap. I secure my shoulder straps on the pack and start the walk to the Pump and Go.

I arrive early, before Gary has come and opened everything up. I let myself in, yet another bell refusing to jingle above my head as the door closes behind me. *This old town is really starting to show its wear and tear,* I think. Sally is there to greet me with a mew and a purr, rubbing up against my legs. I bend down and pet her, running my fingernails across her back, just the way she likes it. Flicking on the lights, I set my backpack on the floor in the corner and go to fill up her water bowl. After I set it on the floor, I decide to grab one of the Styrofoam cups from the slushy machine and cut it down, so it is more like another mini bowl. Taking it back behind the counter I fill it with some whipped cream from the cooler. She starts happily lapping it up, white foam coating the edges of her whiskers.

"My farewell treat to you, girl."

I grab the receipt pad and a pen and start to write to Gary. I can't help feeling a little cowardice, writing notes instead of telling people in person about my leaving, but this seems like the only way I can do it without breaking down, or backing out. I already have enough apprehension as it is. Plus, I have made a promise to myself that I am going to start prioritizing my well-being, too. If this is the way I need to do it at first, then so be it.

I tell Gary how grateful I am to have worked for him and to have learned all that I have about cars from my experience in his garage and his patience with me while I healed. That I am heading out on an adventure with Kasha, and I am not sure when I am coming back, so this is my official notice. I apologize for the abruptness of my departure, but an opportunity presented itself, and I needed to jump on it. I hope he understands. I tell him that I am leaving the key to the shop under the paint can that seconds as a doorstop out front and to wish me luck.

When I turn to go, I notice an envelope sitting next to the cash register with my name on it. Tearing open the edge, I notice it is my paycheck. My final paycheck, I suppose. I shove it back in the envelope, crease it down the center and pop it in my back pocket. Giving Sally one more pat, I pick up my bag, switch off the lights, and lock up the front door. Before I leave to meet Kasha and Jack at Darla's, I slip the key under the rusty paint can, like I told Gary I would, and walk away. Closing a chapter in my life.

Kasha

Today is the day we say farewell to South Brook and the ones we love here, pack our things, and prepare to set off on our grand adventure to the coast. I am so happy and excited. I feel like I have butterflies in my stomach, and my fingers and feet are itching to do something. Anything. This energy is electrifying, and I feel like I could skip the whole way there. This is the best I have felt in a while, and I know this is exactly what Gabriella and I need right now. I am sure I should feel some melancholy for leaving my family and Darla's, but my joy for finally shaking this dusty town off my boots is currently outweighing any feelings of remorse. I can't help but wonder if this is how my brother felt when he finally left.

I lace up my combat boots over my fishnet stockings, feeling like I have really nailed my look today, with my cutoff shorts, tank top, and black choker. I wrap my oversized flannel around my waist and add fresh mini braids to the top of my head. I shove some random outfits and necessities in my old army duffel as I prepare to leave.

I peek into the munchkins' room first. The three of them are all still tucked up in bed, dreaming the morning away. My young siblings look so calm and peaceful in their beds, covers snuggled around them, teddy bears and dollies shoved under their arms, serenity on their little faces. It is a peace that I know won't last. As soon as one wakes, hungry for breakfast, the chaos will ensue. I feel a smile tugging on my lips, thinking about the hustle and bustle that is the morning routine in the Owens home.

Next, I head down the narrow hall to Ma's room. She is still asleep, too, covers knocked off the bed and in a pile at her feet. Her golden hair rests across the pillow, as if blowing in the wind, satin nightgown ending at her folded knees. I stand there taking her in for a moment, trying to memorize her. She is so beautiful and has worked so hard in her life... never complaining, always providing. I have always told her I want to be just like her when I grow up, but I want her character, not her life. I walk over to the side of the low mattress and gently, silently place a cool kiss on her temple. She shifts slightly but doesn't wake up. Tiptoeing back out of the room, I slowly close her door, leaving it open only a crack, just how she likes it. It offers privacy but allows her to hear the Animaniacs when they wake. I know Ma and the littles won't miss me, not really. In a way I have been gone for a while now, so this change, I think, won't sit too heavily on them.

I told Gabs and Jack that we should meet at the diner just after first light. I thought that sounded cool, 'after first light,' like something from one of my mystery novels. Gabs wanted to leave bon voyage letters to her dad and Gary before heading over. Later today we are planning on going over the travel details. Jack is working most everything out, which makes things nice. It allows us to focus on the excitement of the trip and not stress over the nitty gritty part of travel. A part of me is still concerned that Gabs will want to back out and stay, even though I could see the shift of determination in her eyes the other day after I did my absolute best to try and convince her everything will be fine. I am set on not giving her any reason to doubt her decision and I plan on arriving at the diner early. She is suspicious enough.

Tossing my green canvas duffel bag over my shoulder and adjusting the strap across my chest, I start the walk to Darla's. I'm embracing the pep in my step, the song in my soul, and the gentle morning sun just beginning to warm and light my face. The sky has a light pink and lavender hue to it as the day starts to rise, the sun just beginning to crest the edge of the mountaintops. The morning has always been my favorite part of the day. When the sun is just warm enough to energize you, the air still crisp from the night behind it, you feel like you can breathe. Like anything can happen. The birds are chirping in the nearby trees, and I want to sing along with them. I can't believe this is finally happening. That we are finally going to the Cliffsides. These are not quite the circumstances that I had originally thought would allow us to take the trip of a lifetime, but things work out one way or another, I suppose. I don't believe it is healthy to dwell on the could've and should've been situations. There's nothing you can do about them, so you might as well pull yourself up by your bootstraps and move on. Make your own destiny.

"Onward and upward," I say to myself, and I can't help the laugh that escapes me.

Jack

I sit down at the petite writing desk in my room at the B&B. It is a tiny, simple thing that is small enough not to be intruding in the humble room, with a single drawer and matching wooden chair that tucks in neatly underneath it.

Unbuckling and popping open my leather case, I pull out some paper and a fountain pen I brought with me on this journey. I need to write an update on how the job is going and give headquarters a heads-up that I will be returning to Cliffside Manor soon, with two in tow. I think they will be pleased, even if my return has been delayed. There are some circumstances that cannot be rushed; they always arrive at their intended destination eventually. Hopefully. Management should understand.

I feel the scrape of the pen on the calloused paper, and I take my time scrawling the words across the stationery. I have always believed that anything worth doing is worth doing well.

As I write, my mind drifts to the girls. It will be a slower trip home than usual, considering the unconventional way we will be traveling, but a part of me is looking forward to the journey. I have sorted all the details out for our journey and plotted the route. The girls and I are planning on sitting down so I can go over everything with them this morning. I sense that Gabriella can tell that something is amiss, but I don't believe she knows the crux of it. Kasha and I had an in-depth conversation a couple weeks ago at her fire pit about how we desperately needed to get Gabriella on board with our plan. Kasha was initially against it, not wanting to lie to Gabriella, but I made myself clear that there was not much choice in the matter. We need her to come along if we want it to work.

Mrs. Carver stumbled over and over an apology yesterday about needing to head out for a few days to celebrate her granddaughter's graduation from college. She said the date just snuck up on her and she feels like a terrible host for leaving a guest unattended. I tried to assure her that it was fine, that I would only be staying another night and that the milestones in a loved one's life should be celebrated with those they love. She hemmed and hawed for a bit longer about her guilt but ended up cooking me enough food and pies to serve a small army. Cooking is obviously this woman's love language, and I can't help but imagine the late Mr. Carver being anything but stout around the middle.

To be honest, I am looking forward to the quiet of the day, and it works out perfectly with our approaching departure. I plan to have Kasha and Gabriella stay here in one of the other guest rooms tonight, so we can leave before the sun is up in the morning. Mrs. Carver will be none the wiser, though I don't think she would mind other than that she won't be able to talk their ears off and bake them desserts. She asked me to leave the house key in the cookie jar that is shaped like a hen, on the kitchen counter, then just turn the bottom lock on the front door so it's secured behind me in the morning. I assured her that I could do that and thanked her for her hospitality.

I finish the letter with my monogram on the bottom and fold the paper in half, creasing it down the center. I slide my feet into my sandals and shove the key into the front pocket of my jeans. Grabbing the maps I've marked methodically—plotting the journey across the state to the coast—I head downstairs. I need to be at the diner soon, but I have one more stop to make first.

I need to talk with Jewel Pickard.

Gabriella

Kasha has a heaping pile of blueberry pancakes, a plate of bacon, and a pot of tea waiting for us when I show up at the diner. She is sitting at one of the wooden picnic tables out front. The faded yellow umbrella is still closed from the previous evening, but it is better this way, allowing the morning sun to warm us as we sit.

I smell the scent of the pancakes and bacon, and I start salivating, my stomach rumbling in response. I didn't realize how famished I was.

"Girl, you are no longer a waitress, you don't need to serve us anymore. Though I do appreciate your foresight immensely."

"I thought we would celebrate with a breakfast fit for queens. Recently unemployed queens."

At this she pours us each a cup of tea, steam swirling into the air above the hot liquid, and we clink cups.

"To being unemployed."

"To going on an adventure. Nothing but positive changes are headed our way," she adds, confidence lacing her voice.

As we sip our tea that is so hot that I am sure that the tip of my tongue will be singed for a day, we notice Jack strolling up to our table.

"Good morning, ladies," he says, sitting down next to me, bench straddled between his legs. I try not to notice how good he looks, how his jeans hug him just right.

"This looks amazing," he continues. I feel my cheeks heat at his comment, feeling like he is inside my head. He thankfully doesn't seem aware of my current embarrassment, instead piling pancakes and bacon onto his plate. *How can he eat that much?*

While rubbing our purple-stained pancake bites through the puddles of maple syrup coating our plates, we discuss the logistics of our trip. Jack asks if we have packed yet, and we simultaneously gesture to the bags at our feet. He explains how Mrs. Carver has headed out for the week, something about a granddaughter's graduation, and that we can stay at the B&B tonight, so we can leave before the sun and not disturb our families.

The commuter bus that runs from South Brook to Merced will arrive at the bus stop at four a.m., just outside the Pump and Go. We will need to arrive early, bright-eyed and bushy-tailed, so as not to miss it. It is about forty-three miles to Merced and will take us about an hour and a half to get to the train station there. We should have roughly an hour before we need to make our connection, jumping on the train. At the thought of riding on a train, Kasha and I both let out a little squeal, clapping our hands excitedly. Jack just rolls his eyes and continues.

"The train ride will last just under six hours, and we shall travel about two hundred miles," he says, and I can't help but smile at how he is informing us about the time and the distance. Like we have another option. "It will drop us off at our stop in San Luis Obispo. From there we will get on another bus for the next couple hours, taking us thirty-eight miles north. That is as far as public transportation can take us."

I nod, knowing what he is about to say next, knowing that he will be looking at us to make sure we don't have any reservations about the final leg of the journey. I school my expression and hold the teacup up to my lips, allowing the steam to heat my face.

Jack continues, "Once we disembark from the final bus, we will walk the remaining six and a half miles to Cliffsides. It should take us a couple of hours, depending on our pace."

"So... we should arrive in the late afternoon?" Kasha clarifies.

"Yes, so long as everything goes smoothly, which I expect it will. I have already told the house to expect us and when. We should have a hot meal waiting and your rooms should be prepared."

Kasha and I exchange a look, eyebrows raising at the thought of a mansion with staff. Kasha and I lock eyes, and hers are sparkling with the excitement that I feel bubbling up in my center. I start laughing, unable to hold my smile in. I am not sure who this guy is, how he lives in a rumored-to-be haunted mansion on the coast or how he stumbled into our lives. The one thing I do know is that this feels right. Nerves are just nerves, and they are natural. I need to enjoy the moment. If Kasha trusts Jack, then so do I. I trust Kash with my life.

Chapter 13

The Trip

As we stand at the bus stop anxiously awaiting its arrival, I find myself shivering. Whether my trembling is from the cold of the dark morning or from my nerves for the trip, I can't tell. Hands fisted around the straps of my backpack I begin to pace in front of the bench, trying to shake the fluttering that has seized my body.

The bus stop is only about six paces from end to end, and I can't bring myself to go any further as I walk back and forth. Jack is sitting on the bench that is located under the bus stop's metal canopy, one leg crossed over a knee, reading the morning paper he brought with him from Mrs. Carver's. He appears to not have a care in the world. Kasha has dropped her canvas army duffel bag at her feet and is leaning nonchalantly against the pole that supports the canopy, staring off into the dark vegetation across the street, lost in her own thoughts.

None of us talk. It doesn't feel like we need to. The dark stillness of the early morning seems to demand our quiet, implying the feeling that anything said would be both frivolous and too loud.

I glance down at my delicate silver watch, mentally noting that the bus is not late and that it should arrive in the next six minutes. The thought makes the butterflies in my stomach skip and jump.

I couldn't bring myself to eat anything for breakfast this morning before we left the B&B, both my jitters and the time of the day making it difficult, so I brewed myself a cup of peppermint tea, hoping that would both fill and settle my stomach.

Jack wasn't kidding when he said that Mrs. Carver left enough food to feed a small army. After we returned from the diner yesterday and got settled in our assigned rooms at the B&B, we dug into some lunch. I opted for one of the turkey sandwiches that was premade in the fridge, with all the fixings I could possibly want, stacked impossibly high, and a bag of potato chips from the pantry. Mrs. Carver also had a pitcher of freshly made lemonade in the fridge that was heavier on the "ade" than on the "lemon."

We had spent the day relaxing, trying to enjoy the solitude of our last day in South Brook. Jack went upstairs to his room after lunch, claiming he had to do some things for work. Something about reports to write. Kasha and I didn't press him. We were just grateful for all that he was already doing for us. *There is more good in the world than evil, Gabriella. Remember to trust in that.*

Kasha spent what seemed like hours on the tire swing tied to the big sycamore out front, and I folded myself up in one of Mrs. Carver's rocking chairs on the front porch with a book I found in the living room. I didn't need to look on the back of the chair or feel the JP branded into the wood to know that it was one of the chairs Pops had made. I slowly ran my hand over the armrest, the feel of the wood beneath it simultaneously making me feel melancholy and proud to be rocking in it.

This peaceful revery continued until dinner, when we again ate enough food to feel gluttonous, then topped it off with a peach pie that had been resting on the counter. Before Mrs.

Carver's son-in-law came to pick her up to take her to her granddaughter's graduation, she told Jack that if she returned home to pie still on the counter, she would be most offended. So, we did our best to polish off the sweet tenderness of the pie, crust flaking with every stab of the fork.

With a weight pressing on my chest, I can't shake the need to hear Pops's voice before we pull out. I know I only have a few more minutes until the bus arrives, so I fish for some loose change in my pocket and make a dash for the payphone a few strides up the road.

I slide my lone quarter into the slot and press each button on the cold keypad, my hand gripping the receiver tightly as I hold it to my ear and listen to it ring on the other end.

"Hello?" Pop's voice is rough and groggy on the other end. Like I woke him from a deep sleep. Then I realize that is probably exactly what I did.

Before I let my racing heart and shame for calling so early get to me, I say, "Hey, Pops, it's Gabby."

"Who's there? Hello?"

"Pops, it's me. Gabby. I… I just wanted to say… I love you."

Silence.

"Pops? Can you hear me?"

"Gabby?"

Automated voice, "You have one minute remaining. Please deposit additional change to continue." I frantically fish through my pockets, looking for another ten cents, but come out empty handed.

"Pops! Can you hear me?"

"Gabby, is that you?"

Silence.

Beeping. The line was disconnected.

I stand there for a moment, the cold touch of the handset in my grasp as I listen to the finality of the beeps on the other end of the dead line. An icy chill creeps up my arms, settling in my core, making me shiver.

Slowly, I hang the phone up on its metal receiver with a definitive click that causes tears to prick behind my eyes. Turning slowly, I gather my resolve and begin walking back toward Jack, Kasha, and the impending bus.

As I approach our small group, I hear the rumble of the bus engine before noticing the headlights streaming through the trees, coming our way. I check my watch again—3:58—more out of nervous habit than anything else, trying to shake the melancholy creeping in. I wish I could have had a conversation with him, even if it was brief. But I know in my soul that I should be grateful to even have heard his voice at all.

As the bus makes its approach, Jack fluffs and folds his paper, standing and tucking it under his arm. Kasha pushes herself off the support pole and grabs her duffel, sliding it onto her shoulder. The bus pulls up, right on time, the brakes letting out a high-pitched squeal as it comes to a stop next to us. The door hisses open as the driver's hand pulls the lever, hydraulics doing their job. As it opens it feels like more of a transfiguration, bathing us in light too bright for my eyes at first, than a source of public transportation.

Stealing a deep breath, I look to Kasha and meet the wide smile already smeared across her face. Automatically we grab each other's hands, giving a tight, quick squeeze, and step onto the bus.

The inside of the transit bus is pretty much how you would expect a city bus to look. The seats are two rows of two and are blue with a faux leather strip running down their centers. Jack hands the driver our fare, and we make our way down the aisle, settling into a few seats in the back two-thirds of the bus.

There are only a couple of other people on the bus, in addition to the portly driver, at this time of day. One appears to be a maid, who is sitting at the front of the bus, with her dark hair coiled into a tight bun and a tan raincoat over what looks to be the collar of her aproned uniform. Her tub of cleaning materials and worn cotton purse sit on the seat next to her, her white-shoed feet crossed at the ankle underneath her. She glances up for a weary second when Jack hands the driver our toll.

The other person looks like a teenager, but it's hard to tell with his sunglasses on despite the sun not being up yet and the dark hoodie pulled low over his head. He is sprawled on one of the seats in the back like he owns the place, headphones over his ears, the cord running down his chest to the Walkman on his lap. He is either indifferent to our arrival or asleep.

Kasha and I slide into two seats on the left side of the bus and wedge our bags between our feet. Jack takes the seat directly across the aisle from us, placing his leather satchel and folded newspaper on the empty seat next to him. I watch as he removes his soft-brimmed hat and sets it on the pile of his belongings, absentmindedly running his hand through his hair.

The doors let out another puffing sound as they close. The bus lurches forward, and we are on our way.

The ride doesn't take too long, and the time is spent looking out the windows, watching the trees and hills go by as the sun starts to peek over the mountains at our backs. My nerves have shifted from trip anxiety to wondering if I am doing the right thing. I still have a twisting feeling in my gut, but now I also have a heaviness in my heart. I wonder how long it will be until I see Pops again.

Shortly after the thought enters my mind, we are in the city, and I am fully distracted by the vastness of it. Traffic, lights, and buildings are in every direction I look. People are littered about, even at this early hour of the morning. The motion of everything is overstimulating, and I am very glad I am not driving.

We pull up to the train station and prepare to climb off the bus, grabbing onto the support poles and hoisting our bags over our shoulders. Stepping off the last bus stair and onto the curb of the sidewalk outside the station, my heart starts racing.

"Kash, we are at a train station! Can you believe it?" My excitement is muffled by my awe.

"I know, I know! I am so excited! I can't believe this is happening! Jack, where do we go next?"

Smiling at our joy, he pulls the tickets out of the inner breast pocket of his jacket and says, "I'll go check us in. You girls can head around that way." He points in the direction of a sidewalk that wraps around the side of the building. "There

TES

should be benches and concession stands next to the track if you are hungry I'll only be a few minutes, then I'll come and meet you. We have some time before the train arrives, so just make yourself comfortable or stretch your legs, but stay close."

We nod, link arms, and head off in the direction Jack indicated.

The train station is a tan, one-story building, with a food vendor window on its back side, facing the tracks. There is a wide platform that drops a few feet to the tracks below, with old-fashioned lampposts and metal benches spaced throughout it.

Folks are milling around with coffee, a bagel, or a newspaper in their hands. No one has the appearance of intermixing or talking to strangers; everyone keeps to themselves as they wait for the train to arrive.

The crowd consists of commuters mainly, on their way to work. There are a few groups of what appear to be travelers like us. They are easy to spot because they stay huddled together, like one of them will get lost, never to be seen again, if they venture too far from the group. They are wearing brightly colored shirts with the locations of different places on them. Bulky cameras hang from a few of their necks, and they sport wide-brimmed sun hats on their heads and have loads of baggage at their feet. It makes me glad Jack told us to pack light, not just considering our upcoming hike, but because it keeps me from looking too much like these people. Like a tourist.

Kasha and I each get a muffin from the concession window; hers is blueberry, mine pumpkin. We walk over and glance down at the rails as we peel back the wrappers and take a bite. My muffin is delicious, with a buttery glaze on top and an overpowering flavor of cinnamon. *I should grab another one for the train ride, before we board,* I think to myself. *Never hurts to have a backup snack.*

I jump as I feel a tug on the back of my sweater. Turning around I look down into the deep brown eyes of a little boy, no more than probably four years old. His hair is disheveled from a night of sleep, and it looks like his mother hadn't gotten around to combing it yet. And he fidgets with the hem of his Teenage Mutant Ninja Turtles t-shirt.

"Excuse me. Can I have your muffin?"

"My muffin?" I ask him, unsure if I heard him correctly with his slight speech impediment.

"Yes. I want a muffin."

"Well, no. I am sorry, this is my muffin and I already started eating it. See," I turn the muffin so he can see where I have taken a bite. "You wouldn't want this muffin."

"Oh, man... Okay." After a beat he adds, "Are there any muffins left? I *really* want one." At this he drags out the word really, in a long dramatic fashion that would have anyone with a soft heart thinking that this child is near to starvation. The act has a smile naturally forming on my face.

"Yes, I believe there are more muffins. Many different kinds, too," I tell him. "See that window, right over there? That is where they have them."

"Oh goodie!" he exclaims and dashes off in the direction of the concession stand window.

"I am sure that one will keep his mother on her toes," Kasha tells me and we both chuckle at the encounter.

"What do you think it will be like? Cliffsides, I mean," I ask Kasha as we stand there eating our breakfast.

"I suppose it will be lovely. Like something from a book or a painting. Waves crashing along the shore, salt air on our faces, blowing our hair. Jack said that they sometimes host balls. Could you imagine? Us, going to a ball?" At this she gives a little sway of her hips, opening her arms wide, her smile contagious.

"I'm not quite sure how we got so lucky. I feel like I'm just waiting for the other shoe to drop. You know? Like this isn't real," I add, a bit dubiously.

"Hmmm..." Kasha pauses for a second, mouth twisting to the side. "Two things. First of all, why does the other shoe need to drop? I think we have been through enough, and this is Fate's way of rewarding our grace. Besides, we have already had this conversation. Remember?

"I know, I know," I say, trying to sound more nonchalant than I feel.

"Also, it is laced with old, mysterious history. When I was looking up places to go when we first started planning our trip a few years ago, I fell down the preverbal rabbit hole."

"Proverbial," I correct her.

"Yeah, yeah, whatever. Anyway, the article stated that this place was abandoned a few years after the original owner died in a fishing accident. It claimed that no one wanted to buy it on account of too many odd things happening whenever prospective buyers would go to look at it. Well, the lack of sale was attributed to some supposed hauntings, not to mention the fact that it remained crazy out of the way of any type of civilization. A money trap. It is kind of cool that it has been restored back to its glory days, though."

I nod. "Makes me wonder how Jack ended up with it."

"Inheritance." I jump slightly as I hear the deep timbre of his voice.

"Sorry," I try to add quickly, not wanting him to think we were talking about him. "We were just discussing the manor, and..." I find myself trailing off, not knowing what exactly to say. Everything that comes out of my mouth just sounds like rambling. I take a bite of my muffin to shut myself up and notice Kasha trying her best not to laugh at my blunder.

Jack's eyes dance between the two of us for a second, his fedora tipped low over one eye to block the morning sun, before he adds, "It was actually my dad's. I grew up there. He was the fisherman lost at sea. The stories of it sitting abandoned for years are true. I was away for a while, and the marine weather took its toll, making it look worse for wear." He pauses for a second, a seriousness coming over his features, throat bobbing as he swallows. But just as soon as his discomfort appears, it vanishes, replaced by mirth as he says, "As far as it being haunted, I suppose you will just have to see for yourselves."

Just then the announcement came on that the train to San Luis Obispo was arriving and that all passengers should begin to make their way to Gate D on their designated platform. Jack gestures for us to follow him, and we tuck in as the crowd begins to shift, finding the areas where they need to be to board the correct train cars.

Once we receive the go-ahead to board, I follow Jack, stepping over the gap between the platform and train, making my way up the narrow stairs behind him.

We have a whole car to ourselves for the time being. Apparently, the conductor seats the passengers together in the cars intended for their designated stop. This helps to eliminate confusion and the shuffling of people on the train for each destination. Half of the car has regular seats that look like they recline, and the other half has love seats facing the large windows down the side of the train. I hope we have a private train car for the duration of the ride.

When Jack takes our bags from us and lifts them up to store in the overhead compartments, I try not to look at the sliver of his stomach stretched flat, peeking out from under his shirt, as his arms reach above his head. *No, Gabs, now is not the time, but damn.*

To distract myself from the, um, view, I wander over to one of the wide viewing benches facing the windows. The seats are red velvet with little gold accents along the stitching, reminding me of Christmas. Kasha must have had the same idea, because she mentions feeling like she is riding on the *Polar Express*. Unable to hide our smiles, we curl up together on one of the double viewing benches, legs tucked under our bodies. We are prepared to take in every piece of the landscape from here to San Luis Obispo.

The train slowly starts to chug forward, and I have an overwhelmingly childlike sense of bliss washing over me.

"I quite literally feel like a kid on their way to the North Pole to see Santa," I say.

Kasha in the seat next to me says, "I know, this is so cool! I'm actually happy that the train ride will take us the majority of the day. I don't think I'm going to want to get off."

We watch the hills slowing turn into the flatlands of the valley. The grass is a golden brown from the hot summer sun. Fields of almond trees, hay, and citrus all roll past for miles upon miles. We shoot through oil fields, with hundreds of pump jacks looking like dinosaurs repeatedly dipping their heads to drink from the dry ground at their feet.

Jack comes to stand behind my bench seat, leaning forward and resting his arms on the back so his face is closer to mine, gazing out the wide windows at the panoramic view in front of us. I glance up, meeting his sparkling eyes, then down at his lips that are only inches away from mine.

"Here," he says, reaching over and handing me another pumpkin muffin.

"How did you know I wanted another one?" I ask, surprised.

A smile tugging at one corner of his mouth, he says, "You looked like you were enjoying it before we boarded. Besides, it never hurts to have backup snacks."

Shocked into a brief moment of silence, I feel my cheeks sting and my heart start beating a little faster before I say, "Thanks," and quickly turn to look out the window. I suck in my lips to try to hide the stupidly large smile that is threatening to be released.

He walks over to another chair and props his feet up on the footrest, crossing them at the ankles. Reclining his seat, he tips his fedora down over his eyes, smile still pulling at the edges of his mouth. He interlocks his fingers over his lap, elbows resting on his hips, and appears to go to sleep.

When I turn back around, Kasha is watching me watch him with a wicked grin on her face. Apparently, my expression says it all. I playfully slap her arm and shove a bite of muffin into my mouth, turning back to the scenery zooming by.

My favorite part of the locomotive journey begins when we start to hug the California coastline. As we twist through a winding valley of vineyards, grape vines rolling over hills as far as the eyes can see, the ocean peeks out to give us a tiny glimpse from time to time. Watching the pristine rows of grapes whip past gives me a dizzying sensation. I want to run my fingers across them, like a child would do with a stick along a picket fence, and hear it clink with the movement.

After waking from his nap a few hours later, Jack appears with a stack of premade salads in his hands. "I got these from the lunch car. Thought we could eat something before we disembark. We're getting closer. It will be a quick bus ride, and then we are on our feet. Hope you gals are ready to stretch your legs."

"I will be after I eat something. Good thinking, Jack," Kasha responds, reaching out to take the garden salad with ranch dressing.

I opt for the Caesar and thank him, crunching a fat crouton before I even take a bite of the lettuce. The three of us sit there in the wide, comfortable seats eating our salads, watching where the mountains meet the sea.

Before we know it, the train pulls to a stop at a beautiful Spanish-style building. The station is a smooth, white-stucco, single-story complex with a red-tiled roof. Jack stands and reaches up to hand us down our bags. Walking down the narrow stairwell, we step off the train, leaving one fantasy world and stepping into another.

I crane my neck to look up at the big palm trees that surround the station, spinning in a slow circle to ensure that I get the full view. The green of the palm fronds stands out against the light-blue sky, scattered with white clouds above us. There is a slight ocean breeze that hits us, making me antsy to see the water and to get to our destination.

I am snapped out of my reverie when Jack tells us that the bus stop is just around the corner. Everything seems to be running on time, so that gives us about twenty minutes to get there. After we toss our empty salad containers in the metal trash can on the platform, we head in the direction he mentioned.

The bus ride to San Simeon is quick in comparison to the train ride, especially considering the Christian high school choir group that kept us entertained throughout the trip. A small group of kids sat in the back of the bus on their way to Hearst Castle, singing hymns the entire journey. Kasha chair-danced and clapped her hands along to the rhythm as Jack and I tried to stifle our embarrassment and laughter. Hand clasped over my mouth to keep from laughing out loud and causing a bigger scene than Kasha already was, I tried to distract myself with the view. It was harder than it looked, mainly due to her constant bobbing in the seat next to me.

Finally, the bus comes to a stop. The end of the road, the driver states, and we begin exiting, one at a time. The first thing I notice is the change in atmosphere. The temperature is a lot chillier here than at home or even at the train station, and I pull my black knit sweater tight around my center.

Then there is the smell and feel of the air. It feels fresher somehow. The salt from the sea and the moisture coating my senses make me abundantly aware that I am at the shore.

"You won't need that once we start moving," Jack notes, hinting at my secured sweater.

"Well, then I suppose I'll take it off once I start to warm up," I respond, detaching my cap from the loop at the top of my backpack and shoving it on my head. "Until then, I'm cold."

"Oh, she's always cold," Kasha interjects matter-of-factly. "It wouldn't surprise me if she wears it all the way to Cliff-sides."

"Okay," Jack says as he turns to Kasha, fists resting on his hips. Gesturing back in my direction with one hand he continues, "If she wears it halfway to the manor, I have to carry your bag the remainder of the way. If she takes it off, you'll carry mine. Deal?"

A nefarious grin starting across her face, Kasha reaches forward and clasps Jack's hand with a hearty slap. "Deal. I like nothing more than an easy bet."

Turning to me, he adds, eyes narrowing, "Now, no cheating to help Kasha out. I will be able to tell if you start to get too hot."

Tossing my hands in the air, I say, "Don't look at me! This is between the two of you. I'm just going to do my thing."

Raising an eyebrow and considering me for a second, he grunts and nods as we start walking north. I can't help the twinge of jealousy that flutters to life in my center at their banter. Old doubts about the two of them resurface. But I quickly try to stomp them down.

There is a dirt trail that weaves along the side of the road, hugging the shoreline. We continue to hike along in a single-file line, Jack leading the way and Kasha taking up the rear. The path is slender, with knee-high amber grass swaying in the breeze along the sides. There is a light dusting of dirt that is kicked up from our shoes, but the cool ocean breeze quickly carries it away.

It is amazing how loud the ocean sounds when the waves are crashing on the sand and rocks to our left. I thought that the river at home was loud, especially after the snowmelt, but this is different. Occasionally, cars pass us on the main road, adding to the rumbling, rolling sound of the sea.

After walking for about an hour, Jack stops abruptly and spins to face me. I come to a rough halt, as to not plow into him.

"What was that?" I ask, feeling like there is something that I should have noticed and begin looking around. Heart skipping a beat, I think about the knife strapped to my calf.

"You're not hot?" he asks incredulously.

"No," I say. "Quite comfortable, actually." My sweater is still on, but it hangs open down the front, exposing my white tank top and a sliver of midriff.

He stares at me for another moment, face serious, and then looks past me to Kasha. I turn back, too, and see that she looks like the cat that just ate the canary. Without a word she slips her duffel over her head and reaches forward, handing Jack the strap.

He grunts and drapes it over his own shoulder. Adjusting his grip on his satchel, he weaves his jacket through the straps of Kasha's duffel bag, spins around, and continues walking.

I turn to look at Kasha, and we both start laughing. "Thank you, good sir," she adds with a mock salute and an enthusiasm that she obviously feels.

He doesn't bother saying anything or turning back around. He simply raises his hand in the air, giving it a little wave, and keeps walking. Our giggles don't stop for another thirty paces.

We continue in comfortable silence until we hear the most horrible honking and growling sounds, accompanied by a terrible smell.

"What on Earth is that?" I exclaim. Kasha doesn't answer but rather heads off at a sprint toward the cliffhang and the source of the noise.

Cupping his free hand to the side of his mouth, Jack shouts loud enough to be heard over the bellowing from below. "Stay up here! Don't go down!"

As we stand on the edge of a sandy drop-off, the largest, strangest-looking creatures I have ever seen are sprawled across the sand on the beach below us. They look like seals but appear to be five times their size, some of them with their long proboscis noses swaying back and forth as they wiggle their gigantic bodies over the sand. A few of them lift their heads into the air and let out a loud gurgling before moving surprisingly fast over the beach, slamming their bulbous chests into each other. Others are passed out in the sun, and still others emit a clacking sound from deep within their throats.

"What in the Heavens are those things?" Kasha asks, mouth agape. "They look like monstrous sealions."

I have never seen her at such a loss for words. I also cannot believe that she is standing there with her mouth ajar. The creatures have a scent that you could taste, and I pull the sleeve of my sweater over my fist and cup it to my mouth, having it act as an air filter. It only helps slightly. The smell is that of chemicals, decomposing fish, and feces. It's almost as overpowering as the noises that continue to erupt from the beach.

As we stare down at them in pure disbelief, Jack explains, "Those are elephant seals. The males and females come to sandy inlets, called rookeries, to mate, molt, and sunbathe. They spend the majority of their lives in the ocean, eating fish, squid, and sometimes sharks, but this stretch of the central coast houses them year-round. It's important to remember that they are extremely huge and are also wild animals. The females, especially, will attack you if you get too close to their pups."

After taking in the strange creatures for an extended period of time, we press on down the trail. As we walk, Kasha and I begin rapidly firing questions to Jack about the elephant seals, and he struggles to keep up with our back-and-forth questions.

"Why do they smell so terrible?"

"Because they are obese creatures of the sea."

"The noises, is that how they talk to each other?"

"Yes, depends on the season and their sounds, but..."

"Why were they on the beach?"

"To soak up the heat of the sun, breed, molt, and care for their young."

"Could they eat us?"

"Well, I wouldn't recommend getting too close."

"Oh my God, Gabs," Kasha says to me. "Did you see how ugly they were? Are the males the ones with the funky noses?"

"Yes –"

"Ha!" she interrupts Jack. "Gabs, we thought the selection of men were terrible back at South Brook!"

At this we all start laughing so hard that I have to stop to catch my breath, leaning forward and placing my hands on my knees. Once my lungs feel like they can hold air again, I stand, wiping the tears from my eyes with the backs of my hands.

That's when I see it.

Sitting on a coastal overhang is the Cliffside Manor.

Chapter 14

First Impressions

"Wow," the word escapes my lips as a whisper as I look down at the mansion from the edge of the bluff.

It sits on a small peninsula, a single gravel road turning off from the main highway and weaving down to the manor below. A myriad of tree types span the property. From tall, narrow Italian cypress trees lining the fence along the property's entrance, to king palm trees with swaying fronds dotting the area closer to the house, and big, shady sycamores spread throughout the pastures adjacent to the main building. The house sits like a sentinel, watching both land and sea. It's built close to the edge of the bluffs; there are waves crashing along the stony shore below it, and there are tiny, rocky islands off its coast. One of the larger, rocky islands holds the lighthouse Jack mentioned when we were sitting around Kasha's bonfire, back in South Brook. The lighthouse sits proud and erect, staring out to sea, a wide, blue stripe encircling its top, in contrast to its otherwise stark white paint.

The mansion appears to have been built in the Queen Anne style, with a steep cross-gabled roof, large dormers, and a big wraparound porch. It has wood panels for its siding that are painted a muted gray, with crisp, white trim and a stone-gray roof. I can't help but think how it must blend into the foggy coastline when the marine layer rolls in thick and moist off the water.

Off to the northern side of the property, there are large, fenced-in pastures and a barn. Multiple horses are out in the sunny fields, grazing. At the sight of the horses, I am overwhelmed with giddiness, feeling like a child. Already in awe of the house and view, I have a profound sense of eagerness to walk the remaining way down the hill to the estate.

After we've all spent a good while admiring the beauty of the house—waves crashing on the rocks below its terrace—Jack's fingers brush against mine. He links his pinky with my index finger and, in the voice of someone at peace, says, "Welcome to my home."

"Jack, this is incredible," I say, still barely able to find my voice, a warmth spreading through my soul at our contact. "Are those your horses?"

"Yes, you can go and see them or go for a ride, if that is something you would ever like to do. I used to raise them for sale, but they are simply pleasure horses now. I find them beautiful, and just watching them brings me joy. But first, we should probably head down and wash up. Clarence should have supper ready for us soon."

At the thought of supper, my stomach lets out an audible gurgle.

"Who is Clarence?" Kasha asks as we make our way down the dusty path toward the house.

"Clarence works for me. He has been like a member of the family since before my dad passed away. He helps keep everything running smoothly, both when I am home and when I am away for work. He is a kind, grandfatherly figure, and I have never been able to pin down how he does everything he does in such a calm and efficient manner. I think you both will like him. If you have any questions or needs while you are here, he can assist you with them."

We complete our descent, and Jack opens a large, rusty gate at the entrance of the property, which lets out a screech with the movement. As we head down the gravel drive that seems to go on for a quarter of a mile, I am struck by the smell of the ocean and the horses. It is a lovely combination, and I find myself already never wanting to leave.

Just as the house comes into a clearer view, the largest and scariest dog I have ever seen comes bounding from around the side of the terrace, heading directly toward us. Kasha and I instinctively huddle together, arms weaving tight through one another.

Jack's face breaks into a huge grin as he starts laughing. "That's Sam! He's completely harmless. There is nothing to be afraid of, unless you are deathly allergic to drool and tail wags. He was the runt of a litter of pups we had a long time ago, and I couldn't find it in me to sell him off. He has too much personality, this one does. Don't you, boy?"

At this, Jack drops his and Kasha's bags and leans forward, giving Sam big rubs all around his floppy ears. Sam's mouth is agape in what looks like a big canine smile. Drool spools down from his jowls, his long, pink tongue dangling out of one side of his mouth. He hasn't stopped moving even as Jack pets him. His front paws move in a constant one-two-three, one-two-three waltz, and the tail looks like it could knock you unconscious if you're not careful.

Cautiously, Kasha and I untangle from our protective huddle, and I step forward to say hello. Sam goes stone-still, ears perked, eyes making direct contact with mine. I reach forward, stretching out the back of my hand in his direction so he can give it a smell, heart pounding in my chest. As if in a flash, his face is on mine, his gigantic, wet tongue sliding across the side of my face, from my jugular to my temple. Holding my breath, eyes pinched shut, and panic lodged in my throat, I stumble back, a muffled scream erupting from my tightly sealed mouth. Once I realize that I am not being mauled to death and eaten by this enormous Hellhound, I crack open one of my eyes to see Jack and Kasha in stitches of laughter and Sam looking up at me like I am his new favorite plaything.

Slime is still coating my face when Jack says between gasps, "I think he likes you."

One eye and my mouth still fastened shut, I tentatively reach up and wipe my face with the sleeve of my sweater. It comes away wet and sticky.

Utterly grossed out but unable to be mad at the silver eyes staring up at me, I tell Sam hello, but I add that he needs to work on his manners.

Continuing to laugh, Jack agrees, picks up a stick that looks like it was once a small tree branch, and tosses it up the lane for Sam. Sam takes off in long, bouncing strides after the stick, fully entranced with this new game.

We arrive at the manor shortly thereafter and follow Jack up the small flight of stairs that leads to the wraparound porch and front entrance. The craftmanship of the veranda is stunning, with detailed notches carved into the railing that sweeps around its perimeter. It is obviously handmade, and I feel myself gawking.

At the sound of the double front doors opening, I spin back around to be greeted by a tiny, round man in a fully tailored suit. He has stark, white hair combed to the side, twinkling, green eyes, and a face that looks like it could hold all the confidences of the world.

His gloved hands are clasped politely behind his back as he says, "Welcome home, Mr. Finnley." He inclines his head just slightly in Kasha's and my direction. "And this must be Ms. Pinkard and Ms. Owens. Pleasure to meet both of you. Welcome to Cliffside Manor. Please do come in. I am sure that you are both famished and in need of a washing up after your long journey here."

"Thank you. It's nice to meet you. A bath and dinner sound lovely," I manage to get out. "But you can call me Gabriella."

"And I'm Kasha," Kasha interjects quickly at my side.

"As you wish. I am Clarence. Please don't hesitate to inform me of any needs that may arise." Extending his arm out wide, palm up in a welcoming gesture, he says, "Please, ladies, this way if you don't mind. I will show you to your rooms."

We cross the threshold into the manor, and I am just as speechless, observing all the intricate details and finery of the interior, as I was looking down on the house from the bluff. Framed ancient pictures, yellowed with age, hang from the dark-stained, wood-paneled walls, and there is a white-and-burgundy rug that blankets the wooden floorboards at our feet. In the entryway there is a slender table that holds small, glass figurines and a crystal vase filled with wildflowers.

I strain my neck forward, trying to catch a glimpse down the hall, through one of the many open doorways, when Clarence takes both our bags from us and begins to lead us up the grand staircase. Kasha is close on my heels as we ascend.

Once on the second-story landing, Jack pauses before saying, "I hope you enjoy your rooms. Take a minute and wash up if you'd like. I will see you downstairs shortly for supper."

Then he heads off down the banistered hallway in the opposite direction of where Clarence is leading us.

We watch him go for a second before Clarence clarifies, "I will tap on your door when you are expected to come downstairs for supper. There is a tub with soap in each of your rooms and fresh clothes in the armoire, should you be inclined to wear something other than what you packed. There is no big hurry, though. Dinner won't be served until later."

Clarence walks us just a little farther down the upper corridor and stops at two doors mirroring each other across the hall. Opening one door wide, he delicately places Kasha's bag within the entrance. "Ms. Owe—forgive me. Kasha. Your room." Twisting on his heel and taking a step to the side, he opens the opposite door, setting my backpack just inside the threshold, though he never crosses it himself. "Gabriella. See you ladies shortly."

He silently and politely dismisses himself, leaving Kasha and me standing in the entryways of our respective bedrooms. We glance at each other as Clarence makes his departure down the hallway. Smiles spreading across our faces, we slowly close the doors to our rooms.

The space feels more like a small suite than a bedroom; it's almost the same size as our living room and kitchen back home. The bed is up against the wall nearest the door, with an ornate oak bedframe whose posts reach almost as high as the ceiling, a soft yellow floral bedspread, and matching pillowcases.

The other side of the room tapers off, becoming smaller as I near the large window, where afternoon sun pours in from outside. This must be one of the dormers, I think to myself. As I take in how the shape of the room has changed, I feel like this space is its own special separate nook. Facing the window is a vintage-looking sofa upholstered in more floral print on a beige background; there's an ornamental wooden railing along its edge and Flemish Scroll legs. A small coffee table is placed across from it, housing a book. I peer down at the cover: *Wuthering Heights* by Emily Bronte. *A good book,* I think to myself. I remember having to read it in our high school English class. I have always leaned toward the Gothic novels of the Brontë sisters more than the ornate societal descriptions of Jane Austen.

Reversing slightly, I head into the open doorway to my left that leads into the attached bathroom. The floor is beautifully tiled with small, white, hexagonal tiles framing brown ones that are woven into a leafy mosaic. Bleached subway tiles coat the walls near the tub and sink, and oak paneling covers the remainder of the bathroom. Under the small window on the far wall is a clawfoot tub.

I head over to the brass fixtures suspended over the side of the tub and stand there with my hands on my hips, pondering the functionality of the faucets. I fuss with the spigot until the temperature feels right and then stick my hand under the running water to plug the tub.

As the tub fills, steam beginning to encircle the space around me, I take down my hair and brush it out, then resecure it higher up on my head, intending to keep it out of the water. Stripping out of my travel-worn clothes and leaving them in a messy pile on the floor, I quickly stash the knife in between the couch cushions and dash back to the filling tub. I step over the side of the bath and dip my toes into the toasty water, then slide down until all but my head is submerged. Water lapping at the back of my neck, I close my eyes and revel in the sensations of clean, hot water. Absentmindedly, I reach over and grab the lavender soap from the hanging shelf on the side of the tub and start lathering my body. I lie there in pure bliss until my skin turns pink and the water begins to cool.

Standing, water sloshing about my calves, I grab one of the fluffy towels and wrap it around myself. I dry my body just enough, so I don't slip on the tiled floor and break my neck, and I head back out to the bedroom.

Curious, I walk across the room and open the large, teal-painted armoire in the corner. Clarence and Jack were right. There is a large assortment of clothes, ranging from everyday wear to evening gowns. Pulling some out for closer inspection, I notice that they are all in my size. This puzzles me, my brow furrowing and eyes narrowing in skepticism. *How are all these clothes already here and ready and in my size?* It is odd, to say the least. But I try to push the negativity from my mind. *Think rationally, Gabriella. I am sure Jack just called ahead and told Clarence what we would probably need upon our arrival.*

I pull an olive-green sundress over my shoulders. It fits snugly around my bust and hips, with delicate shoulder straps that crisscross over my back, and it flares out just slightly at my knees. I continue to rummage through the armoire until I find a pair of nude flats and a matching cream shawl. I have just slipped my feet into the shoes and wrapped the shawl around my shoulders when there is a knock on the door.

"Miss Gabriella, dinner will be served downstairs in the dining room in approximately ten minutes."

"Thank you, Clarence. I will be right down," I say back through the closed door.

Heading back into the bathroom, I pull my hair back out of its tie and run the brush through it, leaving it to hang loose down my back. There are no mirrors in sight, so I just hope for the best and turn to leave, opening the bedroom door to begin my way downstairs.

I find Kasha standing outside my door in a form-fitting, burgundy minidress, hair twisted up, exposing her long neck.

"Girl, you look lovely," I say, taking her in.

"Why, thank you! So do you! Oh, my God, Gabs, I love that color on you!" she exclaims, taking my hand and spinning me around so my skirt puffs out around my legs with the motion. "I have a whole closet full of clothes that I would have bought myself if I had the money. And they all fit perfectly!"

"Same," I say. "If I could afford them and had the style sense to buy them, that is."

Laughing at the good fortune we find ourselves in, we head downstairs. Once on the first-floor landing, we ponder which way the dining room is. After randomly entering what looks to be a library, then a sitting room with a large fireplace, we find a room with a long table set with formal tableware for three. Jack is already occupying one chair.

Upon seeing us entering the room, Jack stands. Clarence seems to appear out of thin air, pulling out our chairs across from Jack and motioning for us to sit.

"Good evening, ladies. I hope that your accommodations are to your liking," Jack states, resuming his seat.

"Yes, this place is amazing. Thank you."

"And thanks for the clothes," Kasha adds enthusiastically. "They are amazing and fit like a good pair of worn shoes."

Jack gives me a quizzical look, eyebrows pulling together. I shake my head slightly, signaling him to let it go and trying to stifle the smile that is threatening to turn into a full-blown laugh.

The table is covered with a white cloth, and sky-blue napkins are placed next to the set of white porcelain dinner plates, trimmed in gold. There are crystal glasses filled with ice water, and we have more silverware than I have ever seen set on a single table. I feel like I am suddenly out of my depth.

Before I can contemplate the cutlery for too long, Clarence reappears at our sides. With gloved hands he pours Kasha and me each a glass of white wine and a red one for Jack. Then he promptly places small garden salads in front of us, salad dressing in a silver boat on the table, and disappears through swinging doors and back into what I assume is the kitchen.

After we have finished our salads, we are treated to a delicious dinner of roasted chicken, potatoes, and fresh garden vegetables. Jack explains how everything we are eating tonight, excluding the wine, comes from his property. The hens and vegetables are all homegrown and processed here.

After removing our dinner plates and replacing them with dishes of ice cream, mint leaves intentionally placed on their sides, Clarence withdraws back into the kitchen. I look up at Jack. "Is it just us and Clarence? This place seems so big, and poor Clarence is waiting on us hand and foot. Surely, we can help out around here during our stay."

He smiles and takes a sip of wine. "It's no trouble at all. Trust me, Clarence enjoys fussing about. And to answer the other part of your question, there are other guests here and more staff members. I thought that it would be nice and relaxing to enjoy a more private setting for your first night here.

"You are welcome to explore the property tomorrow or relax around the manor," he continues, "whatever you feel like doing. I only ask that you do not venture to the third floor of the house. Everywhere else is fair game. There is a beach trail that winds down the bluff to the sea. Just watch out for elephant seals," he adds, eyes sparkling. "You are also welcome to go and see the horses. If you want to ride, just ask Gus to saddle one of the mares for you. You will probably find him napping in the barn."

"That sounds incredible. Thanks!" I turn to Kasha who is nodding in rapid agreement.

As we polish off our ice cream and wine, the exhaustion from the day starts to set in. Kasha and I offer our appreciation again and excuse ourselves, retiring for the evening. As we head upstairs, the light from the setting sun pours in through the windows, casting everything in a pink glow.

My eyelids are already becoming heavy with every step closer to the fluffy bed that I know is awaiting me. At the top of the stairs, I give Kasha a big hug, then cross the threshold of my room, clicking the door shut behind me. Warm and full, I kick off my shoes and collapse into bed, allowing the peaceful oblivion of sleep to carry me away.

Chapter 15

The Manor

The next morning, I awaken to the sun streaming in through the paned windows of the bedroom's alcove. The curtains are still ajar from the day before. I must have forgotten to close them last night. I lie in a nest of blankets and pillows, taking a moment to remember exactly where I am. That was one of the best nights of sleep I have had in a long time, and I find myself feeling revived and ready for the day.

Dragging myself from the comfortable bed, I look down and realize that I slept in the pretty dress I wore to dinner the night before, which is now wrinkled with sleep. Stretching and mussing my hair, I head to the bathroom, stepping out of my dress along the way. I head right to the tall, porcelain sink to brush my teeth. That is when I notice that the pile of dirty clothes that I left on the bathroom floor, along with all the ones that were in my backpack, are now laundered and neatly folded on the console table that sits adjacent to the sink.

Feeling surprised and a tad guilty, thinking of Clarence coming in here at some point to collect and wash my laundry, I grab a coiled washcloth from the shelf and run it under the water. When I see him, I will tell him that I am grateful, but there is no need for him to cater to my every need. I am capable of pulling my own weight and happy to do it.

Wrapping up my morning routine, I slip on a pair of jeans and a white, collared button-down. The top hugs my waist and breasts and sits open at a V a few inches below the base of my throat. Testing the movement of the shirt arms, I am content to see that I still have a full range of motion in my shoulders; the sleeves don't fit too tightly.

I kneel and begin rummaging through the bottom of the armoire until I find a pair of riding boots. It's like this place has everything I need exactly when I need it. Slipping them on, I can't help the bubbling anticipation I feel about getting on a horse again. It feels like it's been years since I would show up at the Garrisons' ranch to ride their old gelding around until dark. I plan on seeing if I can get a quick cup of tea and something small to eat before heading straight to the barn. Gus, I think, is the name of the guy Jack mentioned who cares for the horses. I should probably see what Kasha is up to before I go as well.

I quickly braid my long hair, letting it hang over my shoulder, and then make my way downstairs. There is a delicious smell coming from the kitchen, so I head in that direction.

Tentatively, I push the heavy, swinging, white door open and peek my head into the room. Kasha is standing at the counter with flour on her nose and dough covering her hands.

Looking up at my entrance, she beams. "Hey, girl! I hope you slept well! I slept like the dead. This is Ms. Gladis Smith, but she said I can call her Gladis." Here she tips her chin in the direction of the woman of ample build in a cornflower-blue dress and white laced apron, cinched around her expanding middle.

Her graying hair is coiled up on her head, cheeks rosy from the heat of the oven. With a knowing smile she says to me, "Good morning, Miss Gabriella. I do hope you had a restful evening."

"We're making lemon scones," Kasha chimes in enthusiastically. "You seriously must try one. They are Heavenly! And I helped!"

Laughing lightly, Ms. Smith adds, "That she did. And a natural you are, Miss Kasha. Here, Gabriella, pull up a chair. I will put on a pot of tea for you."

"Thank you, Ms. Smith."

"Gladis, please. The 'Ms. Smith' is not necessary," she says, a smile warming her face.

"Gladis," I correct myself. "I'm surprised you trust Kasha not to burn down your kitchen."

Kasha flicks some flour from her fingers in my direction, sticking out her tongue, when Gladis's back is turned to light the stove.

"Oh, I'm not too worried about that. Besides, I have my eye on her," she adds as she turns around, a sarcastic grin alighting on her lips. "She is right, though; you must try one of her scones. They are delicious if I do say so myself. In fact, I may not allow her to escape the kitchen so easily now that I know she has a talent for baking."

I look over to Kasha, who for once in her life appears to be blushing, looking down at the rolled dough in front of her.

Just as the tea kettle starts to whistle, I stand and walk over to the pile of lemon scones that sit alluringly on a platter, picking one up and placing it on a napkin. Taking it back to my seat on the high stool next to the counter, I take a bite. I am hit with the sweet, buttery flavor, which blends perfectly with the tanginess of the lemon drizzle. It is tender and instantly begins to flake with my modest bite. Letting out an audible moan, I close my eyes, relishing the flavors. Hand cupped under the remaining portion in my other hand, I look up at two sets of expectant eyes. "I think this is the best scone I have ever eaten," I add, speaking around the remaining bits in my mouth, and I genuinely mean every word.

Kasha claps her hands and lets out a little squeal, sending both flour and Ms. Smith's eyes into the air. I pop the rest of my scone into my mouth with a laugh and begin sucking the remnants of frosting off the tips of my fingers.

Ms. Smith hands me a cup of steaming tea and asks, "So, my dear, what does the day have in store for you?"

"Well, I was going to see what Kasha wanted to do, but I was hoping to walk over to the stables and see the horses. Maybe even go for a ride if I'm lucky."

"Oh, you will be lucky enough. I'm sure those horses would be thrilled to have the exercise. If I was a gambling woman,

I would even bet that Gus, the stable hand, would be just as happy to have you take them out for him. What about you, Kasha, dear?"

Kasha looks quickly between Gladis and me before she says, "Well, I was hoping I could spend some more time here in the kitchen with you. I am really enjoying myself. I feel like I'm discovering a passion I didn't realize I had."

"I would happily welcome the help," Gladis reassures her.

"You don't mind, do you, Gabs?" She peers over at me. "I can come see the horses with you another time, if you'd like."

Smiling at my best friend, I assure her that I don't mind at all. If she keeps baking like this, I personally will help Gladis chain her to the kitchen sink. The mood is light in the warm kitchen, and I feel at home in such a new setting.

Finishing my tea, I grab another scone and make my exit. I practically skip down the stairs of the terrace, feeling rejuvenated. I have a pep in my step that wasn't there before. The morning sun beats down on my face, but the air is cool with a light breeze coming off the ocean, setting the day at the perfect temperature.

I head down the dirt lane, pastures sprinkled with scraggly oaks on either side of me as I approach the barn.

My steps slow as I peek into the barn. As soon as I cross the threshold, I inhale the smell of horses and hay and close my eyes relishing in the beautiful, rustic scent.

"Hello?" I ask as I make my way deeper into the barn, peeking into the different stables as I walk along. "Gus? Is anyone here?"

I admire a buckskin that turns to look at me from the far end of the stall, but it doesn't bother to come any closer. I turn to the opposite stall and approach the big bay, who has just poked his head over the stall door for a scratch on his muzzle. He is overly friendly and keeps lifting his lips into the air with every motion of my fingers on his upper lip.

Leaving him behind, I head toward the adjoining stall, whose gate was left open. It has a few rakes, a wheelbarrow, and a large pile of hay occupying it. Wedged into the pile of loose hay, there appears to be a dark shape lying near the top. I step farther into the stall, and I notice a skeletal figure in the heap. It is curled into a fetal position, with its back to me. The vertebrae of his spine appear fully exposed through the back of the soft blue shirt. Lumps of every bone are visible through his thin top, and a hip bone protrudes out of the top of his brown canvas pants. The exposed bones of what was once an arm flop down as he shifts on the hay, and I see the different bones covered in rotten tissue and the exposed ligaments pulled tight over the forearm and decomposing hand. My hands fly to cover my mouth as I pinch my eyes shut and let out an involuntary scream.

Suddenly there is a boy standing in front of me, holding my shoulders. "Ma'am? Ma'am? It seems like yous have had a fright. Are yous okay? Do yous need me to fetch Mr. Jack for yous?"

I blink at this boy holding me in place, his slight Southern accent laced with a speech impediment. I peer around his shoulder toward the haystack, but the image is gone. I step away from him to have a closer inspection, feeling both terrified and perplexed. There is nothing there, barely an indentation where I saw the corpse.

Taking a deep, shaky breath to steel myself, I say, "I am sorry. I thought I saw something. . . No, there is no need to find Jack. I'm all right." *I must've imagined it.* Shaking my head at my irrational delusion, I turn to face the young man standing in the storage stall with me.

"I'm looking for Gus. Do you know where I can find him? Jack said to talk to him about seeing the horses and going for a ride," I say, trying to regain my composure.

"Why, yes, ma'am. That's me," he says enthusiastically, pointing a thumb right at his chest, a large grin spreading across his freckled face.

He looks no more than fourteen, with a mop of messy, rust colored hair, hazel eyes, and a spattering of freckles across his nose and cheekbones. He is tall and lanky, like most boys his age. He's wearing a soft, blue button-down shirt, cuffed at the elbows, and brown canvas pants. I feel my heart freeze in my chest as I gape at this boy, eyes going wide, not knowing if I should flee or if I am truly going mad.

"I's know, everyone looks at me like that when they first meet me. I's young, but a guy needs to start somewhere in life, and Mr. Jack was kind enough to give me a chance. He says I's a natural with dem horses." I can hear the pride in his voice as he lifts his chin.

Snap out of it, Gabriella. Get a hold of yourself. You just stumbled on this boy sleeping in the hay. For God's sake, there is still hay in his hair. Your eyes are playing tricks on you.

"That sounds lovely," I manage to croak out. With a little more composure, I add, "I used to spend every free moment I had on my neighbor's ranch, growing up. I have always loved horses."

TES

"Theys honestly one of da Good Lord's greatest creatures. I's think I's got a mare that yous will just fall in love with. Please, come with me, Miss. . .?"

"Gabriella," I supply.

We head out of the stall and down the corridor until we are standing at the paddock of a gorgeous palomino.

"This is Miss Adelaide, but we's call her Ada," Gus says with such reverence in his voice that I understand why Jack has placed him in charge of his horses. "She can be a little temperamental and wants to do what she wants to do when she wants to do, but show me a mare that don't." Here he cracks himself up, sliding his eyes to me to see if I am as amused as he is. "But she's a good mare and wills take great care of ya. I's think the two of yous will get along swell."

He grabs the halter off the hook on the wall and enters her stall. I watch, allowing the smell of the barn to calm my remaining jitters. Ada is a beautiful mare. Tall and slender, with good muscle tone and conformation. Her back is long and straight, legs straight under her joints, and her coat shines golden in the morning light. She picks up her hooves in a delicate dance as she walks. There's a slight curl to her neck, and I can't wait to feel what her gait is like underneath me.

She walks right over to Gus and dips her head into the halter in his hands. After securing the buckle, he gives her a long, slow rub down her forehead, massaging the space under her forelock as she pushes into him for more.

Leading her out of the stall, he says to me, "I's get her groomed and tacked up for ya, Miss Gabriella."

"Actually, Gus," I interject, "I would love to groom and saddle her myself. If you don't mind."

"No's trouble at all, ma'am," he says and leads Ada over to a large, wooden tie rail and loops the lead through the hole in the hitching post. "Alls the tack is rights there," he says, pointing to the tack room doorway. "I's be back in a few minutes to check your girth for yous. Can't have yous slipping off or anything foolish. Mr. Jack would have my head." Smiling, he tips his imaginary hat to me and heads back down the corridor.

Walking over to Ada, I reach out my hand so she can give it a sniff. As she does, I run my other hand down the length of her neck and give it a good scratch right in the nook where her neck meets her shoulder. She leans hard into me and extends her head out, front lip jutting forward with the motion. "Feel good, girl?" I ask with an airy chuckle.

After giving her a quick pat, I head into the tack room and grab a curry comb, soft brush, old hairbrush, and a hoof pick. Dumping the contents into an empty bucket I walk back toward Ada and start to pamper her. I feel a wash of tranquility spread over me as I run the brushes across her sunny coat and down her long tail. Horsehair and dust start to coat my skin and clothes.

Once I'm satisfied with her gleaming coat, I take the bucket of supplies back and start searching for tack that I think will fit her. The saddle is not too hard to find; it sits on a wall mount with a brass placard labeled Adelaide. Pulling the saddle pad down and tucking it under one arm, I use my other arm to remove the saddle. I grab the back of the seat and wedge the tree under the horn on my hip to help me carry it. It doesn't take me long to remember the motions of tacking a horse. My muscle memory kicks in, and before I know it, Ada is saddled and nearly ready to ride.

I turn to find Gus, but he is already leaning up against a nearby post watching me with a kind smile on his young face.

"I think I got it," I tell him, "but I'm not sure which bridle is hers."

"It's the hackamore. She's a gentle gal with a soft mouth. I's grab it for yous."

He is back a couple seconds later with a lovely, braided bridle in his hands. Slipping off her halter, he seamlessly places her nose through the hackamore and pulls it over her ears. He slowly walks around her, checking her saddle, making sure I did everything correctly. With a serious look on his face, he pulls on her girth, making it just a bit tighter.

"Alls righty then, yous be all set, Miss Gabriella. Have a beautiful ride."

"Thank you, Gus," I say as I take the reins in one hand, placing my left foot in the stirrup and hoisting myself up, then swinging my right leg up and over the saddle.

Giving Ada another pat, I pull the reins to the side, directing her down a nearby trail.

We spend what feels like hours exploring the paths along the pastures. Not wanting to venture too far for my first ride, I stay relatively close to the manor, but with the property being so large, it is easy to spend a day out in the open.

Considering the substantial amount of time we've spent warming up at a walk, I only have to drop my reins slightly for Ada to know what I am asking. She's ready to pick up the pace. We trot for a few paces, getting the feel for one another, before she instinctively jumps into a nice, steady lope.

The wind pulls across my face, my body automatically moving in unison with Ada's gait. I have ridden a lot of horses over the years, but I have never felt this instant connection with a horse before. It feels like our souls have connected; our hearts merged. I am surprised by this instant bond.

I lay the reins loose on her neck, giving Ada her whole head. She drops it, tucking in, lifting her tail, and pulling faster. Harder. I can feel her legs ripping forward with each motion, digging at the air in front of us. We run across the field at a full gallop, and I have never felt so free in my life. The golden grass whips below us, cool sea air blowing across my face and making my cheeks tingle. The oak trees in the pasture, the mountains to our right, and the sea to our left blur with our speed.

My legs supporting my weight, hips and back shifting with every pounding hoofbeat, I spread my arms wide, feeling the wind and sun on my body, my heart racing with every stride. I have become an extension of Ada, and I feel her need to race forward. Her need has become my need. I lean forward in my saddle, reins still loose and flopping before her withers, pulling and charging with her. Flying.

After what feels like both an eternity and a time cut too short, we begin to slow our pace, returning to a lope, then a trot, and eventually a walk. Her walk is more of a constant prance, as I feel her dancing beneath me.

I lie forward in the saddle so the horn lays at my side instead of in my gut and hug her, pressing my cheek against her sweat-slicked neck. Feeling her heaving for breath and coating myself in her sweat, I smile into her flaxen fur. Her heat and heartbeat feel like they match my own, and I know she is as sated as I feel.

I spot Jack sitting on the fence line in the distance, so I turn Ada over in his direction.

When he sees me coming, he jumps off the fence and walks up to us. He confidently grabs my reins, bringing my mare to a solid stop before him.

"How's Ada treating you?" he asks as he steps to the side to avoid her still-jigging hooves. "Looks like you were enjoying each other."

He is absentmindedly rubbing his large, callused hand down her curled neck to calm her, his head level with my hips in the saddle. I look down at his blue eyes, his dark hair tussled in the breeze coming off the ocean. I have the sudden desire for him to rub his hand up my thigh and grab my hips, pulling me from the saddle and into his arms.

Swallowing hard and heart racing, I manage to say, "Good. It feels wonderful being back in the saddle."

"That's right, you used to ride, didn't you?"

"All the time while I was growing up. Our neighbors—the Garrisons, the ones with the large cattle farm—had horses.

They would let me ride their old appaloosa gelding, Sundance, after school. I had to practically be pulled from the saddle when the sun would set."

"I remember you telling me now," he responds with a smile. "And it makes sense, you're a natural up there."

"Oh, I don't know about that. Adelaide is a pretty remarkable horse. I have never ridden anything quite like her before."

"She is a rare beauty, for sure." As he says this, he doesn't take his eyes off mine. Electricity snaps between us. *I can't be the only one who feels this,* I think to myself. But I find myself too shy to say anything further, and I silently kick myself for it.

Ada starts tossing her head around, pulling back toward the barn. Her impatience with our conversation is obvious.

"I should probably—" I start.

"Yes," Jack says. "I think she is ready for her wipe down and grain." Looking to the foam that has formed on her shoulders and flanks, he adds, "You gave her one of the best workouts she has had in a while, and I can tell she enjoyed herself. Take your time. I am glad that you two have found one another. Maybe we can take a ride together soon."

"I'd really like that," I tell him and find myself as giddy as a schoolgirl at the thought of dashing through the sycamore trees on the back of a horse with Jack.

"Good. I'd like that too," he says, eyes dancing. "I'll see you back at the manor this evening. There is something I want to talk to you and Kasha about."

Before I have a chance to inquire as to what he means, he has turned to pick his way back across the field, toward the big house.

Later that evening I sit with Kasha on a couple of Adirondack chairs on the terrace, each of us with a chilled glass of wine in our hand. Sipping our wine and watching the sun dip closer and closer to the deep blue horizon, we discuss our day. She tells me all about her time in the kitchen with Gladis and how she taught her how to make a mincemeat pie. It is fun seeing her so happy. I tell her about my ride and how I think I am in love with Ada, the big, golden mare that looks like sunshine and moves like the wind. I also mention my encounter with Jack; how every time I see him, I feel like my heart skips a beat. I never really know what I am saying when I start talking to him.

"Girl, I think you officially have a crush. I'm proud of you. It's about dang time," she says, laughing at me.

Trying to hide my blush with another sip of wine and glancing at the dirt still under my fingernails, I try changing the subject before I get in too deep, thinking about Jack and his broad shoulders and gentle aura.

"Doesn't this place feel like Heaven?" I ask Kasha, blissfulness warming my soul.

There is a long pause. I slowly turn my head to look in Kasha's direction to see why she hasn't responded. Her face is abruptly solemn, like a window curtain drawn suddenly.

"Kash?" I ask. "Is everything all right? Is it something I said?"

After another beat, she says, suddenly serious, "No. I mean, yes. Everything is wonderful, and I agree with you about it feeling like Heaven..." She trails off for a second before continuing. "Gabs, there is something I need to tell you. I am. I am not sure how to star—" Anxiety starts to pool in my stomach at her words. *I knew I wasn't fully imagining things when I felt like she was keeping something from me. We know each other too well for secrets, and I fear that she too is in love with Jack.* My heart plummets at the thought.

"Good evening, ladies," Jack interrupts her as he glances between Kasha and me. I hadn't heard his approaching steps, so it feels as if he materialized next to us. I wonder how much of our conversation he has overheard. He gives no indication of having interrupted when he continues, and all I want to do is hear what Kasha had to say. "It's a lovely night. I just wanted to let you both know that we are hosting a ball in two days' time, to celebrate the new moon. You are both welcome, and if I am honest, I expect you to attend." A smile lights up his eyes as they connect to mine. "Clarence should have laid out a few gown options for you in your rooms. I hope that they are to your liking."

"How exciting! A ball! Kasha and I didn't have the best experience at our senior prom, so this will be like making up for lost time and bad memories," I say, previous conversation slipping temporarily from my mind.

"Why do you celebrate the new moon?" Kasha asks, veering the subject away from prom and I am filled with a tinge of guilt in the pit of my stomach for bringing it up.

"Originally it was an agricultural festival, marking the start of the season and a way for people to bless their future crops. We had Jewish immigrants for neighbors, once upon a time, and they introduced our family to the tradition. It was called

Rosh Chodesh and was a monthly holiday that celebrated the arrival of a new month. It has changed slightly over the decades, and we went from breaking bread made from the first monthly harvest to hosting grand balls. It has become an event of more grandeur since then, but the message is still the same. It signifies the birth of possibilities, and people use it as a time to align with their deepest desires... and dreams. I find that fitting. Don't you?"

As he speaks, his eyes bore into mine, and I feel my breath hitch. A dreamlike essence hovers over me, not just at the idea of attending such a fancy event, but because of what this man seems to do to me whenever we are within close proximity to one another.

The three of us start rambling on about the upcoming event, and Kasha seems like she's forgotten our previous conversation just as easily as I have. How many guests will arrive? Where is the ballroom? Will there be live music? What time does it start?

The anticipation is intoxicating. As the stars start to twinkle in the inky sky, Kasha and I head off to bed feeling like princesses, the new moon looming in the near future.

Chapter 16

The Third Floor

The next day, I head out for what's quickly becoming my morning routine of greeting the day on the back of Ada. She is remarkable. When I ride her, I feel like I've grown my wings back, free like an owl in flight. There's something unbridled about it, something that untangles the knots left behind from the accident. Out in the open, soaring through the grassy fields and weaving through the sycamore forests, I feel like I'm getting my life back. The memory loss, the headaches – they seem almost bearable when I am with her. Ada, and the quiet strength she lends me, fills my soul with hope again.

But I can't ignore the unsettling feeling creeping in about the other guests. Ever since I thought I saw Gus' skeletal form on the haystack, something hasn't sat right with me. As heavenly as Cliffsides appears on the surface, I sense there's a flipside to the coin – something lurking beneath the beauty. My old doubts are beginning to creep their way back into my head.

On our first night at the manor, Jack did explain how he intentionally kept the other guests and staff at a distance – to give us space and privacy while we settled in. At the time, it made sense. But the more I start to pay attention, the more I notice: the guests don't stay very long... and no one ever talks about why. At first, I assumed Cliffsides worked more like a hotel – people coming and going, nothing unusual about it. But then I realized I rarely see them leave. They're just... gone. No goodbyes, no luggage being packed, no cars driving down the winding path back towards town.

Where do they go?

And what is Jack hiding?

He has to have a role in all this, it is his house after all.

Then there is the third floor...

At first, I thought that it was Jack's personal space – his living quarters, and maybe he just wanted privacy. Fair. But that explanation doesn't hold up the more I think about it.

Why the secrecy?

Why is the third floor the only part of the manor that's completely off-limits? And why does it feel like whatever's happening to the vanishing guests... is somehow connected to that floor?

Gathering my resolve, I decide to explore the mysterious, forbidden third floor tonight – after dinner. If something is amiss – or if my imagination really is just running wild – it's better to find out now. The sooner, the better.

My heart begins to race at the thought of sneaking into a place so deliberately off-limits. Still, I set my jaw, steadying myself against the turbulence rising inside of me.

For a moment, I entertain the idea of having Kasha come along with me. But I already know what she'll say – that I am overthinking things again. That I need to stop looking for cracks every time life hands us a win. She'd remind me how much we've been through, and that we deserve something good. That I should just have faith in that.

And honestly, I agree with her. To an extent.

But if something is lurking – if there is something more sinister at play – I need to know.

And I need to know now.

That night after dinner, I excuse myself early, feigning a headache. Except, the pressure behind my eyes is not as fake as I would like it to be. The headaches are getting worse – more frequent, more intense – with each passing day.

Back in my room, I know I need to both prepare and wait for the right moment. I slip off my shoes, opting to explore in my fuzzy socks. *Stealthier,* I reason. I tug on an oversized black sweater and retrieve my knife in its leather sheath, strapping it to the side of my calf with a steady hand that doesn't quite match my racing heart.

I search for a flashlight but come up empty. *Probably for the best,* I reason. *A flickering beam would only give me away.*

With time to kill while waiting for the house to fall asleep, I pace the room, nerves bubbling just beneath my skin. I try to lie down, hoping to calm myself, but the tension coils tighter in my chest. Eventually I give up and move to the small floral sofa by the window.

I pick up *Wuthering Heights,* hoping I can lose myself in the gothic mess of Heathcliff and Catherine – but the words blur on the page. My mind won't stay anchored, drifting constantly to the task ahead. Toes tapping out an anxious rhythm on the floor, I sigh and close the book. Setting it back on the coffee table, I get up and resume my pacing.

The grandfather clock in the foyer chimed eleven times.

Dong...

Dong...

Dong...

Each toll seemed to stretch longer than the last, echoing like a slow, ominous heartbeat through the quiet house.

Now or never, I murmur, attempting to bolster myself.

Moving with deliberate silence, I slip out of my room and into the hallway. I keep close to the edges of the floorboards, mindful of every creak, as I make my way toward the stairwell.

Toward the third floor.

The house is still, wrapped in shadows and silence. I creep up the stairs slowly. Methodically. Placing each foot with care. One step. Then another. My weight shifts forward in tiny increments.

Suddenly, as soon as I step down releasing my weight too quickly, one of the steps lets out an audible squeak. The stair groans beneath me, the sound splitting the silence of the hushed house like a gunshot in the night. I cringe at the noise and instinctively hunch lower, freezing in place. My ears strain to hear any sound of movement that my misstep might have caused.

After what feels like an eternity, I start moving again. My hands tremble. My breathing is shallow—too shallow—and it takes everything I have not to gasp for more air. I try to slow it down, to quiet the ragged inhales, as I push forward up the staircase.

The third floor awaits.

Clinging to the wall as I ascend, I curse myself for not bringing a flashlight—or even a match. Previous rationalizations be damned. The higher I climb, the thicker the darkness grows, pressing in like a living thing. Shadows stretch long and wide, swallowing corners and devouring the light. They form depthless pits in every nook and cranny – onyx voids that obscure whatever might be prowling just beyond my vision. My nerves are strung taut.

When I finally crest the top step, I drop to my hands and knees, slinking onto the landing with cautious precision. But the moment my eyes adjust, my heart sinks.

There's nothing here.

Just a single, closed door.

How strange, I think, pulse pounding louder now. I blink against the darkness, trying to see more – trying to make sense of the space. *One door. No hallway. No windows. Just this.*

Remaining on my hands and knees, I crawl toward the closed door and tentatively reach my trembling hand up grasping the brass knob. It is freezing to touch, so cold that it feels like it is burning my skin. I give it a quick twist, heart thundering so hard my pulse is deafening in my ears.

Locked.

I try again, twisting harder this time. But it is to no avail. Still locked. A wave of disappointment washes over me as I slump to the floor, resting my back against the wall. I stare at the door, thoughts racing, wondering about what I am going to do next.

That is when I see it.

There is a faint glow that begins to seep from under the doorframe. At first, it's subtle – just a soft, amber shimmer – but the longer I sit there watching, the brighter it becomes. Slowly, steadily, it intensifies, blooming into a strange and steady pulse.

Curiosity outweighing caution, I lean down and press my cheek to the rough, ancient carpet, trying to get a glance at whatever is behind the locked door. But the more I strain to see, the more the light swells – now flooding the tiny top landing with a luminous white aura.

Startled, I recoil, bumping hard against the banister behind me. The light keeps building. I throw an arm over my eyes as the brilliance grows unbearable, stabbing at my vision with a pain sharp enough to make me gasp.

Feeling like my jittery nerves are about to fully fray, I am struck by a sudden bone-deep fear – *what if I have awakened someone or something in this house?* Horror racks my body at the thought of being caught. Without thinking, I bolt, fleeing back downstairs to my room. In my frantic state, my stockinged feet slip on the bottom of the stairs, and I land hard on my backside, tumbling down the last two steps.

Panicked and breathless, I scramble to my feet, nearly tripping again in my rush. I launch into my room and slam the door shut behind me. My fingers fumble for the lock, finally sliding the bolt into place with a heavy clunk. I flick off the light, plunging the room into darkness, then dive into bed, yanking the covers over my head like a frightened child.

My heart is pounding, my body trembling as I lie there, trying to calm the nauseating wave of fear still crashing through me. Every creak, every distant groan of the old manor feels amplified – menacing.

Unable to fully process what just happened, I'm swept under by a wave of crushing exhaustion that follows the crash of adrenaline. I stay curled beneath the blankets, wide-eyed and shaking, until eventually, oblivion claims me.

Chapter 17

The Ball

The next day starts off differently than I had intended. Rolling over in bed, I notice the light pouring in from my window and am seized with a brief moment of panic, recollecting my previous night's stunt. But I instantly realize that I must've slept in. I had a frightful time sleeping, tossing and turning all night, unable to relax after my foolish midnight escapade. But *I must have fallen asleep at some point,* I think as I rub the sleep from my eyes and grab my throbbing head.

What was I thinking snooping around, like a thief in the night? And not taking Kasha with me or even telling her for that matter. Now that the sun is up and the unsettling has dissipated, it all seems silly. But even as I try to convince myself of my own nonsense, there is still that lingering feeling in my core that something is wrong.

Groaning, I drag myself out of bed. If I've managed to muck up the morning and don't have enough time for a ride, then I need to at least get out of the house and see Ada. Coiling my hair up on top of my still pulsing head, I toss on a pair of jeans and a sweatshirt and head downstairs.

The house is a bustle for the upcoming ball, staff hustling about in preparation. I quickly and quietly dodge the commotion and snag an apple from the fruit bowl on the kitchen counter and slip out the door. I know the fresh air and simple presence of the horses will help set me straight.

After what feels like never enough time at the barn, I head back to the manor so that I can wash and be ready in time for the dance. Kasha and I have decided not to tell each other of the dresses hanging in our rooms. We want our gown of choice to be a surprise, and we know that if we even mention the options, we have available, we will most likely be able to guess what the other person will wear.

Once I've bathed and scrubbed my skin pink, I wrap one towel around my still-damp body and curl one over my hair, trying to sop up the majority of the moisture. Standing, I begin to inspect the gown options Clarence left hanging on a wall hook.

There is a deep forest-green A-Line dress that would hug the torso and flare out at the hips into a long, floor-length sweep. The bodice is in the Queen Anne style, featuring a heart-shaped neckline and small, triangular cap sleeves that rest delicately on the tops of the shoulders. The fabric features a delicate chiffon outer layer, with deep green leaves and vines embroidered over it—winding up from the hem and trailing to the bodice's breast.

Running my fingers over the fabric of the woodland fairy dress, I glance to the other gown to the left. It is a stunning, midnight-blue silk gown, so dark it looks black until a touch of light reflects off the sleek fabric, highlighting its deep blue tones. There are tiny silver stars delicately scattered over the gown, making it look like I would be wearing a galaxy. It is a slender column gown with thin spaghetti straps and a drooping cowl neckline.

Both gowns would, by far, be the most elegant things I have ever worn in my life. Nibbling on my bottom lip, I decidedly grab the midnight dress off the hook and hold it up to my body. Nodding to myself in silent confirmation, I slip it on, feeling the smoothness of the silk on my skin and the form-fitting cut of the evening gown. It accentuates my breasts before pulling over my flat stomach and resting delicately on my hips. It flows down in a liquid motion, hovering just above the floor, and a slit runs up the length of my right thigh. I find it both stunning and fitting, being covered in the starry night for the new moon festival.

Beneath the gowns lie matching shoes. I slip my feet into the dainty, silver, low-heeled shoes that accompany the midnight gown, fastening the straps across my ankles. When I take a few steps, moving over the room to see how the gown feels in motion, I notice the set of jewelry intentionally laid out on a black velvet cloth on the dresser.

Back in the bathroom, I take down my hair and am happy to see that it has dried enough for me to pull it up in a twist, without it still looking wet. Once I have completed the updo, I pull a few loose strands out around my temples, so they hang down the sides of my throat, then make my way back over to the jewelry. I slide the delicate earrings of diamond droplets through my ears, and they dangle just below my chin, looking like jeweled rain. Next, I tip my head to the side and slowly fasten the fine, silver chain of the necklace. The solitaire diamond, appearing to represent the North Star, as it lies softly on my sternum.

I take a second to look down at myself, butterflies kicking up in my stomach. Instantly I want to know what Kasha is wearing and dash across the hall. I knock on her door in rapid succession until she opens it.

She stands there in a lovely, cream-colored, traditionally cut gown coated in sparkles that shimmer in the light with every slight movement she makes. It has a corseted bodice, with triangular shoulder sleeves, and it fits tightly around her breasts and tapers in at the waistline before flaring out in a dramatic cascade of fabric that swishes just above her ankles. It is finished with over-the-toe, low-heeled matching shoes.

"Oh my God, girl! I am so glad you are here!" she says. "I need your help. You look ridiculously beautiful, by the way. Like a night goddess! I love the dress, and it is so fitting for you! Jack is going to die... I mean there is no way he'll be able to take his eyes off you tonight. And if he does, there is something terribly wrong with the man," she adds with a laugh. She grabs me by the wrist and pulls me into her room, shutting the door behind us.

"Kasha, if I am a goddess of the night, you are a summer queen," I reply. "Just look at you! This dress is stunning on you!"

"Thanks, but I seriously need your help. I have no idea what to do with my hair."

Grabbing her hairbrush, I comb out her long, golden locks, then loosely braid it across the top of her head and down her right temple, wrapping it in a loose but secure chignon that sits between her left ear and shoulder.

"I don't know what I would do without you," she says as she runs a pair of long, pearled earrings through her ears.

We beam at each other, and I reach out and offer her my elbow. She takes it in the crook of her own, and we head downstairs in search of the ballroom.

The ballroom is not hard to find, given the number of waiters in white dinner jackets and bow ties running around with silver platters hoisted high on their wrists, filled with sparkling champagne flutes. Kasha and I each take a glass off a passing tray. As I sip the golden liquid, I feel the bubbles tickle my nose and pop in the back of my mouth.

Following the calm, magical, instrumental music, we enter a large room through wide-open, ornately carved double doors. There is a scattering of white, linen-set tables adorned with shining silver table runners and navy-blue napkins. Centerpiece vases filled with bouquets of white moonflowers, light-blue hydrangeas, and purple delphiniums, with green sprigs spouting up through the flowers, are placed on each table. Around the dance floor at the heart of the grand room, the tables form a graceful ring, ready for the evening's celebration. A large crystal chandelier hangs above, light bouncing off a thousand different glittering facets.

At the far end, near the front of the room, a band clad in formal attire serenely plays a repetitive classical melody as guests begin to make their way in. Women in an array of colorful gowns and men clad in tuxedos, mill around the room socializing, sipping champagne, and nonchalantly searching for their name cards on the tables.

Clarence appears next to us as we survey the room, white-gloved hands clasped behind his back and his white, tailored jacket buttoned snugly over the bulge of his middle. "Good evening, ladies. May I assist you with finding your seats?"

"That would be lovely, Clarence. Thank you. This place is so grand, we weren't sure where to start," I say as we follow him around the edge of the room.

Stopping at a table that sits off to the side and in the far row of seats, he motions to our names scrolled in elegant script on the place cards lying over our dinner plates. I can't help but notice Jack's name card placed to the right of my own.

"Ah, here we are," he says, pulling out our chairs for us. "If there is ever anything else, please let me know. I will be floating along with the tide of people throughout the evening, never far away." With a nod, he is off again, toward the entrance.

Once we settle into our seats, a deep voice behind us says, "You both look stunning tonight."

Standing abruptly and turning, I come face to face with Jack. He stands there in a pitch-black suit, cut perfectly to fit his slender, muscular build, a white button-down beneath it popping with the contrast. His dark hair is combed back, making his blue eyes look all the more daring as they bore into mine.

"No, please, I did not intend to have you get up. I just wanted to express how happy I am that you came and that you look so beautiful tonight."

He leans forward and softly kisses each of my cheeks. I feel the heat of his touch and the champagne race to my head. Then he lifts Kasha's hand, gently bringing it to his lips.

"You are both a sunny day and a refreshing night sky. Did you plan that?" he asks.

Smiling, Kasha responds for the both of us. "No, we decided to surprise one another."

"A happy surprise," I add, "as all the options Clarence laid out for us were remarkable. It was not an easy decision."

"Well, I, for one, am delighted by your choices. Here, please sit. Dinner will be served shortly, followed by a night of music and dancing," he says, smile forming on his mouth.

As we lower ourselves back into the high-backed, cushioned chairs, the music stops, and a loud gong sounds from somewhere out in the hallway. Perplexed, Kasha and I exchange a look as Jack leans in and whispers that it is to announce the start of dinner, to remind people to find their seats.

Servers whisk into the room, trays with large silver domes balancing precariously on their upturned hands. It looks like a dance of its own—they move and twist through the tables, delivering food to awaiting partygoers.

The room is filled with the sound of chatter and clinking cutlery as people begin eating. Wine is poured, and there is an echo of men's and women's laughter. Kasha and I glance over and follow Jack's lead on which fork to use for each serving.

"I have heard that you two have been making yourselves at home, here in Cliffsides, over the last couple of days," Jack says after the soup course. "Please tell me about it."

"Yes," I begin, "and thank you again for your hospitality. Kasha seems to have moved into the kitchen with Gladis."

"Oh, I absolutely love it," Kasha declares. "She has taught me to bake all sorts of things. It's like solving a puzzle, trying to pick out what ingredients to add to what, and to give it that extra oomph, you know?"

"That is wonderful to hear. I may have to add you to the employ if you are that passionate." Jack smiles at Kasha before turning his gaze to me. "And you have been spending every day in the stables, I've been told."

"It's so freeing," I enthuse. "I never felt such peace until I rode Ada. She makes me feel like I have wings." I quickly add, "And Gus has been so kind. I do feel guilty waking him each morning, though. Does he sleep in the barn every night?"

Jack has to pull the wineglass away from his laughing lips before he responds. "By his own design, I assure you. We compromised on a nice loft room, above the barn, but I think he still prefers to sleep in the haystack." Based on the quizzical look I give him, Jack continues. "He was an orphan sleeping on the streets for the majority of his short life. Even before his parents died, I'm not sure he ever had a real bed. My job led me to him many years ago, and I found him curled up in a pile of old newspapers and corrugated paper shipping cartons. I brought him home to Cliffsides and quickly discovered he had a passion for animals and was a natural with the horses.

They always seemed to calm in his presence, being drawn to him. He hasn't ventured far from the barn since." After a sip of wine, he adds, "And please don't feel guilty for waking him. That boy would sleep the season away if we let him."

As we finish our meal, the band kicks back up. Jack stands and leans in, lightly touching the top of my back with one hand. The other hand opens in front of me, and I feel the heat of his breath on my neck as he asks, "May I have the first dance?"

All I can do is nod before he pulls me out of my seat, and we disappear into the crowd. Before we are fully swallowed up, I look back over my shoulder. Kasha lifts an eyebrow at me, playful smile gracing her lips.

As soon as we find the center floor, the piano starts with a flourish, and a beautiful, strawberry-blonde woman in a snug, white, sequined, strapless gown joins the formally dressed band. She cups the silver microphone in one hand and starts singing. Her voice is angelic as she sings a slow, sultry tune in French. I swear she looks and sounds just like Helen Merrill of the 1950s.

Holding my hand, Jack extends our arms, using his momentum as he swings me out slowly into a circle on the dance floor. He pulls me in close, and our bodies come together, as if magnetically drawn toward each other, and we begin to sway to the music. One of our hands is clasped together, guiding us, while my other hand rests on his broad shoulder. I feel the heat seeping through my silk dress where his hand presses against the small of my back. Gliding and moving together as if we are one, the electricity crackles between us, making my heart race like Ada against a storm. I have a heightened sense of every muscle in Jack's body as we move together. Our eyes never leave each other's during the dance, but our bodies and souls take flight.

The magic of the moment gives off the sensation that it is only Jack and me on the dance floor. The lights dim around us, and the room and people nearby begin to disappear. The song lasts longer than a song normally would, making me feel like we are taking the night with us. But as soon as I think of how I never want this moment to end, I hear the exquisite singer carry her final note of the French version of "You Go to My Head," and the piano man tickles the keys in a final flourish.

Even with the music stopped, Jack and I have not stopped moving together. He slowly dips his head to mine, arms shifting to fully wrap around my middle, encircling me. A breath gets caught in my throat as our lips connect in a longing, sensuous kiss.

When we break apart, Jack's voice is gravelly. "You have bewitched me, Gabriella. As much as it pains me, I must make my rounds and greet the other guests, but all I want in this world is to stay with you in my arms for the rest of eternity."

"Jack..." His name escapes my lips.

Raising the back of my hand to his mouth, he holds it there for a beat—two—before giving it a gentle squeeze and releasing it to wade into the throng of finely dressed people.

As I stand motionless in the middle of the dance floor, the world comes back into focus. The lights brighten, the music picks up, and the bodies of those around me start dancing again, no longer suspended in time and lost in the thrall.

The next song has a quick beat, and bodies begin moving rapidly together. Before I am fully aware of what is happening, a man has grasped my hand and is twirling me into a fast-paced dance. I look over toward Kasha, who is already in full spin with another gentleman. Still feeling lightheaded from Jack's kiss, I try to allow myself to get caught up in the joy of dancing, permitting the music to distract me from the spinning in my head and the flutter of my heart.

Kasha and I dance to song after song, never leaving the dance floor, though our partners shift with each of the melodies. I feel alive, lungs heaving and sweat starting to trickle down my skin, and once there is a break in the music, I excuse myself and head toward the bar for a drink.

I stand there while the bartender finishes serving another patron.

Looking down at me he asks, "What can I do you for?"

"Glass of pinot grigio, please."

He turns and looks through his bottles. As he twists back around to me and begins to pour my drink, I catch a flash of scarred, distorted skin pulled roughly over his face. Decaying cheeks and hollowed-out eyes stare back at me. I blink, feeling panic rise within me, but as soon as my horror begins to surface, the vision is gone.

I numbly thank him, spinning on my heel and heading directly to our table. Clumsily setting down my wine, I spill some over the edge and onto the tablecloth. I grab a nearby glass of ice water and take a large gulp. My hands are shaking as I raise the water back to my mouth for another drink, sloshing it as I do. I rub at my temples trying to dislodge the terror from my head. *What the fuck was that? I'm fucking seeing things.*

I am suddenly jumpy. The music seems too loud, every movement and motion drawing my eyes. Everything seems like a threat. I feel like a hunted rabbit. *I need to get out of here.*

Kasha returns to our table, but her big, sweaty smile fades as soon as she looks at me.

"What's wrong?" she asks, concern lacing her voice.

"It's nothing. I thought I saw something." I start to calm slightly, having her here.

When she doesn't respond right away, I go on. "I went to the bar to get another glass of wine. The bartender... The bartender, I swear, Kash, he was dead. It was like a horror film. You know the ones that flash in and out of scenes? Because I blinked and everything was fine. He was smiling, handing me my drink. My head is swimming." I begin to ramble. "It's probably just too much wine, with all the dancing and the heat. You know? I'm sure it's nothing. Never mind. Don't listen to me," I say, trying to force a smile that I don't really feel.

Kasha just looks at me, rosy cheeks fading. Her face is stone white, and her lips form a grim line as her eyebrows pinch together.

"Seriously," I insist. "Go. Dance. Have a good time. That redhead you were dancing with was hot. I'll be okay. I'm going to have some more water. Then I will come back and join you."

"You sure you are okay?" she asks. "I can stay with you. Maybe we can tell Jack. He'll know what to—"

"No, really," I interrupt her, waving my hand in dismissal. "I'm fine. Just a trick of the light."

"Okay..." she says, dragging the word out. "But you promise that you're okay and that you'll hit the floor again?"

"Yup," I try to reassure her, but I can't bring myself to meet her eyes.

She dubiously walks away, glancing over her shoulder a few times before she disappears back onto the dance floor.

I plop down in my seat, back slouching, and take a deep breath, running my hand down my face. Leaning forward, I reach past my untouched wine and grab the glass of water to finish it. I still feel shaken and decide it's best if I go up to bed and get some sleep. Kasha will be mad that I left, but I'm sure she will eventually understand. I pull myself up, feeling unnaturally heavy, and make my way upstairs to my room.

Chapter 18

The Beach

After spending another night tossing and turning, I decide to drag myself out of bed at dawn. Still reeling from last night, and the horrifying realization that even after my brief reprieve upon our arrival at Cliffsides, things seem like they are getting worse. I need to get out of the house and get some fresh air. Clear my head. Not only do I still have a chill running down my spine from the new quirk I decided to pick up—hallucinations, *that's a fun one, Gabs*—but also from the kiss with Jack.

I slip into a pair of jeans and toss a thick, oversized, ivory, cable-knit sweater on over my bra. I retrieve the knife from the cushions of the couch and slip it into my boot. Even knowing the hallucinations are most likely just another side effect of the hard hit to my head—like the memory loss and headaches—the firmness of the hilt and the leather sheath against my skin gives me comfort. And that is good enough for me at the moment.

Without opening the door all the way, I ease myself through the small crack, so as not to have its hinges creak. Turning silently, I click the bedroom door shut behind me. With dawn just beginning to break, the house remains asleep, a soft golden hue creeping through the windows. I assume that many people will remain in their beds for a while, especially after the late night of drinking and dancing. I slide past Kasha's room and tiptoe downstairs. We will need to talk, but right now I need some alone time in the cool morning air.

I hear some noise coming from the kitchen, and I assume Gladis must be starting breakfast or cleaning up from last night. I don't really care to find out which, and feeling like a burglar, I sneak past the doorway and out the front.

Taking a moment to stand on the veranda, I close my eyes and let the chill of the morning calm and refresh me. Something large slams into my leg, buckling my knee and throwing me off balance. I stumble, forced to take an abrupt step to the side to keep from falling. Startled, I look down to see the gigantic Great Dane, Sam, looking up at me expectantly and I can't help the feeling that he can sense my unease. I tousle my hand between his ears and watch his droopy jowls flap with the movement.

"Okay, boy. Want to go for a walk? You can come along. Now, where do you think the entrance to the beach path is?"

As if he understood me, he starts off down the steps, heading for the bluffs. Pausing a few paces ahead, he turns and looks back at me as if I am the silly, slow human who doesn't understand that I need to follow him.

Sighing, I say to both myself and to Sam, "Okay," and start down the steps after him.

The path by the house goes only a few dozen yards before it looks like it disappears behind some large coreopsis bushes, their yellow flowers protruding out at chest height. Trusting Sam, I follow his wagging tail and tall, lanky form through the bushes to the steep trail that leads down to the rocky beach.

As I traverse the path, I notice that someone went through and dug out sections of the trail and placed large, wooden railroad ties across it, making the steeper sections easier to get a foothold on. Where the steep, crumbling edge of the bluff is dangerously close to the path, there are some metal spikes embedded in the ground, with a thick wire cable running through them as a makeshift railing. *Sketchy, but functional.*

While I carefully navigate the downslope, Sam seems like he could care less about the drop-off. He bounds down the path and then back up to make sure I am still following him. Then he turns and races down again. It's like he has done this a million times, and a part of me wonders if he has.

Eventually we reach the bottom, and I make the two-foot leap down onto the stony sand below. Slowly standing up from my crouch, I dust my pebbled hands on my jeans and take in the landscape around me. The air already feels different along the water's edge, thicker somehow. It's as if I can feel the salt from the sea coating my skin and laying heavily in my hair.

The roar of the surf crashing against the rocks echoes off the surrounding cliffs and boulders. It reminds me of pressing my ear to a conch shell to hear the ocean—but standing here on the graveled shore, it feels more like I've shrunk and stepped inside the shell itself. The ground beneath me is rough, covered in coarse sand that feels more like a beach of pebbles than fine grains.

The shore is peaceful, and I feel secluded in the alcove that I have traveled down into. I'm surrounded by sandy bluffs behind and to the right of me, and there are large rock formations to the left and the pounding sea in front of me. I need to walk, so I head toward the rocks. With the tide out, there is just enough room for Sam and me to walk between the rocks and the surf without getting wet.

We stroll along the ribbon of shore, me contemplating the events of the previous evening and Sam splashing in the cold water. I bend down and pick up a big piece of driftwood, throwing it for Sam. He races ahead to happily retrieve it, then drops it at my feet. Now covered in sand that has adhered to the drool bubbles left on it, I grimace slightly before picking it up and tossing it again.

Continuing down the beach, my thoughts drift to Jack, and I feel myself smile at the thought of him. I didn't see him after the dance, after the kiss we shared, but that doesn't seem to bother me - *not really,* I tell myself. I feel like I'm falling for him, and the sensation is both exhilarating and terrifying. I'm afraid that if I surrender to it, I'll never find my way back home. That and my overactive emotions keep telling me that he seems to be holding back. He is still an enigma, and I don't know why I feel like he is not giving me his whole heart. His entire truth. Even with my small feelings of trepidation I smile to myself, swept away on a cloud of new romance, not just because of his generosity and his gorgeous property, but for his sincerity.

I have never met a man with such a tranquil strength about him before. I get the sense that we would be perfectly content in each other's silence, and I find that deeply comforting. He told me that I bewitched him; the smile on my face broadens as I recall his words to me. *No, this isn't just a one-way street,* I reflect.

It all still seems so surreal. Being here. Jack. Then there have been my flashes of horror, I think, and the smile fades from my face. First with Gus, then with the bartender last night. And what is with the off-limits third floor and guests mysteriously vanishing without anyone seeing them leave? *Why am I suddenly seeing death around me? And where do the guests go that no one wants to talk about?* My exploration halted... *Maybe this place is haunted.*

As soon as the questions enter my head, I freeze. Sam is standing stone-still, directly between me and the water, stick forgotten at his paws. His scruff is raised from his head to his tail, and a horrifyingly low, rumbling growl erupts from the depths of his chest. The hairs on my arms rise as I try to see what he is sensing.

When I spot the large elephant seal stalking us from the edge of the surf, Jack's warning comes rushing back about them being aggressive, especially if they have pups nearby. She easily outweighs me by over a few hundred pounds and has a mouthful of long, intense-looking teeth. There are so many large rocks in the shallow sea that the pups could be anywhere.

My eyes dart back and forth, trying to catch any other movement. I slowly approach Sam, giving him a pat on his back to let him know that we will be slowly retreating in the direction we came from. I am intensely grateful I have him with me.

When Sam turns his head to acknowledge me, I swear, his lips are not just pulled back to expose the rows of menacing teeth, but there are no jowls at all. Elongated fangs jut out from his gory, skinless skull, dripping saliva and blood onto the sand. Always large, he seems to have doubled in size, and although his eyes are still silver, they are lacking pupils as they look back at me glowing with a deep and terrifying ferocity.

My heart hammers like a war drum as I jerk away from him. My foot snags on a jagged piece of driftwood—gravity drags me down hard and fast. I slam onto the rough ground, eyes snapping shut, teeth crushing my tongue until the metallic taste of blood floods my mouth.

Before I can catch my breath, at lightning speed, a boney clawed hand has a vise-like grip around my ankle. Whipping my attention away from Sam to what is wrapped around my foot I scream as the elephant seal has morphed into a humanoid corpse. It supports itself on three limbs, with its other arm painfully secured around my ankle. Dark decaying skin pools and melts off of its skeletal form like slimy seaweed. The creature's eyes are huge opaque saucers staring at me... through me... but my attention is quickly diverted to its gnashing jagged teeth, foam building in its mouth. It pauses for a second not breaking eye contact and cocks its head sideways, its neck popping and cracking with the movement, before it starts to drag me towards the sea with inhuman strength.

Panic erupting from me, I try to reach for my knife hidden in my boot. With violently trembling hands, I clutch the hilt and yank it free from my boot. The sea monster thrashes me back and forth across the rocky beach, disorienting me. I try frantically to get a better hold on my knife, as the creature drags me through the icy water and out to sea. The ocean licks at my legs and stomach, spilling into my mouth and blurring my vision. In the chaos my weapon and all sense of survival end up slipping from my grasp as soon as we hit the slick, icy water. I begin kicking and clawing at the sand and rocks, trying to escape its deathlike grip, broken terrified sobs racking my chest. All hope lost with my weapon.

Just when I have come to the realization that this could very possibly be my end, in a flash there is a large grey body at my feet. The growls and snarls are so loud they radiate through my bones, making me quake. Sam is there in an instant, maw arched wide, bloody saliva spilling from his fangs, eyes glowing with rage. He clamps down hard on the throat of the creature as it lets out an otherworldly screech, the sound so violent I clasp my ears, afraid they will start bleeding from its high-pitched bellow.

Instantly, I feel the grip on my ankle disappear and I impulsively start scrambling backwards towards the beach and the safety of the cove. There is violent splashing and a shrill squeal from the depths of Hell itself, so loud that I pinch my eyes closed and cover my ears. When I find an ounce of strength to pry my eyes back open, I notice blood on my hands from trying to shield my ears from the sound. There is a shrill ringing sound radiating in them still and I find it difficult to hear. I can't see Sam or the ghoul anywhere. I start glancing around panic stricken, unable to catch my breath, my heart feeling like it is going to pound right out of my chest.

I continue to crawl backwards, away from the sea, until my back slams hard against a cold, solid rock. I curl my legs to my chest, eyes wide as I try to breathe. *Just breathe. In and out. In and out.* Sam and the demon are gone. I slam my eyes closed again, trying to pull myself out of this nightmare. And begin to rock back and forth. *This has to be a nightmare. I am ok. I am ok. This is just a bad dream. Just a bad dream.*

I open my eyes to see Sam, inches from my face, but this is not the Hellhound I saw a moment ago. It's Sam, with his lolling tongue and floppy ears, head cocked and tail wagging like this is a new game I am playing. A relieved sob escapes my throat as Sam gives me a big, wet kiss on the side of my face. My panicked sob morphs into a choked laugh.

I stand on trembling legs and give him a pat on his head. Scanning the shore behind him, I see there is nothing there but the ocean lapping tranquilly along the stoney shore. All is calm and quiet, like nothing even happened. Still shaken, I second guess what I just experienced and roughly rub my hands down my face. Sucking in a heavy breath to steady myself, it now seems like a good time for us to leave. Still quivering from the encounter, I start heading back toward the inlet and the trail that leads up to the hill, with Sam at my side.

As soon as we make our way through the narrow path around the boulders, barely avoiding the rising tide, I spot Kasha standing on the beach. Sam dashes off toward her, leaping in the air, vying for her attention and happy to have even more company.

I shake my head, trying to dislodge the terror still etched into my bones. *It had to be another hallucination. I mean, really, there are no such things as monsters – and just look at Sam... The happy, playful oversized pup. Get ahold of yourself, Gabriella.* I chide myself.

Laughing, Kasha swings her arms in wide motions around his head, imitating rough play. This only seems to animate him more, to the point that he starts barking at her and jumping in the air. Grabbing a nearby stick, she launches it through the air, and Sam is off like a bullet after it. As if the last few minutes never happened. *Because they couldn't have.*

"Careful," I say as I approach her, voice still a bit unstable. "You may not want to throw it again, once you see the condition that he returns it in."

"Ha! I'll take my chances," she says. She is suddenly serious, though, as she continues. "Say, what happened? You just disappeared last night. Then you were gone without a trace this morning. I was worried. I'm glad Gladis spotted you heading down here. Otherwise, I would have never found you."

We sit down in the softer portion of the pebbled sand and watch Sam play with the piece of driftwood. I pull my knees toward my chest and hug my forearms around them trying to gather myself before I answer.

"I didn't want to wake anyone. I needed to get out and try to clear my head. I didn't sleep well."

"Men will do that to you." There's a playful smirk on her face. "But in all seriousness, are you okay? You don't want to go home, do you?"

"No, no... I love it here... I do," I tell her. While still trying to understand what just happened. *Was it even real? Or was it just another one of my flashes?* "In fact, I am happier here than I have ever been in my life. But I can't shake the feeling that something is terribly wrong."

"What do you mean?" Kasha asks, giving me a sideways glance.

"I don't know. Things just seem off at times, like there is this ominous weight sitting over the property, and it only shows up in flashes and bursts. Things will be fine one moment, and then the next they're not. But before I can process anything, it's all back to normal. I feel like I am going out of my mind." When Kasha doesn't respond, I continue. "I am starting to think that those rumors about Cliffside Manor being haunted are more than just rumors. I am seeing things, feeling things, Kash. Just glimpses... moments... But... they feel so real."

TES

Kasha is unusually quiet as she listens to me. "What sort of things?" she asks. Her lips are puckered, and her eyebrows are drawn together in concern.

"Death? Ghosts? Demons? I'm not sure exactly. I know it sounds crazy, but I am getting these hallucinations of people turning into corpses. Then there is sweet Sam here." I nod my chin in the direction of the playful dog, splashing harmlessly in the surf. "There was an elephant seal, at least that is what I think it was, aggressively stalking us just now. We must have come near some of its pups and didn't realize it. Anyway, when I touched him to signal our leaving, he turned to me, and I swear Sam was taller and scarier. Not the playful Dane you see now. Kash, he looked like a Hellhound... But I tripped and ended up falling. I swear I was being pulled into the ocean by a sea demon, but then when I opened my eyes, he was the floppy-eared dog you see now and there was nothing there but the lapping waves on the sand. I must have just tripped and fallen in the water when I got startled. I don't know, but I am soaked now and confused. I... I'm struggling to remember..."

We sit there, silence stretching between us for a moment, and Kasha looks to be deeply contemplating what I have just told her, brow furrowed. I distract myself from this feeling of foreboding by watching Sam sniff and then roll in some sea kelp that washed up on the shore, like nothing happened. *Because nothing did happen. What if I was discharged from the hospital too soon?* Even with my head spinning from everything going on, I can't help but think that dog is going to stink and will need a serious bath when we get home.

Interrupting my thoughts, Kasha says, "This seems serious, Gabs. I am happy you are happy here! I really am, and so relieved, too, because I love it here and don't want to go home. But girl, where you go, I go. You know that, right? Despite that, this is some seriously spooky stuff. I believe you. I really do, but I think we should tell Jack. This is his place after all. I think he would have some insight into it." At the look I give her, she goes on quickly, "I know you guys have something starting between the two of you, and I am absolutely. Freaking. Thrilled. But I really don't think that he would judge you about these visions. I honestly believe he can help. You know, shed some light on the whole thing."

"No. Kasha, please. I really don't want to say anything to Jack. Not yet at least. It was hard enough telling you that I think I'm going crazy. I can't. I won't tell Jack. I am sure it's no big deal. In fact, I'm sure it is just leftover trauma from my head injury. They say that severe head trauma can cause delusions or hallucinations. Yes, I'm sure that is all this is. I mean, I was in the hospital for a while after the accident, right? How about this... Please, please don't say anything to Jack, and I promise I will go see a doctor. If I have any more episodes, we will get a ride somehow, I can even take Ada, and go into town and find a doctor and let them know about it. You know, see what they have to say about everything. See if it's something I need to be concerned about. In the meantime, I think I just need some rest and relaxation. You know, good ol' traditional medicine. Maybe even a glass of wine to calm the nerves."

After what feels like an eternity of silence radiating from Kasha, she forces a small smile and says, "Yeah, wine and rest. Okay, but we are having a big one."

I give her a tentative smile back as we rise to our feet, dusting the sand off our bottoms and hands. I give her a hug and can tell that she is not satisfied with our conclusion, but I know she will honor my wishes. That's what best friends are for, after all. Support, trust, and keeping one another's secrets.

Chapter 19

The Ride

After an evening of wine therapy with Kasha, I stumble back to my room for a night of hopefully blissful and dreamless sleep. Then I notice an envelope on my end table, my name written in elegant script. Without hesitation, I tear it open and try to adjust my blurry vision on the classic handwriting. It is from Jack. He wants to go for a ride together, first thing tomorrow morning.

Still feeling slightly numb from our afternoon indulgence, but suddenly more grounded, I press the note to my heart. A smile warms my already flushed checks, as I curl into bed, drifting off almost instantly – dreaming of horses, wind in my hair, and a certain dark-haired, blue-eyed man.

I wake bright and early, sunlight streaming through my bedroom window in soft golden ribbons. Excited for my ride with Jack, I fling the covers off and spring out of bed, more eager than I've felt in days. I need a win right now – and nothing beats horses and Jack.

I dash to the bathroom, quickly freshen up, and splash cold water on my face to try to quell my throbbing head. No headache or former horrors are going to dissuade me from having a lovely day today.

Heading back into the main room, I begin to rummage through the armoire for something to wear. *Hmmm, I need something cute, flattering, but practical. No pressure,* I smirk to myself. I settle for my tried-and-true blue jeans, boots, white tank, and my favorite open flannel. *Comfortable, a little flirty, and entirely me.* I decide to leave my hair down, letting the waves fall past my shoulders to hang just above my hips.

Nervously, I check my watch – half past eight. I should still have enough time for a quick cup of tea and a piece of toast before we make our way to the barn. I don't want to be late for what feels like an actual date.

Heading downstairs, there is a small part of me that is relieved to see that Kasha's door is closed. She is probably still asleep, and honestly, I don't need the eyebrow wiggling and teasing right now. I've got enough butterflies without her stirring the pot. And to think that I once suspected that she and Jack were having a fling behind my back. She has been nothing but supportive of our budding relationship, I should have never doubted her loyalty.

However...

A loud crash cuts off my thought.

I quicken my pace and push open the swinging saloon style doors to the kitchen, heart already in my throat. Inside, I find Jack and Gladis on their hands and knees laughing uncontrollably while trying to mop up the mess of still-steaming coffee, tea, and shattered porcelain scattered across the tiled floor.

"Oh," I exclaim, watching the brown lake spread across the floor, mini rivers sneaking toward the cabinets. "Here, let me help."

I grab an extra dishcloth from the counter and make my way towards the scene.

"Oh, no deary," Gladis tells me, still laughing, "We are enough of a mess. No sense in you dirtying yourself, too. Besides, I've got it under control now."

Jack slowly rises, merriment twinkling in his eyes. "Just clumsy. I zigged, when I should've zagged," he admits with a sheepish grin.

"That you did," Gladis replies, laughing again. "I can't take you anywhere, Mr. Finnley. Now go upstairs this instant and get changed. You have a nice, young lady here waiting to go on that ride with you."

Still chuckling, Jack shrugs. "Sorry, Gabriella, but I need a few more minutes."

"No worries," I say, feeling their good spirits rubbing off on me. "I was hoping to get a cup of tea and piece of toast before the ride anyway."

A smile creeps across my face, and suddenly, I'm hit with a flashback of spilling a milkshake all down Jack's shirt. Maybe he's the one who can't keep himself out of messes.

I laugh outright, catching both Jack and Gladis's attention. Jack tilts his head, like Sam does when he's trying to figure something out.

"What? What is it?" he asks, amusement dancing in his eyes.

I try to speak, but I need to catch my breath from my unexpected burst of laughter. I lean forward, one hand on my knee and the other gesturing that I need a moment to gather myself.

Taking a final deep breath, I manage to say between gasps, "You... You're covered in – look at –" another burst of giggles hits me, "it reminds me of the great milkshake incident back at Darla's. Jack, maybe it's you."

That does it. The hysterics fully take over, and I have to sit down on a nearby stool before I completely lose control.

Jack looks at me, then down at his coffee- and tea-stained shirt, then back at me... then over to Gladis.

"The girl is not wrong, love," Gladis informs him, before she too starts howling with laughter.

"Ha, ha," Jack says dryly, but I see it takes all his self-control not to join in on our amusement. "All right, I can take a hint. I'll go upstairs and change. You ladies enjoy your laugh at my expense," he says, backing toward the door with exaggerated dignity. "But don't think you are getting off so easily, Gabriella. I fully plan on exacting my revenge on our ride."

I merely fan my hand back and forth in front of my face, trying to collect myself as Jack heads out of the kitchen. My fit of laughter subsiding, I turn back to Gladis, who is hoisting herself up from the floor and wiping the joyous tears from her eyes with the edge of her apron.

"Are you sure I cannot help?" I ask again.

"No, dear, it is all but done. How about I make you that cup of tea now, though. I'm in need of a fresh one myself." And we both giggle again.

"Okay," I reply, smiling. "I'll set the toast to pop."

A short while later, Gladis and I are just finishing our tea when Jack returns in a clean shirt.

"Want a fresh brew, love?" Gladis offers.

"No thank you, I believe I have had enough for one morning." Turning to me he adds, eyes still alight with humor, "Ready, Gabriella? I did promise you a ride, and one that would snap you out of your teasing mood."

"Ready," I say, downing the last sip of my tea and rising from my seat. "Thanks, Gladis."

"Have a good time, kids," she calls after us with a wink.

Jack and I start our walk toward the stables. The morning air is crisp, perfectly contrasting with the warmth of the rising sun. I soak in the distant sound of crashing waves against the shore, mingling with the cheerful chirping of the birds in nearby trees.

Jack reaches out gently, and our fingers brush against each other's before we delicately lace them together in a warm and companiable embrace. We continue to walk in silence for a few moments, and I can't help but feel like we are two long lost puzzle pieces clicking into place.

As we approach the barn, a low, guttural growling echoes from within. I glance at Jack, who immediately brings a finger to his lips, signaling for me to remain silent. Hands still grasped; my grip tightens on his as we enter the stable. My breath quickens, and a tremble runs through me. The familiar scent of hay, dust, and horses fills the air—but instead of offering the usual comfort, it only sharpens the edge of my unease.

Then we see it.

Gus is passed out on his usual haystack, mouth hanging open, a line of drool slowly pooling into the straw beneath him. His snores reverberate through the barn, letting out a low rumble that shakes his fragile-looking frame.

I slap a hand over my mouth to muffle the laugh that escapes, just as Jack ushers me out into the dirt breezeway, trying and failing to contain his own smirk.

Whispering he says, "That boy can sleep away his own existence. I don't remember sleeping that much as a teen, but

Gladis informs me that I did. Let's not wake Sleeping Beauty in there. We'll saddle our own horses, okay?"

I nod. "That sounds good, except I think he is more like The Beast than Sleeping Beauty."

We both desperately try to silence our chuckles, as Jack playfully shoves me in the direction of Ada's stall.

Once Ada is well groomed and all tacked up, I emerge from the barn to find Jack, horse in tow. The sun hits me straight on as I exit through the large wooden doors, momentarily blinding me with its golden brilliance, as I cross the luminous threshold. With Ada's reins in one hand, I raise the other to shield my eyes against the radiant light.

Jack's stallion is already waiting. Towering and magnificent, the black horse stands proud in the sun, his arched neck taut with power and his feathered hooves stamping the earth in anticipation. The sunlight dances across his sleek, onyx coat, illuminating it like liquid silver. In certain angles, his dark body shimmers with elusive shades of deep violet and midnight blue, ethereal and mesmerizing. Then, with a shift of muscle, the colors vanish again into rich shadow.

"Wow," I breathlessly comment, as I admire Jack's Frisian stud. "Who is this?" I ask, tentatively reaching up to stroke his silken muzzle. "I don't recall seeing him in the barn before."

"This is Lazarus," Jack replies proudly. "He prefers the freedom of the pastures—he's not one to be cooped up in a stall. That's probably why you haven't met him yet."

"He is stunning, Jack."

At my comment, Ada stretches her snout forward, neck curling to mirror Lazarus' regal arch. Her nostrils flare with each deep breath, ribcage expanding as the two horses acquaint themselves with each other. I hold my own breath, my grip tightening on her reins as I brace for the squeal or kick that never comes. Instead, the horses drop their heads and take a closer step toward each other.

"I think they like one another," Jack says, watching them closely, eyes flicking up to mine for a moment.

Relief floods my body at not having to separate these two spirited creatures. I tuck a strand of hair behind my ear, taking in the horses as they nicker softly, a low rumble vibrating from their chests.

"Maybe they like each other a little too much," Jack adds with a smirk.

I laugh. "Maybe we should run it out of them."

Jack grins at my challenge, then effortlessly hoists himself up and into the saddle of his giant beast. "Challenge accepted,

Miss Pickart. After we get them warmed up, let's see if you and Miss Ada there can keep pace."

"Oh, you don't have to worry about Ada and me," I say. Then, turning my attention to my mare and patting her golden neck, I add, "Does he, girl?"

Placing my foot in the stirrup, I swing my right leg over the saddle and readjust my grip on the reins. As I run my hand through her mane, Ada begins to prance in place, already eager to show off.

"Ready when you are," I call to Jack.

And together, we start out on the trail.

We keep the horses at a walking pace, while riding along Cliffsides' fence line and eventually into the beginning stretch of the trail that leads up into the surrounding hills, speckled with oak and sycamore trees. After a few miles, we pick up the pace, letting our horses trot, their heart rates – and ours – increasing with the rhythm of the ride. We maintain an equal speed, remaining side by side, talking and laughing, sharing the quiet ecstasy of being in sync with our horses and each other.

The further we venture into the hills, the denser the forest becomes. The trail narrows, flanked by towering trees whose canopies filter the sunlight into shifting patches of gold and shadow along the path. It's peaceful in a way that feels sacred.

Out here, surrounded by nothing but trees and life and the azure sky above, I feel the energy of Ada in every stride, coursing through me.

I close my eyes for a moment, breathing in deeply, and savoring the feeling of the day. The scent of earth, crisp air, and horses is intoxicating. Small insects buzz around in a frenzy over the long, swaying grass. The sounds of our horses' hooves on the dirt trail mix with the soft rustling of the leaves and the melodic chirping of birds, as they sing a romantic song to each other from the branches of the trees.

Jack twists around in his saddle to glance back at me, a mischievous grin tugging at his lips. "Would you like to pick up the speed? We did promise to run the lust out of these two."

"Only if you are sure that Lazarus won't hold Ada back," I tease. "This girl has wings, and she is ready to fly."

"All right, let's go!" And giving a quick and loud kissing sound to his horse, Jack takes off at a full canter in front of me.

Ada instinctively accepts the challenge – and not one to miss an opportunity to run – bolts after him. I lean forward in my saddle and begin to move with the pounding rhythm of her stride. The wind licks at my face and whips my hair back in a dance, making it fly like a banner behind me. My heart thuds in tandem with every beat of Ada's hooves. I feel untamed and free, like the owl I once dreamed of becoming – back in what feels like a lifetime ago.

"Go faster or move out of the way!" I shout over the roar of wind and pounding hooves. "You're holding us up!"

Jack's laugh is barely audible above the rush of the ride, fading quickly and swallowed entirely by the sounds of the forest as he pulls ahead.

We race through the hills, dodging low-hanging branches and twisting with our horses through the winding trail. Trees and boulders blur past us in streaks of motion as we tear up the path at breakneck speed.

"Jump!" Jack shouts, seconds before Lazarus leaps over a fallen log blocking the trail.

I barely hear him in time to brace myself, feet firm in the stirrups, legs moving with Ada as she follows suit and launches us effortlessly over the obstacle. A whoop of pure joy escapes me as I land and right myself in the saddle, laughing uncontrollably at the wild, exhilarating thrill of the chase.

In a split second, the forest opens up to a small clearing, the trail widening ahead of us. I blink, momentarily blinded by the sudden assault of sunlight after riding through the thick, shady trees. Seizing the opportunity, I drop Ada's reins, giving her her full head. She knows exactly what I am thinking and surges forward, head dropping as she pulls with every powerful stride. I sink low in the saddle, hovering just above the horn, my hands free and loose on the reins, as they brush the sides of her flying mane. We move as one.

In no time, we're neck in neck with Jack and Lazarus. Jack gives a quick turn of his head to view us pulling up on his right. I savor the brief moment of disbelief and shock written across his face. Swiftly recovering himself, he shoots me a wicked grin before turning his attention back to his horse and the field we fly through.

I can feel his thoughts race through my mind, as if they are my own: *Oh, it is on now.* What seems impossible becomes reality as our horses instinctively find another gear, galloping at full tilt, just as drunk on the thrill of competition as we are.

As we dash through the small valley, I begin calculating my next move. The forest looms ahead once more, fast approaching—and soon, we'll have no choice but to funnel back into a single-file trail.

Suddenly, a covey of quail startles at our thundering approach, bursting from the tall grass in a frantic panic. The abrupt movement sends both our horses bolting sideways in opposite directions, spooked by the chaos. Ada gives a little rear, quickly followed by a sharp crow hop mid-stride. It takes all of my skill to stay in the saddle. My hands tighten on the reins and grip her mane for support, as I use all my strength to try and pull up her head and slow her down. Simultaneously, I adjust my seat in the saddle, having slipped sideways with her rapid movements.

That is when I spot Jack and Lazarus.

Lazarus must have spooked left and, in the commotion, leapt over a small ravine that now separates us. It's a small miracle that Jack was able to both stay on and control his giant, black stallion, and that they managed to clear the ditch without any noticeable injuries.

Still holding his seat, Jack has Lazarus circling tightly to regain composure, when he shouts across to me, "Are you okay?"

"Yes!" I call back. The only thing out of place is my adrenaline, still screaming through my veins.

"Good! Keep riding forward and follow the path. The trails reconnect just a few yards ahead where the ravine shallows. I'll meet you up there!"

"Got it!" I shout, giving Ada's sides a light squeeze with my legs to encourage her forward.

She is still jumpy after our encounter with the quail, and it doesn't help matters that she is now separated from her trail buddy. Anticipating another spook, I gather my reins and secure my seat in the saddle by adding more pressure to my stirrups and straightening my posture. As we reenter the forest at a walk, the sunlight snaps out of existence. The dappling and vegetation becoming thicker the deeper we go. I can no longer see Jack, nor hear Lazarus snorting at losing sight of his mare – but I trust that Jack knows these trails. We will reconnect soon. For now, I just need to keep moving forward.

Out of the corner of my eye, I catch a flicker of movement – quick and shadowed. I whip my head around to track it, but whatever it was is already gone. *Probably a deer,* I think. But I need to know which way it's headed to prepare Ada for another sudden scare.

I scan the woods, trying to get my bearings, but something shifts. The feeling of isolation deepens now—like something is watching.

Then, I see it again.

A dark figure, hunched low to the ground, moves swiftly behind a tree. Ada halts beneath me, every muscle in her body locking into place. I feel her energy shift, her ears perking forcefully forward, straining and alert. She senses it too.

This is no deer.

The dense grove has gone eerily silent. I no longer hear the bugs buzzing, or the birds chirping merrily in the trees. Even the leaves have ceased their rustling with the coastal breeze. It is as if things have frozen in place. I glance around feeling lost, trying to regain my sense of direction.

That is when I spot the shadow again. Quick as lightening it scuttles behind another tree. It is too big. Too fast. *Definitely not a deer,* I think. Twisting frantically in my saddle, I try to pinpoint where the shadowed creature went. My heart lurches at the realization that it is stalking us.

Gathering my reins tighter, I prepare to run if I need to. From the corner of my eye, I see it again – this time it dashes from behind a sycamore in a low hunch then launches upward into the twisting limbs of an oak. My neck whips around as I try to track its motion.

Now it flashes back down crouching next to a boulder.

Getting closer.

Closer.

Ada's perked ears swivel with each flicker of the creature's movement. Her entire body is taut and trembling, coiled with the instinct to flee. I lean forward and place a shaky hand on her neck, trying to calm her. Trying to calm myself.

I don't know what to do. I don't know where to go. Running blindly through the forest feels reckless, but standing still feels like awaiting death.

We take a tentative step forward.

But every time I think about moving again, the shadow creature shifts – emerging in front of us, blocking the trail. *It's toying with us,* I realize.

The temperature suddenly plummets. A sharp chill bites through my flannel and I start to shiver. I let out a long exhale and my breath clouds in front of my face like a warning.

I need to get out of here.

I can't shake my flashbacks to the beach and the sea ghoul. *I wish Sam were here. Where is Jack? Shouldn't he have found me by now?* I pull my hand off Ada's neck to gather the reins, preparing to make a desperate run for it. *Fuck it,* I think, *running blind is better than sitting prey.* I look down at my hand, confused. It feels oddly sticky and warm. I gasp, scream lodged in my throat, eyes going wide. Bits of flesh and fur pull away from her neck, leaving a bloody mess stringing from my palm to where I had touched her.

I blink rapidly, trying to dislodge the vision – only to have it crystallize even further. Ada's once beautiful golden coat has turned a sickly grey, tinged with a brownish hue, and is marred by patches of exposed muscle and bone. I glance down to her legs – blood and pus and decay ooze and drip down from the open cavity of what was once her cannon bone. The skeleton of her leg is now fully exposed. The nightmare mess leaves a puddle of goo on the dirt below her stomping, bloody hooves.

The small amount of tea and toast I had that morning threatens to rachet its way up from my stomach, as the realization hits me – this is another flash. But just like the beach the other day, this feels real. *Too real.* Not like a hallucination at all.

That's when Ada slowly, with a sickening lurch, turns her head to track the movement of the shadow creature. Parts of her skull are visible where the flesh has rotted away, her once honey colored eye gone and replaced by a dark, hollow eye socket. I stare, agape in horror, as parts of her tattered mane and coat fall to the ground in bloody chucks.

I am frozen in terror, my body betraying me. Every muscle locking into place, as if encased in ice. Time seems to stretch in a long, slow pull – slowing down, while my heartrate and breathing accelerate into a frantic rhythm. My limbs feel impossibly heavy and my chest aches with each ragged gasp I desperately try to draw in. Mind racing, I am caught in the grip of fight-or-flight, but I can do neither. I find myself trapped in a state of paralysis.

Eyes bulging, my sight is fixed on Ada's decaying form—I can't bring myself to look away, though every instinct in my body screams at me to run, hide, yell for Jack, to get away. *Run!* But my throat is locked up as tight as my limbs, and the only thing I can hear now is the deafening pounding of my own heart in my ears. I begin to hyperventilate, unable to escape this nightmare. A small, distant part of my mind recognizes what's happening. *I'm having a panic attack.*

There is a muffled shouting sound in the distance, but I am unable to focus on anything but the monster I am astride and the shadow demon hunting me. Then there is movement and hands grabbing at my waist, tugging me from the saddle.

"Gabriella! Gabriella! Gabby, it's Jack. Look at me! Focus!"

A slow and painful thaw begins in my center as I emerge from my fear-stricken state. I blink, disoriented, trying to take in my surroundings. The terror-filled fog that engulfed me moments ago starts to lift, my senses sharpening. My heart still thuds violently against my ribcage, but the tightness in my throat eases, allowing me to draw a shaky, ragged breath.

Jack. Jack is here. Jack came for me. I am safe.

I look over at Ada, who is happily grazing with Lazarus. No longer the zombie horse she was a moment ago. Sunlight trickles in through the branches, birds chirp merrily and chase each other in zest. The forest is alight with life, all menacing shadows of Hell gone. I blink, shaking my head, questioning my own sanity. As my dread fades and the adrenalin ebbs, weakness washes over me, hollowing out my limbs. My knees buckle instantly.

Jack catches me and gently lowers me to the ground. Tenderly, he cups my cheeks in his hands. "Hey. Hey, it is okay. I am here. You are safe."

He tugs me to his chest and holds me until I feel my body relax, and both my heart rate and breathing settle. Gradually peeling myself away, we sit in the tall, swaying grass, his hands now securely clasping my own.

"What happened? Are you okay? When I went to meet up, you were somehow off the trail. It took me awhile to find you."

"I... I..." I start, stumbling over my words as my mind races to catch up with what just happened. "After we got separated, there was something in the woods. Something was following us... I couldn't get a good look at it, but... Jack – oh God. I was so scared. I must have veered off the trail. I am sorry. I didn't realize... I... I..."

"Hey, shhhhh... It is okay. I've got you." Jack pulls me closer to him again until I am sitting on his lap, and safely ensconced in the shelter of his strong arms. He holds me securely for a moment, rocking back and forth in the grass, ever so slightly.

Grounding me. Anchoring me to him, to his calm and peaceful presence.

"Look," he says, delicately tipping my chin up to look into his deep blue eyes, "Look at the horses. They are content, calm. If there was danger nearby, they'd be the first to alert us. Besides, I would never let anything happen to you."

I glance over to the horses happily munching on the fresh grass, tails swishing nonchalantly, as if there is not a care in the world. Deep down, I know Jack is right. Horses are prey animals, regardless of their size. They would sense any threat long before we did. But I can't help questioning what I just saw.

Sensing my lingering unease, Jack continues, "I need you to trust me, Gabriella. Can you do that?"

I gaze back up at Jack, holding his eye contact. His presence is like a soft light in a dark room, settling the raging storm within me as he radiates quiet strength. His calmness washes over me, encasing me in a peaceful stillness. Grounding me in a profound reassurance that I am not alone. *I am safe. And I do trust him. With everything.*

I merely nod, and his eyes dance between mine, measuring me before saying, "Good. Now, let's get these horses and head home. I'm sure Gladis has something warm and comforting brewing for us in the kitchen."

Then, taking both my hands in his large ones, he gently lifts me to my feet, and we collect our horses. Jack holds Ada in place and hovers his hand over me to assist me as I mount my mare before climbing onto Lazarus. I tentatively give her a pat, followed by another nod to Jack, and we head back down the trail in the direction of the manor.

As we approach the barn, we find Gus happily waiting outside for us. Jack dismounts first and hands him the reins before assisting me off of Ada. I manage a weak smile as Gus takes the mare from me.

"Gus, do you mind unsaddling our horses and giving them a rub down? I want to get Gabriella back to the house for some of Gladis' comfort food."

"Not at alls, sir. I's be happy to." Still smiling and whistling to himself, Gus leads our horses into the barn.

Jack takes my hand and guides us towards the house. The sun hangs low in the sky, signaling the approaching evening. I suddenly realize how long we were out. I'm probably out of sorts from only consuming a slice of toast with some tea for the entirety of the day. What just happened, can't be entirely real. *It must have been amplified by my lack of nutrients and old ghost story memories about being alone in the woods. That's it – coupled with the head trauma,* I think to myself.

We walk in companionable silence, and I am grateful that Jack is not pressuring me to say more. To describe more of what happened out there. Because if I am honest with myself, I'm not entirely sure I even could.

We head up onto the veranda, and Jack leads me to the wooden bench that overlooks the ocean. Grabbing the green-and-blue plaid throw that was draped over the back of the bench, Jack gently wraps me in it as I settle in.

I'm feeling warm and safe, the horrors fading further and further from my mind, when Jack says, "I will be right back. Stay right here," and disappears into the house.

Moments later, he returns carrying two bowls of steaming butternut squash soup. Handing me one, I tenderly lift a spoonful blowing on the warm liquid before bringing it to my lips for a sip. It's smooth and slightly sweet, tasting like autumn. Velvety and rich, yet gentle on my still shaky stomach, helping to settle me with its natural earthy flavor.

Jack sits close to me on the bench, cradling his own bowl in his hands. I lean against him, lost in his aura of calm, security, and safety. Shifting slightly, he pulls me closer, fitting me perfectly into the nook of his chest. His arm wraps around me, holding both me and his bowl as he eats. We sit there like that – snuggled together in shared silence and an unspoken comradery – eating our early dinner and watching the waves crash against the rocky shore.

Chapter 20

The Lighthouse

It is a couple days later when Jack asks if I would like to go explore the old lighthouse with him. Just the two of us. Of course, I accept. I feel like I'm going to bubble over with excitement, and Kasha is just as giddy. She peppers me with a million questions from what I am going to wear to how far I am planning on going with the dreamy "stranger." Jack's nickname having never fully left him.

I didn't tell her about the mishap of our ride together, I am not ready to face the consequences of that reality yet. Or uphold my promise to her about talking to Jack or seeing a doctor. So instead, I describe my elegant jeans and light blue sweater in such detail that Kasha rolls her eyes at me and slaps my arm.

"Well, at least let me braid your hair. If you are going to be classically boring, Gabriella, with your wardrobe, I'll need to doll you up somehow. It is definitely a date after all," Kasha tells me as she drags me into her suite and effortlessly weaves a beautiful French braid into my long, dark hair. The blissful feeling transports me to a time when we would sit and play hairdresser as little girls together.

I find Jack downstairs waiting for me with two thermoses in his hands. A smile breaks across his face when he sees me.

"Ready?" he asks. As he hands me a thermos, I tell him that I am, and we set off down the path that leads to the beach. Sam bounds after us, ready to go on an adventure, too.

Turning back to the large dog, Jack tells him in an authoritative voice to stay. Sam throws himself to the ground in a hunch and lets out the most pathetic whine, his mouth making a little round shape with each cry.

"Oh, you will be okay," Jack assures him.

I do everything in my power not to laugh or beg Jack to just bring the giant dog with us. As we begin walking again, I look back one more time and see Sam lay his chin down in the grass in defeat, watching us depart.

Once we're down on the shore, Jack leads me to a small cave, one that I must've missed when I explored this area a few days ago. *Was that really only less than a week ago? It feels like another lifetime.* Inside is a rowboat and a pair of oars. He tosses his thermos in with a clunk and grabs mine from me before doing the same. Walking backwards, he starts to drag the boat across the sand toward the surf.

Just as the water starts to lap at the rowboat's sides, Jack tells me to get in.

"Won't that make it too heavy?" I ask.

"It will make it heavier, but unless you want to get good and wet, I suggest you get in," he says, smiling at me. "I'll be fine. Promise."

Climbing over the edge of the tiny boat and sitting on a small plank, I do as Jack says. I'm not in a hurry to feel the fridged water again anytime soon.

With a running push, Jack launches us into the water and leaps over the side, just as the cold waves lap at his ankles. Quickly grabbing the oars, he rows forcefully against the current. We bob and lurch over the small waves, sea mist splashing my face. I turn back and beam at Jack as he fights the tide and surf, letting out a laugh that is quickly swallowed up by the wind.

"This is the most fun I have had other than being on the back of a horse," I shout as I grip the side of the boat, trying to keep myself steady. *I need to let the horror of that day go. I am not going to allow whatever is happening to me ruin the things I love most about life.*

As we approach the lighthouse, I feel myself frown as I wonder how we will anchor the boat and get ashore. There appears to be no opening in the large rocks that form the base. Steering our small vessel to the southern point of the island, Jack manages to find a small inlet. Getting the boat as close as he can without smashing it to pieces, he jumps out and onto the mussel-covered rocks. He ties the rough hemp rope to an iron stake I hadn't noticed, jutting out from between the slick, sea-worn stones.

I pass him his thermos and reach forward for his outstretched hand. Jack offers me both stabilization and support while I leave the rocking boat and climb ashore.

We scale the rocks leading up to the solid mound of earth that supports the lighthouse, careful not to slip on the wet boulders as we climb. Once on solid ground we walk around the far side of the lighthouse. Jack pulls out a long, ancient-looking key and unlocks the door. Lowering and angling his shoulder up against the old solid wood, he uses the full force of his body to push the heavy door open. The ancient hinges groan in protest with the new, forced movement.

He clicks on a flashlight that he pulls from the inner pocket of his jacket, and I follow him up to the twisting spiral staircase. As we climb the rusty stairs, we pass a few small rooms. I crane my neck trying to peek inside.

"There are rooms in here," I observe. "I thought most lighthouse keepers lived in separate buildings?"

"A lot did. Often, they could even bring their families with them. But because this one is so remote, being out on the rocks without much room to build a separate structure, the keeper lived in these small rooms inside the lighthouse itself. The original keeper of this particular lighthouse had his extended family living back in the main house. Mr. Covell was the first keeper stationed here. When he was originally hired for the job, he brought his sister, Mary, and her family with him. It was her husband, Mr. Covell's brother-in-law, Thomas, who built the main house that we live it today. Cliffside Manor. Except it wasn't as big back then. There have been many renovations since."

As we climb, my thighs are already starting to burn from the exertion.

"This one here was built in 1875," he continues, "when there were a lot more fishermen out along this stretch of coastline. The lighthouse was used to help keep them from smashing into all the rocks that litter the bank. It was a hard job, and the keeper always had to be aware of the weather, oil reserves, and nearby shipping traffic. He had to be able to read, write, and solve basic arithmetic—all things that are taken for granted today, but were not always so common back then."

"Gosh, Jack, you could be a legit tour guide. You are a wealth of information. How on earth do you know so much about this place?"

A deep chuckle rumbles in his throat, and I feel my stomach clench at the sound.

"It's easy because I grew up here," he says. "I used to come up here a lot as a young boy."

"It's so hard to see in here. How could Mr. Covell possibly find his way around or live here like this in the dark?"

"See these wall mounts?" Jack asks, angling the flashlight beam on them. "These held candles. He would light them when he needed the stairwell illuminated, then would snuff out the light when he would go back downstairs for the night. Back then, the keepers always had candles in portable candle holders that made it so they could be carried easily, illuminating the darkness around them. The holders would keep the candles from burning their hands... They also had a basin at the bottom that would catch any melting wax. They would use these in a similar way that we use flashlights today."

As we approach the top of the stairwell, light begins to pour in from above, guiding us toward its glowing reception. Cresting the final step of the staircase, I am left with a sense of awe as I absorb the breathtaking views around me.

As I stand on the narrow section of platform that looks like it's made of new wood, I see that the low walls are covered in soot, and there are 360 degrees of paned windows all around us. The view is remarkable: ocean as far as I can see in front of us, the rocky coastline stretching off into the horizon in both directions at our sides. I take a step around the large beacon located in the center of the small, enclosed space and peek past it to see the surf crashing on the rocks below the bluff. Cliffside Manor sits on the hillside above.

"Jack, this is beautiful," I say, my voice quieted with wonder.

"Yes, it is." As he says it, I turn to look at him, but he is not looking out at the endless, gray sea. He is looking directly at me, eyes boring into mine. I feel a heat rise to my cheeks, and I swallow hard and glance toward the beacon.

"So, how did this thing work?" I ask, trying to distract myself from the sudden tightness in the air between us.

He walks over to me, but because the space is so small, the side of his body brushes up against mine. My skin tingles with his new proximity.

"See this here?" He points to the disc-shaped cylinder near the top of the contraption that sits in the center of a bunch of glass panels. "This is the reservoir, where they would store the oil. Then there is the oil control lever, the burner down there, and this is the damper. The keeper would need to ensure that the reservoir was always full of oil and then safely maintain the flames in the burner using the damper. The light from the burner would then reflect off all these mirrored glass lenses, shooting light out of the windows far and wide to warn ships of the rocks and coast nearby. The keeper would have to constantly polish and clean the Fresnel lenses so they would be in optimal condition. If the lenses were not clean, then the light did not reflect as well or as brightly off the panels, putting lives in danger."

Listening to him talk with such knowledge and passion, I gather my confidence, reach over, and silently lace my fingers through his. He stops talking, snapped out of his history lesson, and looks at me, straightening up to his full height.

"Thank you for bringing me here. This is truly remarkable," I say.

"I would do anything for you, Gabriella. Anything just to see you smile at me and to look at me like you are right now."

He bends his head down toward mine. I lift my chin up toward him, and our lips touch in a soft kiss. He wraps his large hand around my low back and pulls me in closer, our kiss deepening with the movement, our bodies pressed flush together. The air feels charged as our kiss intensifies.

Reluctantly pulling his lips from mine, he whispers onto them, "Come, we should head back downstairs before one of us falls off this narrow platform and down the staircase."

I merely nod, and he interweaves our fingers again, leading me down the winding stairwell. Neither of us says a word until we reach the bottom, comfortable in our silence.

Once on solid ground, I halt him by tugging on his hand, pulling him back toward me. Our lips collide again in a heated passion. Slowly moving us backward with each tentative step, I guide him as we enter what was the keeper's old sleeping quarters. The backs of my knees bump up against the old iron-framed bed and thin mattress as I reach up and pull his sweater over his head, our lips only leaving each other's for a brief second. I want more of him. I need more of him. I want to drown myself in his strength in the calm security his presence always gives me.

"Are you sure?" he asks me, voice rough with need.

"I am sure," I tell him.

Delicately lowering me down on to the old keeper's bed, he trails kisses down my throat and collarbone. I close my eyes and lose myself in the ecstasy of his heated touch.

After we beach the rowboat on the shore, Jack hauls it back over into the hidden cave. We ascend the sandy trail leading up the bluff to the house, hand in hand. As we crest the bluff, we are greeting by a barking, tail-wagging Sam.

"Hey, boy," Jack says, giving Sam a full body rub as the Dane's tail whips even more violently. "See? That wasn't too bad hanging back, was it?"

Sam barks in response as if to say, *Yes, it was.*

With a broad smile across his face, eyes still twinkling, Jack turns to me.

"I have to go check on some things around the property before dinner. Do you mind taking this beast inside and asking Gladis to give him some scraps for his supper?"

"Not a problem. Come on, Sam," I say, reaching for him and trying to get his attention to follow me and not Jack. But before I can take a step toward the house, Jack grabs my arm and pulls me in for another long, sensuous kiss.

"See you later," he murmurs.

"See you later," I respond, unable to control the smile on my face.

I head into the kitchen with Sam on my heels and say hello to Gladis, who is already busy preparing for dinner.

"Hi, dear. Have a nice time at the lighthouse?" she asks, giving me a knowing smile topped with an exaggerated wink.

"I did; it was lovely. And Jack knows so much about the history of this place. It's amazing."

"That he does and very well should. Would you like some hot chocolate before dinner to warm you up?"

"I would love some, please and thank you. Oh, and Jack asked if you have some scraps for Sam, for his dinner?"

"You got it. And Sam is always properly spoiled; Jack doesn't need to worry. Now, just don't let this go spoiling your dinner," she says, handing me a mug.

I promise her it won't, and I tell her all about our date. Well, almost all of it. I decide there are some parts that are meant for just Jack and me.

"Oh, I do love young love," she reminisces. "It reminds me of my youth. So hopeful and exciting. You may not be able to tell now, but I was quite the looker back in my day. I had gentleman callers for miles."

Just then Clarence comes into the kitchen, laughing. "Callers for miles, aye? Is that how you remember it, my dear?"

Swatting a dishtowel at him she responds, "Oh, don't you start with me, Clarence Covell."

He grabs her hands, dishtowel disregarded on the counter in a flourish, and spins her around the kitchen. They embrace in a slow dance, rocking slightly together in a motion that displays years of familiarity, to music only they can hear.

"You were a looker, though," he adds as he lifts her hand and twirls her around her kitchen.

"You weren't so terrible to look at yourself," she responds.

"Time can only be so kind, can't it, my dear?" he says with devilish look on his face before giving her a wink.

"Oh!" she exclaims, armed with the dishtowel again, slapping him with every exclamation that comes next. "That is it! Get out! Get out! One of us has work to do, and if you will not help, I want you out!"

As she is forcefully directing Clarence through the door, both of them laughing, I am blinded momentarily by a flash of light.

When I open my eyes, the smile on my face drops. The skin on Gladis's face and arms is puckered and boiling, peeling down and falling off in draping, black chunks, leaving exposed tissue and bone behind. The skin of her cheek is charred and pulled down, melting and exposing her eye socket. Hand flying to my mouth to stifle a scream, I turn to Clarence, to see if he is witness to my horror. He is happily allowing himself to be swatted out the door, oblivious to Gladis's condition or my terror. That is when I notice his hands held up in defense of his face. They are ungloved for the first time I have seen him, and the skin on his hands and wrists is blistered and peeling just like Gladis's face. My hot chocolate sloshes over the edge of my mug as my trembling hands drop it on the counter with a clatter. I sense them both turn to look at me, but my vision blurs, dark tunnels closing in from around the edges as I flee the kitchen and past them both. Just as I push past, I notice their shocked expressions. Their *normal* expressions.

"Gabriella, darling, are you okay?" I hear Gladis shout after me.

I don't respond as I dash up the stairs, taking them two at a time, and stumble into my room. Closing the door behind me, I turn the lock. I slide down the heavy wooden door until my back hits the cold floor, my hands shaking as I clamp them tightly over my open mouth—pressing so hard the skin aches, and I know I'll leave a red mark. Fear and panic swirl inside me like a storm, threatening to spill over.

Then I scream.

Chapter 21

The Betrayal

I take my mug of tea out to sit on the veranda and watch the sun set below the horizon. I am so tired, and it feels like I haven't slept in weeks. I sense the heavy, dark circles that have formed under my eyes, and every motion I make feels sluggish. Then there is my headache. We have had multiple balls since that first night, so I know that this dull ache that doesn't seem to want to leave my temples has stayed with me for months now and won't go away anytime soon.

Just wanting to reclaim some of that peace that I felt when we first arrived at Cliffsides, I lower myself into one of the lounge chairs, pulling the throw over my legs to stay warm.

The seasons have begun to change, getting chillier, but I can't seem to ever be warm enough. There is a constant cold running through me that I know has nothing to do with the approaching winter.

Taking a few sips of my steaming mint tea, I hear the voices of people arguing in the distance. I close my eyes for a second and try to drown them out with the sound of the ocean and the thrumming in my own head.

Slowly peeling my eyes open, I look out to see the lighthouse in the distance. The fog is starting to roll in. The lighthouse stands tall on the rocky island, waves lapping steadily against the boulders below. I imagine it content in its solitude—melancholy, perhaps, but still proud of the vital role it plays. Then I recall Jack rowing the two of us out there. I think of our date and the kisses we shared. I begin to smile at the memory before my mind drifts to the more sinister event of that evening. I didn't tell Kasha about it or about my haunted ride. I know I said I would... that I would go see a doctor... but it seems easier to ignore it than to face what it may be. I am frightened, and I am not ready to tackle my fears yet.

Still sitting and watching the fog creep along the shoreline, giving it an eerie appearance, my attention is drawn back to the bickering happening around the bend. The woman's voice is growing louder and louder, but I can only make out the deep baritones of the man's inflections, not exactly what he is saying. *Must be a lover's quarrel,* I think. *Strange, though, as there are not too many couples here. And now that I think about it, in all the months that we have stayed at Cliffsides, I have never seen anyone, not the revolving door of guests or the staff, be anything but high-spirited and tranquil at all times.*

"We need to say something. This has gone on for too long," I hear the woman exclaim.

There is a pause, filled by something the man is saying.

Then the woman goes on. "I don't care. She is wasting away. I know you see it, too."

The man interjects something unintelligible again.

"It doesn't matter what the repercussions are. I don't care! There is no way that whatever will happen will be worse that what is currently happening."

More deep, indecipherable objections.

In a tone that has now dropped from the high pitch of emotion, carrying a deadly emphasis of seriousness, the woman says, "I hate lying to her. I have never lied to her. This isn't right. I went along with your plan, trusting you, but I can't do it anymore. If you don't tell Gabriella, I will."

I feel my heart clench and then plummet rapidly into my stomach. A lump of stress lodges in my throat, and my pulse begins to hammer hard and fast. *I was right. There has been something going on between Kasha and Jack,* I think with a sickening feeling. *She has been lying to me,* nausea bubbling up from my center.

Rising to my feet, I discard the blanket and tea before I make my way toward the voices, which I now know belong to Kasha and Jack. I am not clear on what they have been arguing about other than it has something to do with me. Something to do with Kasha having lied to me. *She and Jack have lied to me.*

Feeling an overwhelming sense of betrayal, I stride down the porch and turn the corner, coming face to face with them both. They freeze, shock apparent on their faces. Kasha's mouth hangs ajar while Jack's is pulled into a tight, thin line. Pallor starts at their throats and spreads up their faces as they look at me.

"Tell me what?" I ask, deadly serious. My head is still throbbing, and it is starting to make my vision blurry.

Jack starts, "Gabriella, this is not how—"

"Tell. Me. What." I emphasize each word, my voice growing louder with frustration at both the situation and my pounding head. "Are the two of you together?! Is that what it is?"

"What? No..." Kasha starts as she turns to Jack, arms folding across her chest as she does. Eyebrows raised, chin jutting out, she glares at him with her best 'say something or I will kill you' glower.

"Please, Gabriella, sit down." Jack motions toward a nearby bench.

"No, I think I'm good here. Thanks," I say crossly.

Kasha tries next. "Gabs, it is nothing like that. Remember how you told me about the things that have been bothering you? Not just here, but back in South Brook, too?" When I don't answer, she goes on, "The feeling of being ignored, even by people you were close to, like your pops and Gary. Then here with your frightening visions... of Gus, the bartender, even Sam? And think about your headaches and the memory loss after the accident. You were not being ostracized, and you are not going mad. It's because we—"

"It's because we are in a different realm," Jack cuts her off. "The life you once knew is no longer a part of your world. It's like a veil, and we are on the other side. It thins with time."

"You told him about my visions?!" I ask Kasha furiously. "And what are you both talking about? Neither one of you are making any sense. Just out with it already!"

Kasha takes a couple of large, quick strides toward me and takes my hands in hers. She grasps them so tightly that I feel my bones grinding together. "We are dead, Gabs. We died back in the car accident in South Brook."

What? Huh? No. That doesn't make any sense. I try to pull away, shaking my head, but Kasha is gripping my hands too firmly.

"Think about it," she starts again.

"Careful," Jack says, almost inaudibly, to Kasha.

She repeats herself as she shoots Jack another daggered glare. "Think about it, Gabs. People seemed to look right through you, right? Your pops was more distant than ever, unspeakably so. Only Sally, the garage cat, gave you any attention. No one spoke to us on the bus rides here, other than that little boy at the station, and we had the whole train car to ourselves. And your 'memory loss'... Honey, you didn't just forget about being discharged from the hospital. You never were. Then there are your visions of death... Your headaches. You're still having them, aren't you? They're still keeping you up at night." This last part of her monologue is stated, not asked.

"I... I... don't understand..." I start, wanting to reach up and grab my head.

"The night of the accident, I died right away. My neck broke when we were rolling down the embankment. But you," she continues, eyes brimming with unfallen tears, "you were so strong. You held on for so long. You were in and out of consciousness at the hospital for weeks before your body gave out on you."

Tears start streaming down both of our faces. Still grasping Kasha's hands, I look up and over at Jack. "You were there. I remember. You and Kasha." My eyes dart back to her. "You were both standing in the tree line. Kash, you were in the car, and then you weren't. And, Jack, you were there. Why were you there?"

The numbness starts to fade as I feel the anger build, taking over my shock. Realization is starting to dawn on me. Forcefully ripping my hands out of Kasha's grasp, I take a step back, then another, heat rising from my center.

"Why didn't you tell me?" I shout. "Why didn't either one of you tell me? You are my friends. We're supposed to be able to tell each other anything!"

"Gabs..." Kasha tries, but I'm lost in my despair and sense of betrayal. This somehow feels worse than if they were messing around behind my back.

"I mean, you would tell me if I have food in my teeth, right? Then why the heck wouldn't you tell me that I was fucking *dead*?! That seems like a fairly important fact. Agreed? Almost like something someone should know about themselves. Don't you think?"

Jack takes a step toward me, but when I step away again, he stops. "It was a delicate situation and one that needed to be handled with great care. It is not just something that can be stated or brought to one's attention before they are ready," he says, darting a glance back at Kasha, who meets his knowing glare. "The veil between Realms is thinner for animals and children. That is why the cat at The Pump and Go still showed you affection and the boy at the station was able to talk to you. But souls can be very fragile and volatile things. It is easy for them to become full of sorrow. . . or vengeful. The acknowledgement of one's death is something that they need to come to terms with and discover on their own. Kasha and I hoped that bringing you here would help. However, your symptoms were continuing to progress, and rapidly. We were discussing the best procedure to take when you happened upon us. I am so sorry. You were never meant to find out this way."

"And in what way was I supposed to find out?" I ask, incredulous, my voice cracking with emotion and I hate myself for it.

"Kasha and I were there with you the entire journey. We were never going to let you be alone with this, but it's something that you needed to do by yourself. Something that everyone needs to do by themselves."

My words begin as a murmur, but they gather steam, like a freight train, until I am shouting them. "I can't hear any more. I don't want to hear any more!"

My vision swimming, I feel like I can't breathe. I need to get out of here. I spin on my heels, and I bolt. *I can't. I can't. I can't be dead. I need to breathe. I need to get somewhere where I can breathe.*

I run down the deck and stairs, across the fields, to the first place that I can think of that brings me peace. The stables. I need Ada.

As I approach the barn, I slow my pace. My lungs are heaving as I try to catch my breath from the run over here. I attempt to stifle my large gulps of air, taking in quick, short bursts of breath instead, trying to limit my air intake. I'm worried that I am being too loud with my gasps, and I don't want to wake Gus. I don't want to see anyone right now.

I sneak into the barn. The horses are all munching on their alfalfa, tails swishing with contentment. As I step silently on the dirt floor of the barn, I spy Gus in the extra stall, asleep in his haystack. Soft snores emanate from his skinny body. Quickening my pace, I slide past the open pen's door and head for Ada's stall.

She lifts her head, ears perking when she sees me. As slowly and as silently as I can, I slide the bolt on her door, opening it and slipping inside. After securing it behind me, I turn to face her. She is looking at me quizzically, and I walk over to her and rub my hand down the length of her golden face. As I stroke her flaxen forelock, she huffs a puff of warm air in my face from her large, velvety nostrils. Stepping to her side, I lean in and wrap my arms around her strong neck. She lifts her head in slight surprise, then lowers it again, leafing through her dinner. I bury my face in the crook of her neck and take a deep, deep breath. She smells of horse and dust and hay. And I sob hard into her coat.

Beginning to feel calm in her presence, I quickly head out of the stall and grab a saddle pad from the tack room and tuck back inside with her. Giving her another kiss on her shoulder and trailing my hand down her long back and flank in a gentle, smooth stroke, I take the pad over to the far corner of her stall.

The tears dry on my cheeks as I curl up and lie down on the pad, arm folded under my head. Staring off into space, I struggle with everything that Kasha and Jack have told me tonight. *It doesn't make sense. How can I be dead? How can Kasha be dead? We are here. We traveled here. We eat and sleep and dance and talk to people. Kasha cooks, and I ride Ada. Jack and I have shared kisses and dances and the warmth of each other's bodies. I can still feel and experience things. None of this makes any sense. I must be dreaming because this can't be real.*

Lying there in full denial, sleep starts to claim me, but before it does, I know deep in my soul that they are right.

Chapter 22

The Reunion

I emerge from Ada's stall, midmorning, still fuming and feeling broken from my altercation with Jack and Kasha. As I head back toward the manor, I feel nauseous from both their concealment and from the new knowledge of my death.

I force as much power into each step up the stairs to the porch as I can muster. My anger at their betrayal fueling my every move. I stomp to the far end, to where it wraps around the side of the house, offering some privacy from the comings and goings of staff and guests. I am surprised but relieved that this area is not populated by anyone. It is a beautiful and secluded spot, with a couple of chairs and a small end table. It is the part of the house that faces the ocean, and I can feel the mist and hear the crashing of the waves below me. Standing there, looking out at the gray, turbulent sea, I collapse my forearms on the railing and lay my forehead down on them. I close my eyes and try to breathe. I just need to breathe, feeling as if the mist is my tears and the surf is my pounding heart.

I can't believe that they would keep something like this from me. The level of deceit and secrecy that they had to have conspired over to keep the ruse alive is staggering. *Why would they hurt me like that? Kasha is my best friend. Why wouldn't she tell me? How could she just allow me to keep living in the dark? Especially since we're going through this together. I don't understand why she would want to carry the burden alone. I wouldn't. Then there is Jack. I honestly believed we had something real... something that could have lasted. I feel like such a dunce. Send me one good-looking man with a disarming smile and charming manner, and I am duped. Utterly and hopelessly lost and suckered. How easily I am manipulated.* I can't tell if I am more angry at them for their deception or at myself for being so easily played.

I slowly lift my head from my arms and stare out to sea, lost in my own troubles and heartache. I reach up and wipe away some of the tears that have treacherously slipped down my face. I want to remain angry, to hold on to my wrath. It's easier that way. It doesn't seem to hurt as bad when I'm mad. But when the grief takes hold, I'm not sure I will be able to recover from that.

In my state of desolation and depression, I don't notice the man approaching me from behind until I hear him clear his throat. Sighing, frustrated that my bubble of solitude has been popped, I turn to face him. *I should have stayed in the barn*, I think. I feel the scowl gradually lifting from my face, being replaced by a look of confusion. I study the solid figure in front of me. My confusion slowly morphs into a dawning and astonishing realization.

"Pops?" I ask.

He walks with a clear and determined purpose, closing the distance between us, and envelops me in a tight, secure embrace. "I'm so sorry, baby girl," he says, as a sob escapes his throat. "Back home, after your accident, I was just so scared. So broken. I didn't know what to do. I lashed out, and I don't know if I'll ever forgive myself for it. I don't expect you to forgive me for it. For any of it."

It feels so good to be held in my father's arms. My father, not the drunk, broken man I left back at South Brook, but the man who raised me. The man who loved unconditionally, provided for his family, laughed genuinely, and created things from nothing. The man who loved Martha Goode more than life itself. Who loved me. That is the man who has returned to me now, and I feel my heart swell with so much joy and love and relief that it is almost painful.

Tears pool in my eyes and start to slip down my cheeks as I am overwhelmed with surprise and happiness. I weave my arm through the bend of his elbow, grasping tightly to his upper arm with my other hand, never wanting to let this version, the true version, of my pops go again. He leads me down the steps of the veranda to a bench that rests under one of the large California pepper trees. It sits a few yards away from the big porch, its long, spindly branches hanging low and swaying in the coastal breeze, providing us both shade and privacy. We sit down together, not letting go.

"I don't understand, Pops. What are you doing here? Don't get me wrong, I'm so happy to see you and I missed you so very much. I am overjoyed, really, and joy is very much needed right now, believe me... But they say... They say that I am... we all here are..." I struggle to form the sentence that has been playing on repeat, embedding itself in my head since last night. *I am dead. We are dead.* "Pops, they tell me that I died in that car accident. That I am dead. And now you're here? It's all too much. I'm having a hard time, and I just don't understand. Some things make sense, when I really think about them, but Jack and Kasha lied to me. Kasha – she lied to me." I let the last statement hang in the air, the betrayal that I feel still a deep, raw wound. "But a ton of things don't make any sense. How could we travel here? How am I here interacting with others? How can I still feel and breathe and blush and cry? How are you here? How is any of this possible if we don't exist anymore?" I cover my face with my free hand, feeling lost and confused, like a sailboat adrift on a windless sea.

Taking a deep breath, face serious, Pops removes my hand from my face and sets our clasped hands together on the bench between us before he speaks again.

"Well, my darling Gabby, I can answer a couple of those questions for you, but you will need to set aside your anger and the deception that you feel and talk to Jack and Kasha. Jack will be able to explain everything. This is what he does. He is such a kind, good man. I actually had some time with him, back home, before you left. I can see things more clearly now. I understand. Don't give up on him, Gabby. You, too, can comprehend what is going on and you deserve to have the happiness the two of you are building together, even if that timing is now. In the After. I can tell you that neither one of them had any malice intended or planned to deceive you in any way. In fact, they did what they did for your own well-being and safety. Jack will explain if you give him a chance. And I guarantee Kasha is just as torn up about everything as you are. Talk to her, too. Now, as for your question regarding me and why I am here..."

"Oh, Pops, I don't mean it that way," I exclaim, desperate to explain. "I am so grateful you are here. I just don't understand. Wait. You know Jack? You've met him and you really like him? Trust him?"

"I know that is not what you meant, my dear. And yes, I like Jack. I trust Jack. He came to me shortly before he brought you here, with Kasha. I didn't realize at the time that you were leaving. Really leaving. But he helped sort me out. He... it... helped. I can see that now. I believe you should give the man another shot. Give love another shot. As I said, he is a good man, and those are hard to come by. I will stand by you no matter what you decide, but please know that your relationship has my full blessing.

"Now, to answer your question as to why and how I am here. Back home, I felt like I was going mad with my grief after your mom passed away so suddenly. Then after you... I had lost both my girls. I went from a man who had everything in life with our little family, to a man who had everything snatched away from him violently. I didn't want to go on living. I didn't know how to go on living. I fell into the bottle to try to numb my despair, but it only seemed to heighten my sorrow. Nothing seemed to help.

"I still felt you everywhere... in the house, in the yard, even at the Pump and Go when I needed to fill up the truck. I missed you immensely, and I thought that my want and need to have you back was somehow keeping your soul tethered there. Tethered to me. I went back and forth with myself that I was imagining things, that you were gone, but then something would happen. The opening and closing of doors when there was no wind. A light, cold touch on my shoulder in the middle of summer. The feeling of not being alone in our empty house. Then one night, after an excessive amount of drinking at the Post, I blew up in the living room. That was the day of your funeral. And I just couldn't hold on anymore. I started shouting at the empty walls, throwing things, consumed by my drunkenness and sorrow. I am so ashamed now by my behavior. That was also the night when I felt you leave. I swear your energy was there one moment and gone the next. I was truly and completely alone, standing there dumbfounded and bleary-eyed in our living room.

"After that the guilt took over. It monopolized my grief. What had I done? I kept asking myself, over and over. That was when I really allowed myself to believe your soul was lost, had been lost, and I chased you away. What kind of father was I, to chase away my daughter, even in death? My daughter, when she probably needed me the most. I was tormented by it. It ate me alive. It still does."

"Oh, Pops." I choke out the words through a sob, which threatens to break the fragile dam inside of me.

He holds up a finger and smiles gently, signaling for me not to say anything, to just listen. "You asked me how I can be here, if this place is for the deceased. Well, Gabby, it is because I died myself. Only a couple months after you left. Heart attack, they said, but I know it was heartbreak."

The shock hits me like a thunderbolt, and my jaw drops, caught on the words that won't come out. A new ache forming in my stomach as I imagine my father dying alone in our home.

"But that was when your mom came to get me." He says this so matter-of-factly, as a smile forms on his lips, a twinkle entering his eyes.

Our eyes dance between each other's, and I try to register what he just told me. *I couldn't have heard him correctly. I really must be going mad. Confusion is clouding my thoughts.*

The stress is too much. I am not thinking, seeing, or hearing things correctly.

Movement in my periphery catches my attention. A slender figure in blue jeans, dirt smeared on the knees, and a flowing white shirt, long hair hanging down to her midback, walks up to the back of the bench. I stare. Then blink. Launching myself off the seat I share with my pops, realization bolting through me, as I dash around the edge of the bench and into her arms.

"Mom!" I shriek, flying into her awaiting embrace.

We hold each other, sobbing openly. After a moment, she leans back and cups my wet face in her hands, looking into my swollen eyes. "My little girl. I am so happy to see you. Sorry I couldn't come sooner, but there were different plans in the works for you. You are so beautiful, and I have missed you very, very much."

"I missed you so much, too, Mom. But where have you been? Why didn't I see you when I... when I died?"

"Come, let's sit back down with your father," she says, handing me a handkerchief she pulled from the pocket of her jeans. "We have a lot of catching up to do." Sitting back down on the bench, I note with a hint of awe that it bares Pop's initials, JP.

"Much like how you ended up here at Cliffsides, despite needing a good nudge from Jack and Kasha," she tells me with a smile, "I was at my own personal Heaven on Earth. I spent some beautifully sunny days roaming around the Kew Gardens in London, the Kirstenbosch National Botanical Garden in South Africa and the New York Botanical Garden, all the worlds best. I roamed the garden paths, taking in the vibrant colors and life, the fragrant scents, and basking in the peace they gave me. I knew when you had your accident and passed away, my darling girl. It was a fierce tug at my center. I was sad, but I also understood that death is not the end. It is merely the next chapter in our existence. I kept tabs on you but didn't come to you because I knew that you were in good hands with Jack and Kasha. What a blessing to go through something so difficult with your best friend at your side. Plus, I heard all about Jack from my own Ferrier." At the look of confusion on my face, she halts my questions with a hand motion before continuing her story. "He will explain dear, now where was I? Oh yes. I even met Jack once, when you first passed on. He came to me to see if I felt like I needed to be there for you. I declined, not because I didn't want to see you. That is not it at all, I wanted to do that more than anything. But because I knew in the depth of my soul that you needed to go down your own path and that you couldn't have been in better hands. Honey, you had and still have to come to your own conclusions and make your own destiny. I knew things were hard, but I also knew that you would be okay. Tough times don't last, tough people do. I understood that the hardship you were experiencing with your death would still be the best thing for you in the long run."

We sit there in the shade of the pepper tree and talk for hours, until the sun starts to wane. After taking in everything she told me, I tell her all about my life in the time since her death. About how Jack arrived in South Brook and how Kasha and I were instantly drawn to him, as if he had been a part of our crew for years. I tell her about the accident and all about our trip here to Cliffsides. About how nice people here are, about Ada and my rekindled love of riding. I tell her about Jack and me forming a new relationship – about our fight. About my fight with Kasha. She listens with the calmness and attentiveness of a mother. *My* mother.

Sitting here with my parents, as we talk into the afternoon, a profound sense of peace washes over me. We are a triad again. Lost and found. A missing puzzle piece clicking into place.

They tell me that they will stay for a few more days but will then need to depart. As wonderful as Jack's manor is, it's simply not the place for them. Everyone has a different calling in life and in death, they say, and I will need to make my own decisions based on what is best for me. Based on what I need. Mom echoes Pops' words and tells me I need to put aside my feelings of betrayal and talk to Jack. That he will explain how everything works and how my situation at the manor came to be.

It is in this moment when I realize that things don't end, not really. They merely change form. That change is a part of life, and nothing is constant. A smile curves the corners of my mouth as I begin to grasp the concept that death is just another change in life. That you can experience life after death.

That is when I steel myself to go and talk to Jack and Kasha.

Chapter 23

Reconciliation

That night, I sleep better than I have in what feels like months. I awake feeling refreshed and renewed after spending time with my parents. I feel like I am coming to terms with everything – from the concept of my own death to my parent's deaths, to what Jack and Kasha did. I need to talk to them both to hear their reasoning behind everything.

Yesterday, both Mom and Pops encouraged me to put aside my hurt and to have a conversation with them. I trust my parents, so that is exactly what I am planning on doing this morning. Even with this restored sense of peace, I still need to hear their side of the story. I decide I am going to start with Jack.

After going through my morning routine, I rummage through the armoire and decide on a long and loose tan skirt, with a tight-fitting white undershirt that pokes out of the bottom of my sea-colored cashmere sweater. Keeping my hair down and free, I make my way downstairs.

Following the sounds of clinking pots and pans, I walk into the kitchen. Kasha is there, already covered in flour. Her expression is pained, but she stays silent. I meet her eyes for a second before I have to look away. I need to talk to Jack first; then I will hear her side of things. Besides, her actions hurt more than Jack's, and I still feel like I need some time.

"Hey," I say. After a brief pause, I add, "Gladis, you don't happen to know where Jack is, do you?"

"Good morning, dear," Gladis says cheerfully. "I haven't seen him yet, but he is usually up before the dawn and takes his coffee in the study."

"Thanks," I respond and head off down the hall.

I find Jack sitting in a large, mahogany-colored leather chair, head tipped down over loose sheets of paper spread across the wooden desk. There is an old-fashioned brass lamp on his desk, near a quill pen and his discarded coffee mug. Stains drip down

TES

the white porcelain's sides. He looks up when he sees me, and I can't help but notice how drawn and tired he looks.

Silently, I take a moment to observe my surroundings. On the far wall, directly behind Jack's desk, is a floor-to-ceiling paned window that overlooks the rolling sea and lighthouse. Morning light pours in through the open, deep-green velvet curtains, illuminating the spines of books that line the other walls. Bookshelves are built on either side of the room, so high that ladders are attached to tracks running along the top shelves, allowing readers to reach the lofty collection above. And there is a fireplace made of river rock, fire still crackling as it begins to die down, embers glowing softly.

Watching me, like a rabbit would an approaching cat, Jack doesn't say anything as I enter the study and take in the vast room. His eyes tracking my every movement.

"What are you doing?" I ask, my voice loud in the large, quiet space.

"Working," is the only response I get.

"I would like to talk, if you are not too busy."

"I am never too busy for you, Gabriella." He sets down his pen and stands. "Please have a seat. I will restart the fire and get us some refreshments."

"No. I mean, no, thank you. I am okay. I would just like to start, if you don't mind?"

"Not at all," he says, crossing the room to shut the large wooden doors, offering us some more privacy.

I walk over to the large fireplace and sit down on a leather sofa that matches his office chair, tucking my feet underneath me. Jack comes over and sits on the far end of the sofa, putting a respectable amount of space between us.

"Okay, Jack. If you want me to trust you, I need to know the truth. All of it, right now. No more secrets." I hear the strength in my own voice, but I tamp down the feeling of pride, not wanting it to distract me. I also know my own resolve, and I know that if he is anything but honest with me, I will walk away, regardless of how much I know it will hurt. How much it will hurt me leaving him.

Jack takes a moment to just look at me. He's always had a way of seeing deeper into people than anyone should be able to. For a second I am not sure he is going to answer me, and all my angst will be for naught. He leans forward on the couch, eyes now on the dying flames. His hands are clasped between his knees, and I realize this is the first time I have seen his shoulders slouched. I have a pang of guilt for pushing him into something that he may not want to disclose, but then my determination kicks back in, and I remind myself that this is what I need to know in order for me to move on. To make the decisions that Mom hinted at.

Finally, Jack starts talking, and I find myself holding my breath.

"My father was a fisherman. He ran a small ship off our coast, catching anything from rockfish to squid, to halibut and barracuda. Barracuda tends to be a gamier fish, though, and never sold as well as the others. Sometimes he would even dive for urchins. It all depended on what the market needed and what the sea was willing to provide and when. It was just the two of us for as long as I remember, my mom having died in childbirth. Fishing was what put a roof over our heads and food on the table.

"My father came to buy this plot of land for next to nothing with my uncle. California was just starting to boom with the gold rush and talk of joining the Union to become an official state. There was still much hostility with the Mexicans and Indians who had previously occupied the countryside, but in the end their efforts didn't amount to much..." He closes his eyes for a second, as if trying to gather himself to go on. To remember.

"My uncle was hired as the lighthouse keeper here, and once the land was purchased, my father built this house and the barn you see out there by hand. He hired some labor from town, and they came in on horses or with their wagons and supplies. Once we had a homestead, he opened and operated his fishing business while my uncle manned the lighthouse. Father would cart his fish into town, more times than not. He would just pull up to the pier down in San Luis Obispo and sell his fresh catch right there off the docks, out of his wagon.

"In April of 1880"—here he makes quick eye contact, I presume to see if I am shocked or have made a connection with the date, then looks away— "when I was about ten, we had a terrible storm. Dad had gone out in the boat a couple days before. 'One more good haul before the storm,' he'd said. He had a knack for reading the weather. He knew there was a storm coming, and he went out anyway. I was used to being left alone, to fend for myself for days on end, but this time was different. It was one of the biggest storms of the century. The rain came, and it came with the full force of God's wrath. It only lasted a few days but still managed to dump over fourteen inches of rain in Sacramento and sixteen feet of snow in the Sierras. The central coast was devastated. It ended up being a cold storm that originated up in the Gulf of Alaska and whipped its way down the western coast. The local sea level rose eight to nine inches. That may not seem like a lot, but I can assure you that when you have a body of water as large as what sits off our coastline, those handful of inches can be catastrophic.

"Needless to say, my father never came home from that trip. I went from being a young boy to the man of the house in the blink of an eye. I am grateful for my uncle Clarence and all his guidance ever since. Never once did he try to take advantage of the fragile situation."

"Wait," I interrupt. "Clarence, our Clarence here, is your uncle?"

"Yes, he and Gladis helped raise me after my father perished at sea. They were an item my whole life and then following, but they never married. He lived out in the lighthouse and would come in occasionally to check on us or to have a warm meal if the seas were calm. Gladis lived in the house with me and always made sure I was well fed. She was the one who taught me how to grow and process my own food.

"We had enough saved, and with our property already being prosperous, I was able to have us live off the land for the next six years. Then the money ran out. The crops struggled, and the livestock stopped producing as they should. At sixteen I went to work as a logger, up in the Sierras. I left the house in the hands of Clarence and Gladis; I trusted no others.

"Logging was a hard and dangerous job. The conditions were terrible. Not only did we live and work in a harsh environment, but something always seemed to be on the brink of going wrong. Things seemed to happen fast when it came to the act of felling trees. I wouldn't come home for months at a time, and I lived in shacks near the site. We primarily relied on animal power, using draft horses and oxen to drag the trees away to be loaded on trains and processed further in the factories, but due to our specific location in the southern Sierras, we did not have the train access that they did up north. The animals had to pull the lumber for farther distances until we started utilizing flumes. We specialized in chopping down and processing ponderosa pines and sugar pines. We would fell them and prep them by removing the branches and needles. Then we would begin the process of moving them. Flumes were essentially manmade, water-filled troughs that enhanced the natural streams. This helped guide the logs, which were tied together like a raft, so they could more easily be accessed by locomotives farther down the mountain. Many men slipped and fell down ravines to their deaths, had accidents with the saws or chains; some were even in the wrong place as the tree came crashing down. I thought I had grown up when my father died, but I became an old man after logging.

"I would come home from time to time to rest, to take a season off and see how the manor fared. Clarence and I sat down one night, and I discussed with him the idea of opening the ranch up as an inn. It would serve tourists and travelers migrating between San Francisco and Los Angeles. He agreed that it was a good way to bring in additional income, so I wouldn't have to work as a lumberjack much longer. He also assured me that he and Gladis were up to the task of running and operating the endeavor in my stead.

"That spring, just as the snow began to melt, I headed back to the mountains. I was eager to leave logging behind, but I had to put in one more season's worth of work to earn the income needed to start our new venture as innkeepers. Only I ended up contracting the white plague while working that fall. It spread through the camp like wildfire."

At the look of confusion on my face, Jack clarifies.

"The White Plague, also known as consumption, is better known today as tuberculosis. We know now that it is a very contagious bacterial disease that affects the lungs and can be treated with antibiotics. But a hundred years ago, it was a death sentence. It caused severe coughing and made it extremely difficult to breathe. This resulted in severe fatigue, night sweats, fevers, and the sick person simply wasting away.

"In the late nineteenth and early twentieth centuries, consumption killed more people than any other disease. Early on during its spread it killed one in every seven people. In 1899 the government started shipping people who were infected off on trains to the west. Some went to Arizona or Colorado, but many came here to California. It was believed, and later proven, that the sun and fresh air helped to delay the disease and to ease the patient's symptoms.

"Sanitoriums popped up all over the Californian coast and were advertised as trendy vacation spots. Many of these sanatoriums operated as the resorts that they were promoted as, offering tennis, croquet, and naps in hammocks. They even had full kitchens serving multiple meals a day, and some offered social events as well.

"We already had the manor set up to be converted into an inn when I fell ill. Upon my return home, we decided that we could stick with our plan but make the adjustments needed to have it be a sanitorium instead. It only took about a year to become fully operational, and it really wasn't very difficult. The government helped and offered us a healthy stipend that not only covered my unemployment, but also covered the cost of new beds, various supplies, and food for all our incoming patients.

"Cliffsides ended up being the perfect location for an infirmary. It was far enough away from any major cities or towns, offering both the patients and healthy individuals' safety.

"We had beds throughout the house, and many were even placed out on the veranda. The fresh sea air and southern sun were simple, but huge blessings for such ill people. Those who had the energy could walk the ranch and see the horses or head down to the beach and walk along the water's edge."

Jack pauses briefly, as if debating exactly what to say or how to say it.

"Even though it is what ended my life, it was also the best thing that happened to me up until that point," he says quickly, eyes darting in my direction before he looks away. "It allowed me to offer a haven for dozens of sick and dying people, often extending their lives by years.

"Many people stayed in their city homes, and they ended up dying within months – or at most, a year after contracting tuberculosis. But for those who left and spent nine to ten hours daily outdoors, ate healthy fare, and received daily exercise, they could continue to live their lives for sometimes up to ten years after falling ill.

"I passed away peacefully, asleep in my bed in the winter of 1905, two months before my thirty-fifth birthday. Clarence and Gladis were at my side until the very end. After my passing, they kept the sanitorium running for the remainder of the year. They were no longer accepting new patients and were helping those well enough to travel to move to other hospitals during that time. They worked hard, and it was amazing that they never fell ill themselves. I didn't blame them for wanting some quiet after my death."

My heart aches for him as I listen to his story. "Oh, Jack, I am so sorry. Everything that you have gone through, how difficult your life was..."

"Please don't feel sorry for me. It was my path. Everything happens for a reason, and I was meant to experience what I experienced. I had to live through that so I could help all those people back then, give them peace. It taught me how to give people peace today."

At some point Gladis popped in and delivered cucumber sandwiches and tea. I barely registered her in the room as she quickly and quietly dispensed the tray of goodies and left because I found myself so immersed in Jack's tale.

"But that is not where my story ends. A person's story never ends with their death; it merely transitions. But I am getting ahead of myself. Where was I? Oh, yes; 1905 with Clarence and Gladis.

"Once Cliffside Sanitorium closed its doors and became Cliffside Manor again, life was fairly quiet for them. Clarence continued manning the lighthouse, and Gladis kept him fat and happy.

"In April of 1906, San Francisco had a devastating earthquake."

"Yes, I remember learning about it in school," I say. "It was terrible, but wasn't it the fires that caused even more damage to the nearly leveled city?"

"Yes, exactly."

"But, Jack, what does that have to do with Cliffsides?"

"Well, Gladis and Clarence had been an item for decades, as I have explained. One night when she was visiting him at the lighthouse, back in 1906, that terrible quake struck. The epicenter was just two miles off the San Francisco coast and was one of the worst earthquakes in Californian history. Even though it is over two hundred miles from here to San Francisco, it shook us hard. I had been keeping tabs on them since my passing and was instantly there when the earthquake hit.

"Gladis was upstairs in the lighthouse with Clarence, enjoying the panoramic view while he tended the beacon, when it started. The shaking caused the oil from the lamp to spill, and it ignited quickly. The whole top deck went up instantly, taking Gladis with it. Clarence managed to pull her out, even with the shaking and flames. Those were the injuries you saw to her face and his hands..." He clears his throat. "Clarence ended up being crushed by a falling piece of debris that supported the stairwell once he got her downstairs. The lighthouse has been shut down ever since."

I barely am able to get the words out. My hand trembles over my mouth as I say, "Oh my God, Jack, that is horrible. And the ranch? What happened to the manor?"

"It became abandoned. For a time anyway.

"Back when I died, I was offered a choice, much like the one that you and Kasha will have to make. I had to choose which Realm I wanted to spend my eternity in. There are three primary Realms: the Realm of Ascension, the Realm of Life After Death, and the Living Realm. These three Realms function in this world. Most of them we cannot see, and most people don't even realize that they exist.

"The Realm of Ascension is the tranquil Realm of the afterlife, where the consciousness is able to rest. There is no thinking or emotion, no feeling or need. It simply is a calm and gentle consistent state of peace for the soul. Christianity,

Judaism, Hinduism, and Islam all consider this as a Heavenly Realm. Buddhists have a similar concept and may refer to it as nirvana, a state of liberation from the mind's needs, passions, and sufferings, but all these different religions agree on one thing: It is a soul bank and a place of ultimate peace.

"The second Realm is another Realm of peace, but this one still contains the soul's consciousness. This is the Realm of Life After Death. Now, the souls who choose to stay on Earth will stay within this Realm. This Realm is similar to the concept of Heaven on Earth, and it is the one that we exist in now. It is the Realm that all souls enter first upon their death. Whereas some souls will choose to ascend, some will be sent to purgatory to atone for their sins, and others are removed due to a rotting of the soul. Still others decide to stay here. Here they can bear witness to everything that is said and experienced in the Living Realm, but the Living Realm is unaware of their existence. The living world and this Realm coexist on top of each other, like a transparent tracing paper laid on top of a picture. They function separately but are in continuous motion together.

"Sometimes the veil between the Living Realm and the Realm of Life After Death slips, and that is when living souls will experience things of a spiritual nature. From hauntings to sixth senses, to the feeling of a deceased loved one's spirit. This slip of the veil is how the little boy at the station was able to see you and Kasha.

"The souls that choose to remain on Earth, however, are required to lend their helping hands to God. Many religions speak of this, but it is better known in Christianity that we are ultimately working for the Lord. Colossians 3:23-24 states, 'Whatever you do, work heartily, as for the Lord and not for men.'

"This is why I am here. Why Clarence and Gladis and Gus are here after all these years. Cliffside Manor exists only in this Realm. In the Living Realm, it is a dilapidated and abandoned piece of property that, to the still living, only existed over a hundred years ago.

"When I first died, I was offered the choice, like I said. I chose to stay and dedicate my soul's work to the Realm of Life After Death. There are many different jobs and tasks for a soul to do in this Realm. Mine is to help collect souls that have recently left the Living Realm and to make their choices known to them. I was there waiting for Gladis and my uncle Clarence when they died in the earthquake and fire, much like I was there for Gus when he died of starvation in the streets as a young boy. Clarence, Gladis, and Gus all chose to have their souls assist me in offering a place of comfort to the incoming transitioning souls.

"There are many places like Cliffside Manor all over the world. Each one is a little different. That is because there are many different types of souls on Earth, and each one is catered to for their idea of what Heaven on Earth would be like.

"For some, Heaven on Earth is a tropical paradise, with sunshine and warm breezes and scuba diving. For other souls, it is a life in the Alps, with crisp mountain air and stunning views and constant hiking or skiing. For you and Kasha, it was here, on a simple but elegant ranch with the rocky sea, fields of horses, and a warm, homecooked meal in the house every day. Cliffsides became your place of refuge when the idea of it was etched into your subconscious as a place of peace, a sanctuary, back when you were a young girl.

"As I mentioned, it is different for everyone, but one thing that remains consistent is that people go where their souls believe they will find comfort. I just happened to be lucky enough that the sanctuary I run aligned with your idea of Heaven on Earth." At this he offers me a wan smile that doesn't seem to fully reach his sad, tired eyes.

I take in everything he has told me and start to absorb it. As I do, I look at Jack. Really look at him. He seems older than when I first met him, and not just because he is apparently 131 years old... *Or is he thirty-five? I'll need to ask how that works, but either way, he looks like he is tired.* His *soul* is suddenly tired. I realize I haven't seen his eyes twinkle in weeks. Now they are silhouetted with dark circles and heavy lines. His usually neat hair and fine clothes look disheveled, like he hasn't had the energy to put as much effort into himself as he used to. There is a shadow of dark whiskers on his chin, a stubble that I don't fully mind but that seems out of place on him.

"Wow," I say. "Jack, I'm not sure where to begin. This is a lot to take in. Seriously, thank you for sharing it with me. I asked for you to tell me everything, and I feel like you opened up in ways that I will always appreciate. Please know that I am honored by your honesty. But there are a few things I still don't seem to fully understand."

"Okay. Tell me what they are, and I will do my best to clarify them for you."

"First off, I don't understand, I mean fully understand, my death. After our accident and my time in the hospital, I was at home with Pops. I went to work. I drank shakes and ate fries at Darla's. How could that all have happened if I was dead?"

"Oftentimes, people don't realize they have passed away. They will wake up in one spot and not know how they got there, or they will maintain the same routine that they had in their life. Only things feel different somehow, like a gear has slipped, and they can't quite figure out what is wrong.

"The people around them and their surviving loved ones make them feel like they are being ghosted, but *they are* the ghosts, and they are just not comprehending what is happening to them or why.

"It takes time, some more time than others, to come to terms with the realization of their fate. Your delay, I believe, was due to the head injury that caused your death. Many spirits who had a traumatic head injury or who were in a coma don't comprehend that they have died. It is not as clear cut for them. Many of us Ferriers think that this is due to a soul spending so much time caught between the two Realms. It causes confusion."

"Hmmm. Okay, that makes sense, but then why was I seeing horror in this Realm if it is supposed to be one of peace? Based on what you have told me about how the others have died, it seems like I am seeing their deaths. But that doesn't make sense if this place is supposed to offer me a sense of persistent calmness."

"You are right, and it is unusual, but your visions and your headaches, yes, they are connected. They are also linked to your state of death and confusion. The longer the soul spends in the Realm of Life After Death and doesn't acknowledge their own death, the more the lines tend to blur and bend, causing a ripple effect of repercussions.

"You were seeing their deaths. Gladis and Clarence's scars from the fire. Gus's skeletal frame from starvation. Even Ada." When I start to interject, surprised that he knows, he holds up a hand to stop me. "Yes, I know about your vision of Ada's decaying form. You were too shaken for it to have been just from the evil spirit in the woods. And think about the scar on your head and – Kasha's limp – from back in South Brook. Have you noticed that they don't exist here? That ripple effect is also what has been causing your headaches."

I reach up to touch my scar and only feel the smoothness of unblemished skin. I think back to all our balls and recall Kasha not limping. *How did I not notice?*

"That is because a soul will often carry their scars from life with them into death," he continues. "But it often isn't seen by the spiritual eye, unless there has been a glitch."

"What about Sam? I saw him shift, and it didn't look like it was a result of a death."

"Sam," Jack says, smiling again. "How I love that dog. But he is not really a dog, like those you were familiar with in the

Living Realm. He looks like one and is fashioned after a Great Dane to help camouflage his size, but he is really a Hellhound, sent to help protect the ranch. Just like the rest of us, here at Cliffsides, Sam has a job to do. It is his job to trap and corral the corroded and warped souls that have lingered in this Realm. He takes them to a place where they will have consequences for the actions that they committed in their lives and to where they will never hurt another soul again. Sam is just as much a part of the ranch as I am, but where I offer transitioning souls their choice of peace and rest, Sam offers them protection. On the rare occasion that a twisted and decayed soul will pass through onto this sanctuary, it is Sam's job to stop them and remove them. That is what he did that day on the beach with you. Yes, I do know about what happened and I was horrified to hear that you were attacked. But like I mentioned, Sam is incredible and invaluable."

"Wow. Okay," I say, letting out the air I didn't realize I was holding in. "To be honest, I already felt safe with Sam here, but now I do so more than ever. I just hope I don't have to see his real form again any time soon. In fact, I hope I don't see any of those flashes again either."

"You won't. Not now that you have become aware. Both the visions and the headaches will stop."

"So you are like a reaper?"

"Not quite, though they do exist. Their job is more in line with Sam's. My job is similar, but where reapers just collect souls and send them to purgatory or the Lower Realm, I give them a choice."

"Got it. And you are, what, one hundred thirty-one years old? I don't know, Jack, that is quite an age difference. I'm not sure if that will be a deal breaker for us. Talk about robbing the cradle," I joke, trying to lace some humor into our very serious conversation and hoping to see him smile again. A real smile. I needed to hear everything that he has told me, but I can't help but feel like the weariness on his face and in his posture is somehow my fault.

He chuckles. "Although yes, technically, I have been around and have watched time pass for the past hundred and thirty-one years, I am not really one hundred thirty-one years old. Time is irrelevant at Cliffsides. Haven't you noticed how there are no mirrors, no clocks, no calendars? That is because time is not of the essence here. In some sense, it doesn't exist at all. I died at the age of thirty-five, so that is the age that my soul will always appear in its physical form, of my choosing. If you look at it that way, we really are only ten years apart."

Folding my arms over my stomach, I ask, "Last question. Why did it take you so long to tell me all of this? Why did you and Kasha lie to me about it, about my death?"

"Telling someone that they are dead, that life as they know it no longer exists for them, is shocking to say the least. If a person doesn't instantly come to the conclusion of their passing on their own, then it is up to them to come to it in their own time, in their own way. A soul is very fragile, and if it is thrown for such an unforeseen loop, things can backfire, causing the soul to warp. You can take a perfectly beautiful and innocent soul, but it can still spiral out of control, turning it vengeful if it doesn't comprehend. It's basic emotion resorts to anger. Or it can become full of sorrow. You've probably heard of souls haunting places or things or even people... Crying and circling. They become stuck in a never-ending, timeless loop.

"I couldn't tell you, and I made Kasha swear not to say anything, for this exact reason. Due to your head injury, you drifted in and out of consciousness – even dying a couple of times – so you didn't realize that you were dead. Kasha died instantly. I am sure she will tell you about her own experience, but you lingered between Realms for weeks. When you finally did pass on, your soul was lost. Reality around you was fuzzy. If I or Kasha would have just come out and told you that you were dead, it could have sent your soul into one of those spirals. Kasha helped me nudge you in the direction of breaking your soul's routine of the life it led in the Living Realm by convincing you to finally come here, to Cliffsides. I was worried for a while that it wasn't going to happen. I suppose I have your pops to thank for giving you the motivation to finally leave home. He is a good man, by the way. I am happy he and your mom are staying with us for a bit.

"But I digress. I was there in South Brook on a job. You and Kasha were that job. I was sent to you both so I could be there at the time of your passing. To help you both transition. Now that you are here and you have awoken, you need to make your choice."

"Wait. Before you start talking about choices, you made me think of something. If we are dead, if you are also dead, and we are all in this other Realm, how did you appear alive in South Brook? At the train station and on the buses?"

"When you, Kasha, and I would talk or spend time together, just the three of us at South Brook or on the train, we were in the Realm of Life After Death. But as a Ferrier, I can... what is the word? Manifest myself or things. With Mrs. Carver, back at the inn, or with the conductor on the train, I was able to embody my old, physical form I had in the Living Realm. I hated deceiving you, and please know that it was never my intention. Sometimes white lies are a necessity in order to protect someone. Your soul was lost and confused. I had to play a part so I wouldn't send it over the edge. Please know that everything that I have done has been to protect you and to help you along the way."

I let that sink in for a moment before answering, but I know that I don't need to question it. There is this tug in my center that is telling me that he is right. Telling me that he never meant to hurt me—quite the opposite in fact. Bouncing between my gut feelings, my intuition, and the look on Jack's face, I know that I can trust him. That that trust was not broken. Not in the way I was starting to believe it was.

Jack continues. "I know this is a lot to take in, but we do need to talk about your choices. You can either stay here at Cliffsides or at another sanctuary of your choosing or creation. Or you can choose to have your spirit rise to the Realm of Ascension. The choice is yours and yours alone. You may also take as much time as you need to decide. Some people know instantly where they would like to go; for some it takes what people in the Living Realm would call decades. There is no wrong answer and no incorrect amount of time to decide. It all rests within you and what you feel would be is best for your soul.

"I don't expect you to respond to anything that I have told you today. In fact, I hope that you don't. Please take some time to reflect and absorb everything that we have discussed; it has been a lot of information. I also don't expect your forgiveness for keeping you in the dark, but I do hope to have your understanding."

I tell him I will think about everything and let him know of my decision once I have reached one. My anger has dissolved throughout our talk, and true understanding has begun to settle in as I prepare to leave. Still, my mind reels from our extensive conversation, which lasted most of the day.

Upon leaving the study, I peek my head around the door to the kitchen. Gladis is busy preparing dinner, humming to herself as she chops the garden vegetables.

"Gladis, I'd love to take my dinner up in my room tonight, if that isn't too much trouble?" I ask.

"No trouble at all, dear," she responds, looking up from her task.

"Thank you," I say, giving her a small smile.

As I turn to leave, she asks, "Everything okay, deary?"

I hesitate before answering. "Yes. Yes, I think it actually is." And I surprise myself by really meaning it.

I sense that she is looking at me with more sincerity and seriousness than I have seen from her before. She adds, "Good. He's a good man, you know."

"I know," I say, the corner of my mouth turning upward and my heart fluttering with the thought.

I pull myself off the doorframe and head for my room.

I know Kasha is waiting to talk to me—I can feel it—but I am not ready yet. I need some serious time to process everything that Jack has told me today. And processing is exactly what I do as I click the door to my room shut behind me. Stripping off my skirt and tossing on a pair of sweatpants, I curl up among my pillows and I begin to think.

Chapter 24

The Walk

The next day after lunch, I find Kasha in the kitchen helping Gladis decorate what looks like a layered cake they must have baked that morning.

"Hey," I say, hands in the back pockets of my jeans, as I lean up against the doorframe.

"Hey," Kasha responds, expression subdued.

"Can we talk? I thought maybe we could go for a walk."

She turns to Gladis, who says, "Go on, deary. The hard work is done. I have it from here. You need the walk and talk more than I need to eat this cake."

Kasha quickly washes the frosting off her hands and grabs her coat from the peg by the front door as we head outside.

"So –"

"I just –"

We both start talking at the same time as we make our way down the veranda's stairs and toward the path that wraps around the large pastures.

"You go ahead," I say with a reluctant grin.

"Gabs, I just absolutely hate fighting with you. I hate it. I'm not saying what I did was right or wrong, and it ate at me the entire time, but it was something that I had to do. I..." She roughly bats away a fallen tear with the back of her hand as she trails off.

"I know," I tell her.

"You know?"

"I know. I am not saying that I am terribly happy with how things happened. Or that you were even put in a position to have to lie to me in the first place. I'm going to be honest: It hurt. It still hurts, but I do understand."

I reach over and weave my arm through hers. She looks over at me, tears still brimming in her eyes.

"Oh, Gabs, I am just so sorry. About all of it."

"It's okay. Really. All of it," I say, looking over at her. "Jack and I had a talk yesterday. A long one. And he explained everything to me, from his past and the history of this place to how it became what it is today. We talked about our accident and why he was there in South Brook as well as the extent of his job. He explained the reasoning behind my haunting visions and headaches and how my soul was stuck teetering on the edge of falling into an endless loop.

"I'm sorry, too. I should have listened to you when you said that we should talk to him. That he would know what to do. But I was so ashamed. He and I... well, it felt like we were at the start of something, and I didn't want to be the one to jeopardize it. But knowing what I know now, it would never have been an issue. Gosh, Kash... I even thought that you and Jack had a fling going behind my back. You guys seemed to have this thing, this connection... a secret going on between the two of you. I was jealous and felt like I was really cracking up. So, you see, I owe you an apology, too."

"Really? Oh, Gabs... please know that as much as I love Jack, that never was and never will be a thing with me and him. And no, you don't owe me any kind of apology. You were scared. I know you. It tore me up inside that I had some of the answers to help you, but I couldn't give them to you. Jack and

I argued about it. A lot," she says with a bitter laugh. "That was probably the 'secret connection' you felt between us two – constant bickering and disconnect. To be real, I gave him such a hard time about it, I'm surprised he didn't kick me out or sic Sam on me," she says with a laugh. "Wait! Do you know about Sam?"

Smile forming, I say, "Yes, I know about Sam. I think I like him all the better for it, too. He is the ultimate protector."

"Phew, I am glad I didn't blow something else up that I wasn't supposed to. So Jack really told you everything?"

"Yes, we sat in his study and talked all day yesterday," I say, as we continue down the silt covered path, dust kicking up from our shoes as we walk.

With the sea breeze tousling my hair and morning sun warming my cheeks, I skip my fingers down the aging wood fence reflecting on my time with Jack yesterday in the study. I look out into the pastures next to us, not really seeing them.

Kasha blows out a puff of air that ruffles the blonde hair around her face. "That explains why I couldn't find either of you. Well, I'm glad. Hey, no more secrets between us. Deal? It doesn't sit right, and honestly it isn't our style."

"Deal," I tell her. After walking in silence for a few paces and listening to the gulls crying in the near distance, I add with a shrug of my shoulders, "So. We're dead."

"Yup, appears so," Kasha says with a chuckle. "Go figure, huh? Always thought I would grow old, but I suppose everybody assumes that."

"Think of it this way: Now you won't end up like Darla."

We both start laughing as we instinctively grip each other's arms a bit tighter. Feeling thankful to have my best friend with me and to be back on the same page again, I give her arm a little squeeze. I am grateful to be going through death with her. To be able to continue our friendship in the afterlife. *What a blessing,* I think to myself.

"No, I guess I won't end up like Darla," Kasha says, smile still on her face. "And we won't be stuck in that small, dusty town."

"We should count our blessings."

"We should be careful what we wish for," she says, and we both start laughing again.

We continue walking down the dirt path that borders the wood fencing around the seemingly endless pastures. Amber-colored grass sways next to us, and a late autumnal sea breeze tangles our hair. The sun is out, trying to warm the chilled early afternoon, casting everything in a golden hue.

"On a more serious note," I tell her, trying to express as much sincerity as I feel, "Jack told me that you knew instantly. After the crash. I am so sorry you had to go through that alone. I am so sorry about the crash. About… killing us." A sob racks my chest as the guilt of that night begins to overflow the emotional dam I have tried so hard to build up around it.

Kasha stops walking abruptly and turns to face me, all mirth from our previous jokes gone. "Don't you dare carry that," she scolds me, eyebrows pulled down into a frown. "It was not your fault. There was nothing you could have done differently that would have changed things. We went to the show. Yes, we had a few drinks, but no more than we ever do. We were headed up to The Hook, just like we always do. Could we have skipped the show? Sure. Could we have walked home and not gone up to our hangout? Yes. But we didn't. What if those boys weren't up at the Birds' Nest partying? What if they weren't typical stupid teenagers who throw things off the side of the drop-off? What if we drove by a moment earlier or a moment later? And you know what? I would bet your butt that if we were to do it again, do that night over, we would do the exact same freaking thing. Because that is what we did. That is what we always did. No second-guessing the past will change what happened. It happened because it happened, and it happened when it happened. I believe it was meant to occur that night. So you drop that guilt. Promise me. This is absolutely not something you deserve to carry. Trust me, Gabs, I will tell you when you fuck up. That was not one of those times. Now promise me."

"I promise," I manage to squeak out, overcome with emotion.

"Good. Now that that is over with, on to your other point," she says as we continue forward on our walk, arms relinking. "It was hard, but I wasn't alone. I was never alone. Jack was there, and he was truly great. He was there even before the ambulance came for you. He stood with me outside the car and was a calm pillar of strength as I saw myself lying there in that crumpled mess that was once Carly. I was so shaken and so scared, not only for myself but for you. You kept flashing in and out. You would be in the car one second, and then you were standing on the bank with us, yelling at Jack. You were so angry. I had never seen you so angry before. Then the next thing we knew you were gone and in the back of the ambulance, being rushed to Saint Luke's.

"I never left your side, and Jack never left mine. I believe he was waiting for both of us. I paced the hallways of the hospital for weeks while you lay in that bed hooked up to all sorts of machines, flickering in and out of life, constantly fighting. Jumping in and out of the two Realms. Your pops never left the chair at your side either, by the way.

"Then one day you just vanished, and you were home. But you never knew what had really happened. You never questioned when you left the hospital or how you went from injured to the scar on your head, in a blink of an eye. You blamed it on memory loss from your head injury. But it wasn't memory loss, not really. Your soul, no... your consciousness was in survival mode, and it was trying to piece things back together and the only way it knew how to do that was to make you believe that things never changed.

"But, girl, you were so lost. I wanted to tell you so badly, to help you understand, but Jack made me swear not to say anything to you. The mind is such a powerful and fragile thing. He made the dangers of your situation very clear. It frightened me more than I was already frightened for you. I felt like I was being torn in two, keeping you in the dark and watching you struggle because of it.

"But I didn't go through a single moment of that ordeal alone. Jack was a constant presence, and I always felt safe with him there. I am grateful for him in so many ways, even if we didn't always see eye to eye and argued like siblings. You were there, too, the entire time; you just didn't fully know it.

"Do you remember the night you had that big fight with your pops and came over to the house afterward?"

I feel a stone settle on my chest at the thought of that night. "God, Kasha... That night was so terrible. It still hurts thinking about it. Never have I seen Pops so bad."

Kasha stops us from walking again, breeze whipping her hair across her face. She slowly reaches up and slides it behind her ear. The sun suddenly seems too bright and the crashing of the sea in the distance sounds loud to my ears. I reach up and shield the sun from my eyes and look at Kasha's serious expression when she tells me, "That was the day of your funeral."

The realization hits me like a freight train. Everything clicking into place.

"That was why Gary and Winnie were over, and everyone looked so nice. Dressed up. Pops was running around stressed out about needing to find his shoes. Then he wanted his blue tie, not the red one... Oh, God, Kasha. The blue was always my favorite. I thought they had a double date or something. How could I be so blind? Wait. What you said... You made me think it was a date and dragged me out of the house before I could get answers. You and Jack took me out for burgers and fries, and we hiked up to the waterfall."

Kasha grimaces at my accusation of yet another manipulation. "Like I said, it was dangerous to have you find out too abruptly. I was just trying to do what was best for you. We were both just doing what we thought was best for you.

"It has taken its toll on Jack, as well. Lying to you. Watching your condition worsen. From the day of your funeral to the ghoul on the beach – yes, I heard about that – he has sincerely stressed over it all. We have been trying so hard to help you come to the truth on your own, without you discovering your predicament in a negative way... Therefore, making your already fragile condition fracture completely. And believe me I hated every moment of feeling like I was deceiving you. It made me feel sick every time. It still does."

Taking a deep breath, she continues, "Gabs, do you remember that night, after the big fight? You came up on Jack and me sitting around my family's firepit. I gave some story about being outside, and Jack said that he was out for a walk and happened to see the flames and was concerned, so he stopped by to investigate. Well, that was the night that he fully laid everything out for me. He explained our situation, the reality of our new circumstance, how we needed to help you, and how we had to do it very delicately. And he explained the choice that we would eventually have to make."

"Yes," I tell her. "He told me all about the different Realms and how we will need to decide which one we want to exist in from here on. How it is an individual choice that one soul can only make for themselves."

Exactly. He explained it similarly to me." I watch as she nudges a small pebble along the dirt path with the toe of her shoe, her gaze fixed downward. The quiet motion speaks volumes—just as much as anything we've said aloud.

"Gosh, Kash, it is all just so hard," I confess. "What you went through, what we have gone through, is all so hard."

"Life is hard. Death is apparently hard, too. But it is how you handle it that matters most."

"You're right. 'It is not the situation that makes the man, but the man who makes the situation.' Do you remember that quote from school? Who said that? Do you remember?" I ask, pressing my fingers to my forehead, tapping them as I think. "Oh! Wait, I got it! Fredrick Williams Robertson."

"Impressive," Kasha says with a chuckle. "But that is exactly my point. Every person, living and deceased, goes through difficult times. Every. Single. One. How a person reacts in their darkest hours is what speaks the loudest about that person's character. And if I do say so myself, I think that we have come out pretty pretty. Don't you think?"

"Pretty pretty," I say, grinning at my best friend. "Yes, I'd say that."

We take a bend in the trail, and it spits us out near the back side of Ada's stall. Her ears perk in our direction as soon as she catches the sounds and sight of our movement.

As we head over to her stall, Kasha continues, "So... do you know what you are going to decide?"

I let the question hang between us for a moment. "No. I don't. Not yet anyway. It all still feels so fresh, and I need more time to think about things. What about you?"

"Jack said that we can take as long as we need. That this is not a decision to be rushed. So, let's not rush it. I think—"

"Gabriella! Kasha!"

We turn, scanning the nearby barn for the source of the voices calling our names. Then we spot my parents coming toward us.

"Oh, my two favorite girls in the world," my mother says, embracing Kasha and then me, kissing our cheeks. Pops is close on her heels.

"I am happy to see the two of you attached at the hip again," he says, eyes sparkling between us.

"I could say the same about you, Mr. and Mrs. P," Kasha replies.

"It was a nice day for a walk, and we finally had that talk you suggested," I say, turning my smile from my parents to my best friend. *My ride or die.* And I can't help grinning to myself at the humorous irony of our favorite friendship phrase.

"Long overdue, that one was," she confirms.

My pops' eyes are locked on mine as if to gauge my reaction. "I am glad to hear it. We just wanted to tell you that we are planning on heading out in a couple days."

My mom gives his arm a squeeze. "You know, my girl, remember how we told you that we wanted to see you, to give you our love, but how we needed to move on? As incredible as Cliffsides is, it is not our place."

"I remember, and I understand," I assure them. "No need to worry about me. I am okay now. Jack explained everything, and it all makes so much more sense. I feel at peace with it all now." I can't help the swell of emotion building in my core at the thought of having to say farewell to my parents again. But then I reflect on how I have already mourned them and their transition will not be sad... I will not mourn them as they will not be lost. Their transition is not a goodbye forever, death is never the end. It is a celebration, a new beginning. The next chapter. And I am filled with joy that they get to do their next chapter together. Like it always should have been.

"Peace is all anyone ever wanted for you, my girl," my mom says, embracing me in another hug. "It is all anyone ever deserves in this world."

"So," my pops says, looking between Kasha and me, "have you girls made your choice yet?"

"No, we were literally just discussing that, Mr. Pinkard." Looking to me Kasha adds, "I think we still need some time."

"Well, you two, take as much time as you need," Mom reassures us. "It's like Jack says: these things should not be rushed. Your father and I have decided to ascend, but in no way or form do we want that to influence your choices."

"It won't, Mom. I promise. I can see now how everything is as it should be. That each soul requires something unique, and the underlying pulse is about discovering one's own peace and tranquillity in the afterlife. I am so happy for you and Pops," I say, looking between them. "I really am, and I can feel how Accension is what is meant for you both."

"We are so proud of you, Gabriella," Pops says, tears filling his eyes. "Now, we did come out here to see you, of course, knowing that you will always find your way to a barn. But your mother has been nagging me about wanting to see the horses before we transition."

At this, my mom swats his arm. "Nagging? Really, Jewel?" Turning to me, she adds, "I would absolutely love to ride, if you think that the stable boy could manage."

"Of course. Gus is amazing. I am sure he has just the right mounts for each of us," I tell them.

I note the look of horror on Kasha's face, the slight shaking of my pops' head, and the brimming smile on my mother's face as we head in the direction of the barn's double door entrance.

In the barn, Gus has a blue wheelbarrow blocking the gate to the big bay gelding's stall and is whistling to himself as he mucks it out.

"Hey, Gus," I say, trying not to startle him.

"Ah! Gabriella! So good to see yous! What can I help yous with today?"

"These are my parents, Jewel and Martha, and my best friend, Kasha. They would like to go riding with me, if you don't mind?"

"Mind? Not at all. In fact, yous would all be saving me some time and trouble by not having to exercise these beasts today."

"Great," I say. "Any ideas on who they should ride? They're mostly novice, Gus."

"Not a problem," he says, scratching his freckled chin. "I's think I's have the right thought about alls that. Please come with me."

Gus leads everyone through the center of the barn as I peel off and begin grooming and tacking up Ada for myself. He decides to put my mom on a dainty paint mare who looks sweeter than pie, with long, thick, black eyelashes. Pops is given the grumpy buckskin, and they both stand there glaring at each other. Pops with his arms crossed across his middle and the buckskin with his ears back. I find it both fitting and hilarious. Kasha is told that she will ride Charger, the big bay gelding whose stall Gus was just cleaning out.

"Nope. I can't." She shakes her head. "I need to sit this one out. Sorry, guys. I am just not in the right riding attire." She gestures down to her fishnet tights, combat boots, and cuffed shorts.

"Girl, you are in shorts, not a skirt," I tease. "Now get your butt up on Charger! You will be fine. I promise."

"Yes, get up on Charger, Kasha," my pops says, waving a hand. "If this old man can do it—and under protest, mind you—then so can you."

Groaning, she climbs up on the mounting block. "Why does he have to be so big? I think I would be safer on a smaller one.

Can I ride one of those ponies? Yes, I want to ride a pony. You know, something closer to the ground?"

"Ha! Kasha, you know that what they say about horses, right?"

"No, please enlighten me, Gabriella." As she says this, she rolls her eyes and drags out my name in classic, sassy Kasha fashion.

"They say," I emphasize, "that the big horses are gentle giants, and it is the little ones that are the devil in disguise. Besides, what are you worried about? That we will die?"

At this, my pops snorts, and Gus and my mom try to stifle their laughter by sucking in their lips and looking away. Kasha just shoots daggers at me as she tentatively climbs up and onto Charger's saddle.

The four of us end up having a lovely ride around the perimeter of the ranch. They all follow Ada and me as we guide them on the trail. Kasha looks more tense and rigid than I've ever seen her, her hand clamped so tightly around the saddle horn that her knuckles are white. But when she doesn't notice me watching, I catch a smile tugging at her lips as she leans forward, stiffly, to pet Charger's neck. Pops is slowly tipping sideways in his saddle, slouching the entire time. I have to keep reminding him to sit up tall and shift his weight to the left.

Mom looks completely at peace—riding loose and free, eyes closed, head tipped back to soak in the sun, savoring every moment. I can relate.

We ride until the sun starts to set, and I am sure Pops and Kasha will be plenty sore in the morning. Well, they would be if this weren't the afterlife. Returning the horses to the barn for their evening meal, Gus assures me that he can take them from here to give them their rubdowns and dinner. He tells us that we should head back to the manor. Jack will be waiting for us.

As we leave the barn and the comforting smell of the horses, I can't help but think that we experienced a perfect moment today. This place really does feel like Heaven on Earth.

Chapter 25

The Choice

A few days later, I said farewell to my parents as they made their transition.

Jack led them upstairs to the "off-limits" third floor of Cliffside Manor, the one he asked us not to venture to our first night at the mansion. The one that left me with such feelings of foreboding, that I decided to sneak around and explore. Dangerous and stupid. How much things have changed since that night.

It was a happy farewell and one that didn't feel like a goodbye at all, more like a sendoff or a bon voyage. Because that is exactly what it was, I remind myself. Our souls are made of energy and energy can never be destroyed or die. It merely transforms. Dressed in their best and holding hands, they ascended the stairs, following Jack on to their next journey.

Mom looked beautiful in an uncharacteristically long, flowing white dress, and my pops' hair was combed and slicked in a neat and classy fashion. It had been a long time since I have seen either of them so calm, so happy, so at peace. They were practically radiant as they mounted the staircase, and that alone kept the farewell from having a feeling of melancholy.

I stood at the base of the stairs with Kasha holding tight to my hand. Clarence, Gladis, and Gus were all in attendance, dressed in formal attire. Even Sam was there, sitting at full attention at my feet, donned in a white bow tie, ears perked as he watched.

Once they crossed through the glowing archway on the top landing, all was quiet in the house. A tranquility settled in around us.

Gladis headed off toward the kitchen with Clarence and Sam in tow. She was about to start preparing a celebratory early dinner. Jack explained that this is not a goodbye, nor was it something that should be mourned. It is a celebration of their lives, their love, and their choice. We'll be raising a glass in honor of their wonderful qualities and the next chapter of their journey.

Before we all sit down to our meal, I tell Jack and Kasha that I need a moment to be alone. I need time to sit with the feelings that have come up after my parents' transition. Neither one of them presses me about it, and I'm granted some solitude before our supper.

I grab an ice blue cashmere scarf off the wall hook and wrap it around my shoulders and neck. It is wide and soft, offering me warmth and comfort from the cool approaching winter wind. I head out to the edge of the bluffs.

After I meander to the cliff's edge, I sit down in the soft, golden grass and stare out at the churning sea.

I find that my parents' transition – watching as their choice took effect – has given me a sense of peace, too. I sit with my knees pulled up to my chest, arms wrapped around my shins, and readjust the scarf so it is pulled up over my lips. I can feel the heat of my breath on my face as I breathe into the soft cashmere material.

Sitting there with the house to my back and sea in front of me, I reflect. I reflect on my happy and simple childhood. I reflect on my parent's undying love for each other and their love for me. I reflect on Mom's illness, how her death left such a gaping hole in our lives. It created a void that never seemed to fill with time.

I think about all my time at the Pump and Go and everything that Gary taught me about cars and finances. How much I had learned and did all on my own, rebuilding Carly.

I reflect on all the fun and trouble that Kasha and I had together. From dancing, enjoying a glass of wine around her firepit or at Annie's, driving up to The Hook and just sitting and talking for hours on end. The delicious Darla's shakes, mine always a mix of flavors, and the crispy, oily french fries. Us driving in Carly with the windows down and the wind in our hair as the radio blasted.

I reflect on our accident. I have a new perspective on that night and the days that followed. I can see everything so much more clearly now. It is like a curtain has been pulled back, allowing me to see the entire picture at last.

Finally, I think about all our time spent here at Jack's ranch. The balls and meals; the beach and lighthouse; my time with Ada, riding for hours on end. As I reflect, I think of the friendships that have taken root and my budding relationship with Jack – all nurtured here at Cliffsides.

As I sit on the grass covered outlook, I think about my parent's final words to me at the bottom of the stairs. How they told me to allow myself to be happy and to find my peace. "Don't be afraid to have peace, to embrace the love and joy this world has to offer you. Remember to dance, Gabriella."

Then my mind drifts to the choice that I will have to make. *Will I want to rise to the Realm of Ascension, to an eternal tranquility? Or will I want to remain in the Realm of Life After Death? What would that look like? What would that really mean?*

As I sit here weighing my options, realization gently dawns on me. I feel myself settle, heart rate slowing, muscles relaxing as a smile spreads across my face. I close my eyes and relish the feeling. I know what I want to do. I know what is best for my soul. "I promise not to stop dancing," I whisper into the salt air.

I feel Kasha approach before I can hear her. She takes a seat next to me, overlooking the water. We sit in comfortable silence, watching the waves crash on the rocks at the base of the lighthouse. The ocean shifts to a deeper gray that befits the coming winter.

"Are you doing okay?" she asks, her legs folded underneath her, red poncho wrapped tightly around her body.

"Yes, I am," I tell her, turning to give her a smile. "I feel like I have never been more okay. Things make sense, and I feel settled, sated. I have had some time to think about everything that we have been through, everything that we are still going through, and everything that still lies ahead. It feels like a long-awaited puzzle piece finally clicking into place."

"That sounds amazing, Gabs. Does that mean you know what choice you are going to make?"

"Yes, I think it does. But I don't want it to influence your choice at all, by telling you."

"Girl, where you go, I go. You know that, and there is nothing you can do about it. We are best friends for life. . . and apparently for death." She laughs at her own joke. "But even with that being said, I know what my soul needs, and it is you. It is us and our undying friendship, so there is nothing you can say or any choice that you can make that will change things for me."

"Okay." I hesitate for a moment before telling Kasha my plans. Shifting my body to face her in the grass, I look into her hazel eyes, splattered with green speckles, and hold her loving gaze. These are the same eyes that have been with me through all the good and bad in this world; they belong to the only person who knows my every secret and dream. They have stood by me in life and in death. "I would like to stay," I tell her.

"Oh, thank the Lord!" she shrieks, clapping her hands. The sudden burst of sound makes me jump. "I meant that figuratively, but I suppose knowing what we know now, it can be taken literally." And we both start laughing.

"Wait, what? You're okay with that? Are you sure? What did you want to choose?"

"I wanted to stay, Gabs! I really did. But I was willing to Ascend with you, if that was what you wanted. It could have just been another adventure for us. So, tell me, what made you lean that way, toward this Realm? It doesn't have anything to do with the dreamy guy who rescued us from ourselves, does it?" she asks, smirking at me.

An abrupt chuckle bubbles up in my throat, making it sound more like a snort. "It may. I would like to stay and help Jack run the estate. Help the incoming and transitioning souls understand their choices. I want to be able to help those like me, who don't understand due to the trauma from their deaths, feel safe and welcomed. Besides, I would like to spend my life—or my death, you could say—with Jack. So yes, I suppose it does happen to have something to do with the dreamy stranger. I think we have the start of something special, and I want to see where it is going to go. If he will have me, that is."

"Oh, Gabs, that is wonderful! All of it! You will be a perfect spirit hostess, and I will be the maid of honor at your wedding because of course he will freaking have you. I've seen the way he looks at you and how his eyes are always on you, even when you don't notice. So... about this wedding. I want to wear a deep pearl-blue dress. It will remind me of the sea, of this view that we get to spend forever looking at, and of the sky before a storm back home. You do not have a say in the matter, by the way. Just accept it. It is what it is."

"Kasha!" I laugh in protest and shift my gaze to the sea. "We are just dating. Jack and I haven't even talked about our future. Besides, you haven't told me your plans yet. What you want to do with your Choice?"

"Promise you won't laugh? Well, maybe it is okay to laugh a little. The whole thing seems a little outrageous..."

"You mean like you?" I ask, teasing her and bumping her with my shoulder.

"Ha. Ha. Okay, here it is." Kasha takes a deep breath, steeling herself. "I would like to open a bakery. Kasha's Kookies, I'll call it. Gladis said she will help me with the details of setup and that I am a natural with sweets. But the bakery, although fully functioning, well... it will be a front."

"A front? A front for what?" I ask, perplexed.

"A front for a detective's headquarters. I want to become a Death Detective." Before I can even answer she goes on at rapid speed. "You know how I have always loved mysteries? The thrill and the challenge of trying to solve them? Well, this way I can put those skills to use and try to help wayward spirits. I was talking to the others, and apparently, not everyone knows how they died. It's similar to your case, except that they realize they're dead. It is the not knowing how they died or their feeling of unfinished business that keeps them tethered to the Living Realm. It becomes like an itch that they can't scratch, and they are unable to move on, to make their choice, because they are stuck. And, as you well know, a stuck spirit is never a good thing."

"Kash, that sounds incredible and so very you. All of it. What a great way to serve in this Realm. You will be great at it; I know it!"

Before either of us can say anymore, there is loud barking that is increasing in volume as Sam closes the distance between us. He comes bounding up, knocking into me with his big body. Kasha nimbly avoids getting his whipping tail to her face.

"Hi, Sam. Lonely?" I ask. I'm trying to settle his overexcited movements when I notice a rolled note shoved into his collar:

Dinner is almost done. When you are both ready, please come in and join us.

~Jack

"All right, I suppose we should head in. Jack says dinner is about to be served. Are you ready?" I ask, turning to Kasha.

"As ready as ever. Besides, I'm starving. I am looking forward to Gladis' feast. Should we tell the others that we have made our decision? Or do you want to wait?"

"Let's tell them at dinner if you are okay with that. It's a dinner of celebration. The celebration of choice. It feels fitting."

"Agreed," she says with a smile.

We stand and link our arms, Sam leaping and dancing at our sides as we make our way back toward the manor.

Dinner is as extravagant as I could have imagined. The long table is set with an emerald-green table runner and ivory plates highlighted on the pale yellow placemats. Matching green napkins are folded in an elaborate fleur-de-lis design, with shining gold napkin rings cuffed around their centers. All down the middle of the table are crystal vases filled with green, earthy sprigs and white baby's breath flowers. The entire display radiates the theme of new beginnings.

Jack walks over to the phonograph in the corner of the dining room and delicately places the needle on the spinning record. After a small screech of the vinyl, classical horns begin to play a nice, smooth rhythm, and Louis Armstrong's gravelly voice takes over, filling the empty air around us as we take our seats.

The food is laid out across the table, and we pass the dishes around, serving ourselves healthy portions of each decadent option. I sit near Jack at the end of the table, Kasha on my left. Gladis and Clarence occupy the seats across from us, leaning close like lovers. Gus sits at rigid attention, eyes never leaving the passing plates. He is finely polished with his wheat-colored hair precisely combed, freckles on his face popping from his scrubbing.

Stories and memories and laughter are shared as we savor Gladis' delicious efforts. We talk of past times, silly tales, and new beginnings. Feeling content and brimming with both the food and the love, I lean back in my chair and bask in the emotional warmth of the room.

Jack turns to me, teal-blue eyes locking on mine. "You seem like your soul has shifted. It feels more at peace. Would it be too forward of me to ask if you've made your Choice?"

"I have," I tell him. Then, looking to Kasha as the other quizzical eyes of our new family sitting at the table fall on us, I add, "We both have."

"There is no pressure to tell everyone right now. I was merely noting the shift in your demeanor," Jack assures us, taking a sip of his wine.

Kasha gives me the briefest of nods.

"I would like to stay," I tell him. "I want to help those who are struggling and ease their transition as much as possible."

"Stay in the Realm of Life After Death?" Jack confirms.

"Yes. And here, at Cliffsides," I softly emphasize. "If that is okay?"

"Okay? Of course it's okay. You are welcome here always. Nothing will ever change that, Gabriella." A smile forms on his face. I notice his eyes have a slight twinkle to them again, and I think of how much I like having it back. I will need to work on keeping it there. Gus lets out a little squeal of excitement, and Gladis claps her hands. Clarence is beaming, looking between Jack and me.

"And what about you, deary?" Gladis asks, looking to Kasha.

"I want to stay, too. Not right on the ranch, as lovely as it is, but nearby." Looking to me, she adds, "Very nearby. I want to open a bakery and help people solve the mysteries of their deaths, to help them let go. Gladis has been teaching me in the kitchen, and I feel like I can bake people cookies and solve their cold cases, reviving both the needs of the soul and the needs of the stomach. Because Heaven on Earth should offer the answers they are seeking on their deaths, as well as yummy food, to help them let go and move on."

"Oh, Kasha, my darling," Gladis says with tears in her eyes, "that sounds absolutely grand. And you will be great at it, my dear."

"O.D.D.," Gus muses. "Owens, Death Detective. I's likes it," he says, humor dancing in the toothy grin that takes over his face.

Everyone at the table starts laughing at Kasha's new alias.

"Fitting," I tell her, wiping the laughing tears from my own eyes, and she swats me across the arm.

"Well, this is a day for celebration," Clarence exclaims. "I believe it calls for a round of champagne. I will be right back," he says, excusing himself to retrieve a bottle and some flutes.

As the evening winds down with the sound of clanking dishes being cleaned up and put away, Jack asks if I would like to join him outside.

We head out onto the veranda and walk around the bend to the other side of the house, overlooking the sea. Sitting in the middle of the wide porch is a handmade loveseat-turned-rocking chair.

Breath catching in my throat, I walk over to the loveseat. I run my hand slowly over the wood, and I notice the JP branded on the back of the headrest.

Watching me intently, Jack says, "He made it before he left. Said that this place needed a rocker big enough for two, to watch the sunset over the ocean together."

"Pops always had a way of knowing," I tell him, my voice no more than a whisper. Jack starts to walk toward me when I continue, "I hope I didn't overstep in there. That I really am welcome here. With you."

Jack wraps his arms around me and pulls my body flush with his. I tip my head back and look up into those depthless blue eyes of his, our lips only inches away from one another's.

He looks down at me, and I feel like he is drinking me in, eyes sparkling on mine when he says, "Gabriella, nothing in Heaven or on Earth would make me a happier man. I feel like I have waited my entire existence for you. I would give up eternity to touch you. To hold you. Just tell me, Gabriella, what you want, and I will get it for you."

I stare up into his impassioned ocean eyes and say, "You. I want you, Jack."

Then he leans down and gives me a kiss that holds every ounce of feeling and emotion that we have bottled up inside. Heat and passion and love pouring out of our bodies and into one another. Our lips move slowly together, consuming each other, savoring each other. I know that I never want to let him go. That there is a life after death and that I have found my Heaven on Earth. That it is here with Jack.

Acknowledgements

I would like to give a special thank you to everyone that helped me make *A Moment* a reality. I could not have done it without any of you.

To my mom, thank you for being my sounding board, my biggest cheerleader, my first editor and beta reader. You read every chapter as I finished them, then read the entire book again—and again—just because I needed "a second set of eyes" (your poor, overworked eyes). I will be forever grateful for your support and consistent encouragement.

To my husband, thank you, thank you, thank you. If it wasn't for you always pushing me to be a better person and to jump in with both feet, *A Moment* would have continued to only be a dream. Thank you for always being the wind in my sails.

To my friends Patty and Victoria. Patty, thank you for being one of my first beta readers and suffering through the *rough* rough draft. Thank you for your helpful feedback, but most of all for your snarky commentary in the margins of the manuscript. I will always hang on to that copy for when I need a good smile. Victoria, thank you for all your support and insight into being a new author. Your advice has been invaluable.

To my editor, Jessica Hatch. You helped me turn a good book into a great book and I will be forever grateful for your insight and tips.

To my cover designer, Evgeniia Gurcheva. Thank you for your beautiful work. You helped to give *A Moment* the visual representation it deserves. Talented and professional, I loved working with you.

To the myriad friends and family members who let me pick their brains about car accidents, cars, and medical procedures. Markie, Lara, Ymonette, Raven, Helene, Rich, and Tim, you helped me give my hard scenes life and authenticity. Thank you.

To Kate Quinn, Laurie Forest, and Rachel McMillan, thank you for not only answering a fangirl's questions about writing, the industry, and the steps to take as a new author. I am beyond appreciative for your communication, support, and advice. You all helped to guide me in the right direction while building me up. Real queens fix each other's crowns, and you three did just that. Thank you.

Discussion Questions

1. A primary theme in *A Moment* is anything can happen, change, or is possible in a single moment. What are your thoughts on this? Do you believe that everything can truly change in a blink of an eye?

2. Alcohol and alcoholism are reoccurring themes in the novel. How did these aspects make you feel? Did you find Gabriella's father's alcoholism understandable? Do you think Gabriella's own drinking played a role in her and Kasha's accident?

3. Friendship is another central theme in *A Moment.* What did you think of Gabriella and Kasha's bond?

Have you ever experienced a friendship that fierce – a 'ride or die' kinship? Someone that you could trust to do life and death with?

4. What was your first impression of Jack? Did you see him as friend or foe? Which way did you originally lean?

5. Did you suspect that Kasha was keeping a secret from Gabriella? Did you believe the love triangle aspect of the novel?

6. Did you suspect that the girls were dead? If so, when did you start to think that?

7. Who was your favorite character? And what qualities made them stand out to you?

8. What did you think of Gabriella's headaches and horror flashes? Did you view them as symptoms of her traumatic head injury, or did you suspect more?

9. What was your impression of Gabriella's inner voice? The author wrote her thought is italics throughout the book, did that help give her feelings clarification?

10. Let's talk symbolism. There were multiple symbols that surfaced throughout the story: owls and flight, representing freedom, turbulent seas that often reflected Gabriella's inner turmoil. Did you notice this imagery? While reading, were you able to connect that both the owls and the sea represented different aspects of Gabriella's journey—from South Brook to Cliffsides? Discuss.

11. Another symbolic element in the novel was the color palette worn by Kasha and Gabriella. Gabriella was consistently dressed in shades of blue or black, while Kasha often wore vibrant reds and golds. Did you feel these choices reflected their contrasting—and colorful—personalities?

12. If you were given the Choice, would you choose the Realm of Accension, or the Life After Death Realm? Why?

13. If you were to choose the Life After Death Realm, how would you serve or spend your time there?

14. What would your vision of 'Heaven on Earth' look like?

15. In chapter 22, Gabriella realizes that you can experience life after death. What do you believe happens after we die?

About the Author

Having grown up along the Southern Californian coast, TES has always appreciated the rare scenery of her state. Wanting to shine light on the vastness of the state of California and the uniqueness that the landscape offers, she sets her stories to this special backdrop. TES also enjoys tackling the tough and philosophical questions in life while striving to give other childless couples fictional novels that embrace the happiness that can still exist in a relationship without the option to reproduce. It is these two passions, coupled with her personal journey as a childless woman, that have inspired her books. TES currently resides in Ventura County, California, with her supportive husband, who also tries his best to keep her from adopting all the animals.

For more information on TES, A Moment, and future books,
you can go to her website:
https://testheauthor3.wixsite.com/tes-the-author
or say hi on social media at @tes_the_author